SOUTHERN GENTLEMAN

A Charleston Heat Novel

JESSICA PETERSON

ALSO BY JESSICA PETERSON

THE CHARLESTON HEAT SERIES

The Weather's Not the Only Thing Steamy Down South...

Available for FREE in Kindle Unlimited!

Southern Charmer (Charleston Heat #1)

Southern Player (Charleston Heat #2)

Southern Gentleman (Charleston Heat #3)

Southern Heartbreaker (Charleston Heat #4) Coming Fall 2019!

THE THORNE MONARCHS SERIES

Royal. Ridiculously Hot. Totally Off Limits...

Available for FREE in Kindle Unlimited!

Royal Ruin (Flings With Kings #1)

Royal Rebel (Flings With Kings #2)

Royal Rogue (Flings With Kings #3)

THE STUDY ABROAD SERIES

Studying Abroad Just Got a Whole Lot Sexier...

A Series of Sexy Interconnected Standalone Romances

Read Them All for FREE in Kindle Unlimited!

Lessons in Love (Study Abroad #1)

Lessons in Gravity (Study Abroad #2)

Lessons in Letting Go (Study Abroad #3)

Lessons in Losing It (Study Abroad #4)

WHERE TO FIND JESSICA

- Join my Facebook reader group, The City Girls, for exclusive excerpts of upcoming books plus giveaways galore!
- Follow my not-so-glamorous life as a romance author on Instagram @JessicaPAuthor
- Follow me on Goodreads
- Follow me on Bookbub
- Like my Facebook Author Page

Published by Peterson Paperbacks, LLC

Cover by Najla Qamber of Najla Qamber Designs
Photographer: Rafa Catala
Cover Model: Fabián Castro

www.jessicapeterson.com

Created with Vellum

Chapter One

JULIA

The castle was enormous. Foreboding.

Just like the Scot who stood before Charlotte in the Great Hall. His dark, inscrutable eyes roving over her person, like she was his possession.

His to take.

He was a Baron. A rake. A murderer, if the rumors in London were true.

He was also her new husband.

His lordship crossed his arms over the barrel of his chest. He was dressed in naught but shirtsleeves and a kilt. Back to the fire that crackled in the fireplace, the outline of his broad shoulders glowing in the darkness.

His eyes locked on hers. Haughty. A little...heated.

Charlotte pulled back her shoulders. Preparing for battle.

"You understand your duty as my wife, yes?" he asked.

She tipped her head. "I am to provide you with an heir."

"We begin tonight. Ready yourself."

Then he turned and stalked out of the hall, footsteps echoing across the vast, empty space. A man—valet? footman?—cast Charlotte a sympathetic glance before scurrying after his master.

She shivered but managed to keep her spine straight. She would not cower. Even if she did have to sleep with that beast tonight.

It was a business transaction, nothing more, she reminded herself. He needed an heir. She needed safety. And there was no safer place than this fortress in the Highlands.

Its walls kept the monsters of the world at bay.

But what, she wondered, about the monsters within those walls? Who would protect her from them?

She'd have to do the job herself, she decided.

I pull up to the barn and hit the knob on my car stereo, killing the audiobook of *My Romp With the Rogue*. It's the third book in my friend Olivia's historical romance series, and so far, it's pure deliciousness.

I've always loved romance. In fact, I love it so much that I teach a class on it at the College of Charleston.

But lately, I've been especially obsessed with the genre. Romance novels are just the comfort I've needed after my dad passed away last year. Mom passed two years before that.

I miss my family, more than words can say. But romance makes me feel less alone. It makes me feel hopeful.

Stepping out of my car, I notice there's a shiny, hulking Yukon Denali parked next to me. The thing looks like it could eat my Mini Cooper for a snack. Everything about it screams aggressive, from the huge wheels to the giant chrome grill.

It has to belong to one of the venture capital guys backing Rodgers' Farms, my newest interior design project. I went to grad school at NYU, so I ran into corporate banking types plenty. All sharply cut power suits and pretentious need to splash out obscene amounts of cash.

Judging by this guy's flashy car, he's no different. Yeah, I'm a professor of romance, so I know all about the danger of judging a book by its cover. I don't mean to fall into the same trap. But seriously, just how big and shiny and chrome-covered does your car need to be?

I check out the dilapidated barn in front of me. It's a hot mess, from the peeling red paint to the gaping holes in the roof.

It's also charming as hell. Character galore and plenty of history to go with it, I imagine. Tons of potential.

Exactly the kind of project I love—a historic property we can restore with a thoughtful modern twist. A space we can put our own mark on.

By day, I'm a professor of twentieth century literature (and romance!). I've been enamored with the bohemian ideals and lifestyles of literary greats since I could remember. On the side, I take on select interior design projects. My dad was an architect, and the two of us shared a passion for all things design related. Working on projects like this is my way of keeping Daddy close to my heart.

I accepted this particular project because Luke, the owner, is my good friend Gracie's boyfriend. He loved the design work I did at her downtown coffee shop, Holy City Roasters. I was his first pick to design the farmer's market and storefront he's building out here on his farm on Wadmalaw Island. He grows the freshest heirloom produce and mills the tastiest grits in the area, and he plans to sell them in this barn.

But first, we have to give the space a significant face-lift. Which is where the venture capital people come in. They'll provide the money, while I'll take care of the creative side of things.

The barn door, hanging by a rusted metal hinge, is open. Looping my tote bag over my elbow, I step inside to see Luke and another man standing in the middle of the open space. As usual, I'm running a few minutes behind.

"Hey, Julia!" Luke says, offering me a smile before pulling me into a hug. "How you been?"

"I've been all right," I reply. I'm smiling, too. One of my favorite things about Luke is his thick Southern accent. It's authentic and charming, and I have no problem seeing why it affects Gracie so much. "Excited to get started here. Luke, your property is absolutely stunning."

Stepping back, he tucks his hands into the front pockets of his faded jeans and nods proudly. "Thank you. Gracie and I've been workin' real hard to get it in shape."

My skin prickles with a strange, warm awareness.

The heat of the other man's gaze, I realize.

Turning my head, I find a pair of icy blue eyes, rimmed with long, dark lashes, locked on my face.

"Y'all know each other, right?" Luke is saying. "Julia, this is Greyson Montgomery."

"We've exchanged emails," I reply. "But we've never actually met."

Greyson and his brother Ford are the founding members of a venture capital firm here in Charleston. They raise private money to invest in the city's booming hospitality scene. Restaurants, bars, shops like Gracie's, markets, hotels—you name it, Montgomery Partners is involved.

I've worked with the firm before, when they helped Gracie realize her dream of expanding Holy City Roasters. Ford was my point person for that project; I never saw Greyson in person.

"Greyson Montgomery," the man says, holding out a hand. "Montgomery Partners."

I take it, giving it a firm shake. It's huge and warm and engulfs my own.

His eyes are still locked on mine.

"Julia Lassiter. No fancy business name to show off. But I'm here to design Luke's new storefront."

Greyson's grip is firm, too. Not enough to hurt.

Just enough to make my pulse jump.

The fact that he's ridiculously good looking isn't helping matters. He's tall, dark, and handsome personified. Brown hair neatly parted and combed. Scruff just as neat, trimmed close to his square jaw. Striking eyes and Superman shoulders that strain against his crisply tailored suit jacket.

Greyson is dressed in what I call the Southern man's power suit. Gucci loafers. Custom collared shirt and Ferragamo tie. Shiny alligator belt, the sterling silver buckle monogrammed with his initials. Not much different from those arrogant banking types I knew in New York.

Meanwhile, I'm in platform clogs and a long, floral-patterned prairie dress. Hair a frizzy, wild, wavy mess on the account of Charleston's ever-present humidity. A stack of mismatched bangles on one arm, and a tote bag printed with the cover of *A Room of One's Own* by Virginia Woolf hanging from the other.

Greyson is *still* looking at me.

What is this, some kind of staring contest?

My lips twitch. I'm game.

"So you're the designer who went $15K over budget on the Holy City Roasters project," he says. "Won't be happening here. I'll personally be overseeing every detail, down to the last square foot of countertop and gallon of paint. Understood?"

I don't know whether to laugh or deliver a smart, stinging reply.

I go with the stinging reply.

"You mean the project that's been featured in local and national publications? The one that won a major design award? That pops up on social media so often, and led to such a boom in business, that Gracie Jackson is contemplating opening up a second Holy City Roasters location? You talking about that project, Greyson?"

I hate his name. Very private school prepster.

But for some reason I like saying it.

He tilts his head. The ice in his eyes sparking with curiosity. Heat.

Like I've piqued his interest and pissed him off, all at once.

"That's the one, Julia."

His words lilt with a gentlemanly Southern accent. *Ju-ya*. Electricity zips up my spine. Apparently I like it when he says my name, too. Voice rumbly and deep.

"Then you've seen firsthand why quality craftsmanship and timeless materials matter. It's important we preserve the history of places like this"—I gesture to the musty interior of the barn around us—"so that we preserve their stories, too."

Greyson finally drops my hand.

"It's important we turn a profit. Period. No one's going to pay any mind to those stories of yours if this business is in the red before it even opens. We have a budget, and you'll be sticking to it. I want to see Rodgers' Farms succeed just as much as you do, Julia."

His eyes flash. Humor? Almost like he knows how much I like it when says my name.

Okay. This guy is pompous, sure. But apparently he's smart too.

Wickedly smart.

Electricity thrums between us as I hold his gaze. He towers over me, at least a foot taller and twice as broad.

"They're not my stories," I say. "They belong to everyone. And this business is going to go under if we don't differentiate it from others in the area. Which we do by creating not just a farmer's market, but a destination that has a real sense of place. A real respect for history."

"Profit," he says, crossing his massive arms.

"Preservation." I cross my arms, too, just to fuck with him. "The extra time and money is always worth it in the long run."

His gaze moves to my arms. "When was the last time you looked at a P&L statement?"

"When was the last time your greed didn't suck the life out of a priceless historical structure?"

"Julia, it's a *barn*." He glances at Luke. "Meaning no offense. But let's not forget we'll be selling grits and organic produce here. This isn't Harrod's."

"No, it's not. It's a barn that I'm going to turn into the south's preeminent farmer's market and gathering place," I reply, taking a step forward.

"We," he corrects. He doesn't move forward. But he does lean toward me. Close enough for me to see the pink flush creeping its way up his neck. "We are going to do that. Where do you think the money for this work is coming from?"

"If *we* do the renovation right, we can rent the barn out for events—weddings, rehearsal dinners, concerts. It's a mess now, but if you had any imagination, you could see the possibilities for so much more."

I don't mention that I already have a wedding lined up for the space. Olivia and her fiancé Eli are getting married, and they said they'd love to have the reception here.

Greyson's eyes flick down, then back up. "I have plenty of imagination."

Doubt it.

"Why are you so involved all of a sudden?" I say. "You weren't around for the Holy City Roasters project."

"Simple. We were juggling six other projects at the time, so I put Ford on Holy City Roasters. I'll be your point person going forward. I can be hands on when the occasion calls for it."

"I'm sure you can. Though I doubt it's as satisfying an experience for those involved as you think it is."

"It's what I do for a living."

"Condescend?"

He smirks. "Satisfy." I catch a whiff of his aftershave. Smoky. Bergamot, maybe? "I'm very good at it."

"You know when you pay people to tell you these things, they don't count, right?"

"As a matter of fact, Julia, most people pay me. Literally. I've raised a hundred and seventy-five million dollars from investors this year alone."

Shit he's good at this. Sparring. Spiting.

Bragging about how much money he has.

So arrogant.

But damn, that cocky grin he's wearing is *so wicked.*

The literature professor in me does appreciate a good villain.

A man with a story.

Warmth pools between my legs when I think about his repeated—and pointed—use of my name. Like he's practicing it. Getting it just right, so when he snarls *Ju-ya* as he takes my hair in his fist and slams into me from behind, I come from the gravelly sound alone.

I blink. That's an explicit little fantasy right there.

I like it. Too much.

I haven't been laid in—God, has it really been six months now? Maybe that's why I'm so keyed up all of a sudden. I had my regular hookups on repeat for a while. Once those petered out, though, I wasn't in the mood to date or see new people. Not after losing what was left of my family.

But now I'm feeling that tingle of interest again. Which is just perfect, considering this guy is my new—if temporary—boss.

Oh. And an asshole. And totally not my type. I usually go for bookish guys. Bohemians. Free spirits like me, preferably with foreign accents and a fondness for poetry.

"Please, y'all." Luke takes a step forward, holding up his hands. "Please don't make me call the authorities."

Greyson blinks. Extinguishing the heat and humor in his eyes as quickly as they appeared.

Replaced by that ice again.

My stomach dips.

He lifts his arm, his sleeve pulling back, and checks the enormous chrome Rolex on his wrist.

"I have another meeting. Y'all have the budget and timetable. Julia, please respond to that email I sent you this morning. My investors are eager for a schematic of the barn's new layout."

Without another glance in my direction, he stalks out of the barn. As if he can't get out of here fast enough.

Talk about hot and cold.

Yeah, there's definitely a story there. One I'm suddenly curious to know more about.

Luke lets out a low whistle beside me.

"You can put up your duelin' pistols now." He cuts me a glance. "You okay?"

"Oh, yeah, I'm fine. That guy's just..." *Ballsy. Blunt. Intriguing.* "A total dick."

"I don't disagree with you. But I've done my research, and he's the best of the best. Just promise me this project won't end with a homicide, okay? I can't weigh in on preservation versus profit, but I do know murder sure as hell isn't good for business."

I smile. Nudge his shoulder with mine. "I promise. Just like I promise to do my best to make your dreams for this place come true."

"You're the best of the best, too," he says. "And if there's anyone who won't let a guy like Greyson push her around, it's you."

"That's kind of the best compliment ever. Thank you."

"Thank you for your help," he says. "I'll see you later, Julia."

"See ya."

On the drive home, I listen to *My Romp With the Rogue.*

Callum was not expecting much of his bride.

He certainly wasn't expecting to find her waiting for him in a transparent chemise, gauzy and fragile and so damn arousing it made his blood roar.

She sat by the fire in her chamber, book in hand. When he cleared his throat, announcing his entrance, she turned her head and met his gaze.

Nothing fragile about the look in those blue eyes. They were steely. Determined.

Brave.

She set down her book and stood, plastering the fabric to her body.

Her nipples were pebbled, fine points, and very much visible through the chemise.

Just like that, he was hard. Painfully so.

It made him angry.

"Do you provoke me?" he growled.

The minx didn't even blink. "Isn't that the point?"

"Are you not afraid?" he asked, stepping out of the shadows into the light of the fire.

She did not flinch. Barely moved a muscle. Not the usual response he got to his presence.

"Are we going to keep asking each other questions without answering them?"

He would not smile.

Would. Not.

"You should be afraid," he said.

"I am not." Her eyes flashed. "Shall you punish me for it?"

Oh, he'd punish her all right.

Punish her by making her as hot and needful as he felt.

Punish her by making her shake and moan.

By making her take him into her mouth on her knees.

Callum reached out. Took her breast in his hand. Her breath caught when he ran his thumb over her nipple.

"I shall indeed," he said.

He gathered the chemise in his fists and pulled it over her head.

The flash in her eyes burned hotter.

Whew. Nothing like some play on power dynamics to get *me* hot and bothered.

Only when I reach between my legs later that night in bed, I don't imagine it's Callum the angry Scot touching me.

I imagine it's Greyson the cocky venture capitalist.

He'd say my name. He'd pull my hair.

And then he'd make me come.

Chapter Two

GREYSON

She's infuriating.

Everything about Julia makes me feel like I'm on the verge of bursting an artery. Or bursting out of my pants.

Case in point: I catch a whiff of her perfume—just a hint, sweetening the otherwise dusty air as I step inside the barn—and I'm already at half-mast.

Motherfucker. At least it looks like no one else is around. The parking lot is deserted except for her bright orange Mini Cooper.

One month. I've been around the woman all of one month. But mercy, it's felt like a lifetime.

I stupidly allowed myself to flirt with her the day we met. I was just so drawn to her. Her honesty. Her sharp, shameless wit. Moth to a flame and all that bullshit.

But I won't make that mistake again.

I do not mix business and pleasure. My firm—and my family—are on the line, and in my right mind, I'd never put them at risk by fucking an employee.

Too bad I'm not in my right mind around Julia. Probably explains why I haven't just put my brother, Ford, on this project. That, and I don't want to put too much on his plate. As a single dad raising his three-year-old daughter, Bryce, he's always juggling a lot.

I still have to try to keep this woman at arm's length. For her sake, and for mine.

Luckily—shockingly—we make a decent team. We argue a lot over the budget, but we somehow make it work. When I push her, she (mostly) manages to find creative solutions to problems or ideas that would otherwise put us in the red. My contractor reports she always shows up, even if she's late. His sub-contractors adore her.

Julia is talented, hardworking, and clearly flexible.

Unique as hell, too. It's her quick mind. Quick mouth. The way she dresses like some sexy bohemian Stevie Nicks goddess. How fearless she is when she's calling me out or coming after me. The truth doesn't scare her, and apparently neither do I.

Girl does not give two fucks about what I think. About what anyone thinks.

I give too many fucks. About everything.

We couldn't be more different if we tried.

But I swear, fighting this bizarre, hugely inappropriate, hugely inconvenient boner I have for her has turned me into a legit monster.

I roared a lot to begin with. Now—

Now I'm one of Khaleesi's dragons. I breathe fire and bring instant death upon anyone who crosses my path. I'm a broody jerk when I go too long without seeing her. I'm a broody jerk when I do see her.

It's a vicious cycle. One I can't seem to break, as evidenced by today's visit. I don't need to be here. But Julia was on the schedule this afternoon for a site visit. I told myself I came to double check the HVAC install and have a conversation with her about reworking some budget stuff.

Deep down, I know I'm full of shit.

Julia is standing in the center of the barn, facing away from me. Bent at the waist, elbows on a sawhorse as she looks down at the plans draped over it. One booted foot taps softly against the worn floorboards in time to a silent song. Wild, wavy blond hair everywhere.

When my eyes fall on her ass, simultaneously cute and luscious, just like the rest of her, I consider impaling myself on the pitchfork beside the barn door.

A fitting end for a heartless schmuck like me.

Instead, I stare. Julia usually wears long dresses. But today she's wearing one that's short—weather is warm for this time of year. Seeing her bare legs makes me want to pull my hair out. Then pull her bottom lip between my teeth.

Would she bite back? Or would she whimper? Surrender?

I groan. A sound I manage to turn into a growl, thank fuck.

Julia glances over her shoulder. She straightens, crossing her arms.

She doesn't greet me. Looks at me instead, waiting for me to explain why I'm being extra dickish before we've even said a word.

I think about you too much. I want you too much. I need to stay away from you but I can't, and it's driving me insane.

"Cabinet estimate came back," I blurt. "It's triple what we have budgeted. A storefront selling grits and collards doesn't need custom cabinetry done up in high gloss European paint."

Julia straightens, narrowing her eyes.

"Luke just harvested his biggest corn crop yet. He's going to have a lot of product to sell. Whatever cabinetry we install has to hold up to serious wear and tear. You put stock in here—and use crappy paint—and I guarantee within a year you'll be replacing it. Whatever we spend on cabinets we can make up for with countertops. I selected a honed black granite that's reasonably priced—the place stocks it, so we don't have to buy whole slabs—but very durable. It'll look great with the cabinet color. I also found some brass hardware for cheap at an antique place over in Mt. Pleasant."

She never holds back. Never tempers her words with politeness or patience. Granted, neither do I. But I appreciate her no-bullshit attitude. It's refreshing.

And arousing.

And *infuriating*.

"Cutting costs on two hundred square feet of countertop isn't going to put a dent in the extra ten grand custom cabinets will cost us. We hired you to stick to budget. Rework your proposal and have it in my inbox by tomorrow morning."

"No, you hired me to make this place feel special." Julia puts a hand on her hip. "And I usually make the budget work, don't I? Why haven't you learned that yet? Be honest. Did you really come all the way out here just so you could be rude to me in person?"

I tilt my chin toward the duct work above our heads. "I came out here to check on the HVAC."

Only half a lie. A lie that Julia picks right up on.

"The HVAC," she says, leaning her head to the side. "It was installed last week. You've been out here twice since then."

See? See how quick she is?

God*damn* it.

I look at her. She waits for an explanation. Patiently. No judgment in her eyes. Just annoyance.

Annoyance and a hint of something else. For a crazy heartbeat I imagine it's arousal.

Shaking the idea from my head, I'm overwhelmed by the need to apologize to her. For being such a miserable jerk. For making life difficult just because feeling things pisses me off.

But that would open up a can of worms I do not want to revisit. Too soon.

Too late, really.

At last, Julia digs a silver tape measure out of her coat pocket—she's wearing this beat-up, teeny tiny leather jacket over her dress—and shoots me one last look. Blue eyes alive, set of her shoulders determined.

"Whatever," she says. "Just don't get in my way, all right?"

She turns, taking a quick, angry step past me. But in her hurry, her boot catches on a loose floorboard. She stumbles forward with a gasp.

I tear my hands out of my pockets and lunge to the right, determined to block her fall with the bulk of my body.

My left arm hooks around her waist. I catch her, my other arm curling around her back as I try to reverse her forward momentum by pulling her against me. She's a little thing, petite, so it doesn't take much effort. But my heart still pounds as her body collides with mine, her warmth seeping through my shirt.

My body leaps. For a second I just stand there, Julia in my arms. Both of us breathing hard.

For a second, she lets me hold her.

A second I read way too much into. Poor thing nearly broke her face. She's startled, that's all. Startled into stillness.

Her lingering in my arms has nothing to do with her feelings on how well our bodies fit together, despite their difference in size. It has nothing to do with the hot wash of energy that floods my skin and the air around us.

Tension so thick it hangs between us like the humidity on a hot July day.

So thick I can hardly breathe.

I'm sorry, I want to say.

"You okay?" I say instead. I don't recognize my voice.

"Yeah," she breathes. "Yeah, I'm fine."

Her hand unfurls against my chest. The movement is small but trusting.

My heart clenches. Swelling with a protective urge I haven't felt in ages. Julia is not helpless. Girl's got a spine of steel. But here in my arms, she's vulnerable. Open.

Real.

"You sure? How about your ankle? Can you move it?"

Her hair falls across her face as she looks down. Lifts her leg and rolls her ankle, making the muscles in her calf ripple against her smooth skin.

Lord. Have. Mercy.

"Feels fine."

I let out a silent sigh of relief. "Good. Julia, please be careful."

She looks up at me. Eyes curious as they move between mine. I've noticed she likes it when I say her name. The blue in her eyes—it brightens.

Her hand is still on my chest.

"You know, that's only the second time I've heard you say 'please.'"

I clear my throat. Swimming in ferocious need, heat gathering between my legs.

I'll make you say please.

I'll make you beg.

"You said it yourself," I manage. "I'm rude. And rude people don't say 'please.'"

"But you just did."

"Be honest. Did you come all the way out here just to call me out on my bullshit?"

She grins, digging her teeth into her bottom lip.

Loooooord.

I should not flirt with this woman. But I can't seem to help myself.

Not when she's touching me like this. Not when I've made her smile. A smile she's turning on me. Warmth like the sun spreading through my skin.

Considering I've lived under a cloud the past three years, it feels really fucking nice.

"Surely you've picked up on two things about me," she says. "One, I am *making the budget work*. And two, I very much enjoy calling you out. Sometimes I think you do it on purpose—you throw me these lay-ups, just to see if I'll rise to the occasion."

It's like we're playing truth or dare, and we keep exchanging truths.

Wrong that I want a dare?

"I've never met anyone as quick or full of conviction as you are, I'll give you that," I say.

"I'm anti-bullshit," she replies. "Can't help it."

"I like that about you," I say without thinking. "There are way too many superficial people in the world. In *my* world, at least."

"You included?"

I grunt. Search her eyes. "Me included."

"Actually." She arcs a finger lightly over my lapel. "I don't think you're very bullshit-y at all. You just don't share your story. The real story. You hide it, don't you? Why?"

My heart blares inside my ribcage. My lust burns hotter, even as my stomach contracts.

How did Julia pick up on that?

And how do I keep her from digging any deeper?

By sheer force of will, I step back, unwrapping my arms from around her body.

Her body.

My body.

I'm on fucking fire.

And I'm going to be in trouble if I don't get out of here.

"Keep an eye on that ankle." I spear a hand through my hair and look away. "I—meeting—be in touch—"

I stalk out of there like the place is in flames.

I start my truck. The engine roars to life, air conditioning blasting through the vents. I settle my hand on the top of the steering wheel. Hold it in a death grip as I take a steadying breath.

Better.

That's marginally better. Good enough to get me through the rest of the day at least.

I put the truck in reverse at the same moment the back driver's side door opens.

My stomach falls a hundred stories when I glance at the rearview mirror and see Julia slide into the backseat.

She closes the door behind her.

Our eyes meet in the mirror. Hers glimmer.

Oh, yeah.

Oh, *fuck*. That's arousal in her gaze.

I think.

Then again, I'm a lunatic when it comes to this woman, so my radar is questionable at best.

"What are you doing?" I ask. Grinding my foot into the brake pedal.

Her eyes bore into mine. A beat passes.

"Exactly what you think I am," she replies.

My stomach drops another hundred stories as understanding dawns. Is this happening? Is Julia really propositioning me?

"I don't fuck employees."

"I don't fuck bosses. Or assholes." She takes a breath. "Tell me to get out, and I'll leave. It's just—Greyson, the tension between us...it's eating me alive."

I don't want her to leave.

I should. I really, really should ask her to go.

But I don't. I can't.

I mean, I can fuck Julia and still keep a safe distance, right? Anything more and I'd be playing with fire. But casual sex? It's never been a problem before.

Above all else, I don't want to hurt her. Which will inevitably happen if the sex turns serious.

But we're both adults. She just said I'm not her type. And this is not my first rodeo. Hell, maybe fucking her will make this dragon boner finally go away. Why not give it a try? Worst case scenario, one of us catches feelings and we end it. No big deal. This project will wrap up in less than six months anyway.

"Tell me to leave, Greyson," she repeats, more forcefully this time.

A voice inside my head tells me I'm being an idiot. It tells me Julia is different, the way I feel about her is different, and that I am going to burn us both to the ground.

But I shove the truck into park anyway.

Julia's breath catches. My dick goes full salute.

"You'll stay," I reply, eyes locked on hers.

I turn off the ignition. Unbuckle my seatbelt. Reach across the console to open the glovebox. Inside, there's a pack of Marlboro lights, a half bottle of local rye whiskey, and a handful of condoms.

Ford calls it my sinner's chest.

I call it being prepared for whatever life throws my way. Good days, bad days. Celebrations.

Opportunities to fuck the woman I want so bad I can't see straight.

I grab a condom. Climb out of the car and open the back door.

Julia blinks against the late afternoon sunshine that slants across her face. I step forward so that my shadow keeps the sun out of her eyes. She blinks again, head tilting back as she looks up at me.

Her perfume—not flowery, not musky, just pure delicious poison—surrounds me. My cock throbs.

"Just sex," she says. "Just once."

"Just sex," I say.

But I can't guarantee just once.

Chapter Three

GREYSON

I take off my jacket. Hang it on the back of the driver's seat.

"Scoot over," I say, unbuttoning my sleeves and rolling them up to my elbows.

I'm pleased when Julia does as I tell her. I slide into the backseat and close the door behind me.

Turning to her, I wrap my fingers around her wrist. Her pulse flutters against the pad of my thumb.

"Come here," I say.

She meets my eyes. "Who says you're the boss outside the office?"

One side of my mouth curls into a smirk. "I do. Now do as I say and get on my lap, Julia."

Narrowing her eyes at me, she studies me for a moment.

"Then why was I the one who called this meeting?" she replies, climbing onto my lap. Thighs straddling mine.

My hands find her waist. "Because I needed your consent. Now that I have it, I'll be calling the meetings from now on."

"But you said just once." She sinks lower. Face inches from mine.

Lips full and soft. Begging to be kissed.

"*You* said just once. I know better than to make promises I can't keep."

She looks at me. Touches the tip of her tongue to her upper lip.

I want to scream.

"We'll see about that," she says.

Thighs straddling mine, she sinks onto my groin. Rolls her hips side to side as her center meets with the head of my cock through our clothes.

Her eyes on mine the whole time. Unafraid. Wholly focused. Watching my reaction.

A bolt of heat slices through my middle.

"Fuck," I groan, my hands kneading into her sides. She wraps her arms around my neck, shaking her waves back from her face. "Julia. *Julia.*"

I lean in for a kiss, tilting my head. But she catches me, placing a finger on my lips.

"No kissing."

"What?" I pull back, crushed. I want to taste her. Every inch of her skin. Body. Everything. "Why the fuck not?"

A shadow passes across her eyes.

I'm more curious than I should be about what it means.

But then she blinks, the shadow replaced by mischief. "Because you'll be using your mouth for other things."

"What about your mouth?" My gaze moves to those full, pink lips. "What will you be using that for?"

"Use your imagination. Or do you not have one of those?"

I chuckle. "Already told you I have an imagination."

"Then show me," she challenges, rolling her hips. Even through our clothes, I can feel the lips of her pussy parting over my cock. Caressing it. "Greyson, show me how creative you can be."

I glide my hands up to her tits. Cup them. Her eyelids get heavy when I give them a squeeze, making her nipples harden.

I groan, this time at her responsiveness.

Makes me wonder how long it will take to get her nice and wet. Soaked.

I want her soaked.

My guess is not long at all.

Hooking my finger in the tie at the neck of her dress, I undo the knot. The front falls open, and I pull it down and to the right, revealing her bra. It's light green and lacy, the cup itself sheer. Showing her pale pink nipple.

Gaze on hers, I lean in and cover that nipple with my mouth. Suck it to a harder point through the lace.

Her skin smells so damn good.

She lets out a pant.

I move my mouth up her chest. Glide my fingers into her hair and fist it. Give it a quick, solid tug.

She gasps, her head falling to the side. Baring the tender flesh of her neck to me.

I sink my teeth into her skin. A tiny bite, followed by tongue, lips. Her hips roll against me harder now. More insistent. Needier.

With my other hand, I hike the skirt of her dress up over her hips. She's wearing green panties that match her bra, transparent lace.

Her pussy is neatly groomed, but not completely bare.

My dick begs for mercy.

I reach down and pull her panties to the side. Her folds peek out from between her lips. I glide my thumbs between them and open them. Revealing a cunt so perfect and pretty I growl.

Literally growl.

I look up at her.

"You gotta let me kiss you here," I say, running my thumb over her clit.

Ah, fuck. She's already soaked. As ready as I am.

She nods, breathless.

Putting my hands on her hips again, I lift her off my lap.

"Sit up against the window. Spread your legs."

This time, Julia doesn't fight me. She sits, back to the window, and shimmies out of her panties. They end up somewhere on the floor.

I hope she leaves them there.

Julia is naked from the waist down now, and she's not shy about it. Legs parted, she reaches down and touches herself.

"Don't," I warn. "You come without me, and you'll pay. You understand me, Julia?"

In reply, she bites her lip. Furrows her brows. Keeps circling her fingertips over her clit.

"Then hurry up," she pants.

It's awkward, but I manage to half get on my knees, half lay down on the bench. Meeting her eyes, I loosen the knot of my tie.

Then I lean down. Curling my hands around the backs of her knees, I hold them open and kiss her cunt. The way I'd kiss her mouth —deeply, impatiently, well.

I'm shaking with the effort to hold back.

I swirl my tongue around her clit, and she cries out. Digs her fingers into my hair, urging me to keep going. I suck her. Nibble. Use my thumbs to play with her slick flesh while I lick my tongue inside her.

My dick presses urgently against the fly of my pants.

Her hips buck against my mouth. She's touching her tits, touching me.

Eyes closed. Completely lost to the moment. Uninhibited. Hiding nothing. Literal naked honesty.

Jesus, she's beautiful.

I want to keep going. More than I want my next breath. But I'm going to come in my pants if I don't get inside her soon.

I've wanted her for too long.

I've waited too damn long.

Mouth still on her pussy, I reach blindly on the seat behind me for the condom. I find it. Kiss her clit one last time.

I fall back on my haunches and hold the condom out to her. Opening her eyes, she takes it.

"You," is all I can manage as I unbutton my pants. Don't even bother with my belt.

I pull out my dick and hold it in my fist, getting back up on my knees. Julia opens the condom packet with her teeth. Legs still spread —still propped up against the window—she rolls it down my length using firm, short strokes.

I'm growling again.

"I want to fuck you," I say. Because that's all this is.

A fuck.

That's all this is.

That's it.

We're safe as long as it's *just a fuck*.

She gives my dick another tug. Harder this time. Making me fall onto my hands on either side of her hips, my tie dangling between us.

"Then fuck me," she says.

Need—I'm wild with it. My vision goes red, then blurs. I straighten, grab her by the backs of her thighs, and yank her toward me so that her back is flat against the seat.

I pull her again, closer. I wrap her legs around my waist. My dick bobs over her groin.

Taking it in my hand, I position myself at her entrance. Lean down on my other arm.

We meet eyes. Hers are heavy lidded. Cheeks and chest flushed.

"Greyson, please," she whimpers. So honest in her need.

Why does she have to be so fucking real? Why can't she pretend or hide or fake it just once?

I rear back. Eyes still on hers.

I buck my hips and surge forward, sinking to the hilt in one rough, fast motion. Her tits bounce. Head falls back. The tiny gold chain around her neck flies up to catch on her chin.

"Yes," she breathes. "God, that feels good. You feel so good."

I bite the inside of my cheek. She feels better. Tight and sweet and soft.

My need overtakes me then. I hammer into her, gutting strokes that rock the car.

It's messy and it's fast. Backseat fucking in its purest form.

Just what it needs to be.

I reach between us and curl the pads of my first two fingers against her clit. I do it again. Again, and this time I swivel my hips while I'm inside her.

One of her legs starts to shake. Her pussy flutters around me. Her hands land on the window behind her with a *thump*.

She's close.

I look at her. "You first."

"I don't—"

"You *first,*" I grunt.

Her hips surge against my fingertips.

While I rock into her, I watch her reactions. She furrows her brow, lost to her rising pleasure.

I'm lost in her.

Her hips surge again. She cries out. My balls tighten.

She comes. Clamping down on my cock, squeeze after squeeze that has me growling so loud I bet they can hear me on the next farm over, twenty minutes away. Her body arches hungrily upward, hands clawing at my shirt. Like she's desperate for something only I can give her.

I lean down and cover her body with mine. Holding her against me as best as I can while she rides out her orgasm, cheek to cheek. My nose in her hair, strands of it fluttering as I let out one hot breath after another.

I want to kiss her mouth. My chest aches with the desire to turn my head to the side and capture her lips with mine. I want to soothe her. Taste her. Drink her in.

I thrust once, twice.

And then I'm coming, too. So hard it hurts. I empty myself in a handful of hot spurts. I suck in a breath through my teeth, my heart hammering against my breastbone. I can't breathe. Can't see.

Julia's hands are clutched in my shirt at my sides.

I want to keep holding her. But I can't.

Just a fuck.

Propping myself up on my hands, I pull out of her. The motion makes cum leak out of the condom onto her thigh.

I pause. Heart still hammering.

Her hands are still holding me tight.

I reach down. Smear a little cum across her skin with my thumb.

Julia watches me do it. I wait for her to call me out. It's weird. Wrong. Possessive in a way I have no right to be.

But she doesn't say a word. Just wiggles out from under me, reaching for her panties and pulling her dress down over her hips.

I fall back onto the seat. Feeling equal parts sated and fucking *flattened* by a new, searing sense of hunger.

I'd hoped—foolishly—that having sex with Julia would satisfy my need for her. Make this inconvenient crush go away.

Now I see it's only made me want her more. Again. Right now.

I'm hungrier than I was before.

My hand trembles as I tie off the condom.

Whatever. It doesn't mean anything. Probably just need some nicotine.

"Cigarette?" I say, grabbing a napkin from the center console.

Julia smoothes back her hair. "Yeah. Sure."

We stand in front of my car, the late afternoon light catching on Julia's hair. Her eyelashes. I light her cigarette. Light mine. For several heartbeats, we smoke in silence.

"Why did you do that?" She brings the cigarette to her lips and looks at me. Inhales. "Mark me. With your...you know."

"I didn't mark you."

I take a long pull. Feel the tension in my muscles releasing.

Smoking is a shit habit. But I took it up after my divorce to help deal with...well, everything. I've been hooked ever since. It's the only thing that relaxes me anymore.

That, and brown liquor.

"What was it, then?" she asks.

I shrug. "I don't know. Felt like doing it. So I did."

"Do you have other kinks? Or is that the only one?"

Glancing at her, my pulse skips. Of course she wouldn't call what I did weird or wrong or disgusting.

She'd call it a kink. And be totally nonjudgmental about it.

I drop my cigarette on the ground and tamp it out with the toe of my shoe.

"I should get going."

"Let me guess. Meetings." She tamps out her cigarette, too. "Did I make you late?"

"I'm never late. Unlike some of us."

She grins. "Hey. I'm juggling one and a half jobs. Cut me some slack, will you?"

We meet eyes. Hers are lit up. Lips curled into that pretty grin. Cheeks still pink.

What should I do here? Hug her? Kiss her cheek? We just fucked in the back seat of my car, for Christ's sake. In front of a barn. What's the post-coital protocol for that?

I don't want to be a dick. But I also don't want to give her the wrong idea by pulling her close when I should be keeping my distance.

I need to keep boundaries clear.

Awkward silence stretches between us.

"Welp," Julia says at last, crossing her arms. "Guess I'll see you around, then."

I'm rooted to the spot. Afraid if I move I'll just throw her over my shoulder and toss her back into my car.

"Yeah," I say. "See you around."

She moves past me. I hear her car door closing, her engine start.

Dust billows behind her car as she drives away.

I smoke another cigarette—doesn't make me feel any more relaxed—and head to my meetings.

Chapter Four

JULIA

Three Months Later

At first I think it's just a bad hangover.

But hangovers don't last a week, even in your thirties. They definitely don't make your boobs hurt.

The inkling that something isn't right hits me mid-week. I bury myself in my work, hoping the weird moods, nauseous bloating, and overwhelming exhaustion will go away.

It takes me nearly face planting into my laptop, narcoleptic style, on Friday afternoon for me to finally Google my symptoms.

Pregnancy is a possible culprit.

My stomach seizes at the word. A creeping sense of foreboding moves through me.

"But that's impossible," I blurt out loud, eyes glued to my screen as my pulse kicks into high gear.

Sure, my "just once" with Greyson has turned into a pretty regular thing. The sex is delicious, despite him being a class A-asshole. Hell, maybe that's part of why it's so good. Up until now, I've never really had hate sex.

I had no clue what I was missing out on.

He is the only guy I've been with.

We've fucked in backseats. In bathrooms and on building sites. No matter where we are, however, we always, *always* use condoms.

I *do* regret not being on some kind of birth control myself. My body didn't respond well to the pill. I should've gotten an IUD inserted at that point, but because I'm a lazy idiot, I kept putting it off. That fills me with such regret now—not being more intentional about keeping my uterus baby-free. Stupidly thinking that trusty (heh) old prophylactics would do the heavy lifting. To my credit, I remember reading somewhere they're 98% effective or something crazy like that.

I Google condoms. They're 98% effective *when used correctly*. I run through every encounter I've had with Grey in my head. As far as I can remember, there's never been a snafu.

Although I cringe when I think about our first hookup—the one where I ripped open the condom packet with my teeth. That wasn't the only time I did that, either.

Still. 98% means there's a 2% fail rate. Are we really that unlucky?

The chances that his sperm somehow snuck through all that latex are slim. Then again, this is Greyson Montgomery we're talking about. If anyone has take-charge-son-of-a-bitch sperm, it's him. And now that my mind—really, my anxiety—has caught on the possibility, I know I won't be able to relax until I know for sure.

I take a brisk walk up to the Walgreens on Coming Street. I practically run home. Heart pounding so hard I feel dizzy as I look down to make sure I pee on the test strips and not all over my hand.

A single blue line immediately appears on both tests. *Not pregnant.*

I let out a breath.

I set the timer on my phone for the recommended three minutes.

Turns out my relief is short lived. Less than a minute later, the second line appears in one screen, then the other, each one forming a cross.

Pregnant.

I start to shake. Hard. Throat swelling. I read the instructions over and over again, hoping that I missed something, that the lines are too faint.

Nope. Even a faint second line—and mine are definitely not faint—means you're knocked up.

"You idiot," I say, addressing myself and Greyson and maybe God too. "You big, stupid idiot."

I throw the cover on the toilet and fall down on it, hard, hand on my head. A hundred emotions slam into me with the force of a hurricane. Shock screaming loudest.

The kind of shock that rocks you to your core.

I'm shaking, full body tremors. My hand slides to my mouth.

It's not a sure thing, a voice inside my head says. *The tests could be wrong.*

But I know—in my gut, I just know—that I'm pregnant, and that my arrogant, dickhead boss is the father.

"Julia, sit down," Gracie says, brow furrowed as she pulls out a chair at a table toward the back of her coffee shop, Holy City Roasters. "You look really pale. Are you okay?"

I nod at the chair across from mine. Swallow the lump in my throat.

"You're gonna want to sit for this too."

"Uh-oh." Eva cuts me a glance. "The last time you said that, you were calling to tell me you'd met a French footballer at a discoteca and that the two of you were running away to live, and I quote, 'that fancy as fuck David Beckham life.'"

Olivia grins. "I've heard the stories about that guy."

I laugh, the tightness in my chest loosening the tiniest bit. I knew calling my girls was the right move, even if I do feel guilty for high jacking their Friday night. I met Gracie through my neighbor Elijah—she's his younger sister—but the two of us really became close when I was designing the interiors for her shop. Olivia, the author of *My Romp With the Rogue*, has been my friend since grad school.

Eva I've known forever. We met when I was home one summer from college, and we've been inseparable ever since. She's a pit master —a master of the barbecue pit, how cool is that?—and lives in Atlanta now. While she's not in Charleston all that often, she does come to visit her parents every once in a while. They own a cute barbecue place out on Sullivan's Island. Lucky for me, she's in town this weekend.

"Armand will always be the one that got away," I reply, sighing. "God, he was hot."

"I thought y'all barely talked," Eva says. "You barely spoke French, and he didn't know a word of English."

My smile grows wistful. "It was a magical time."

Gracie sets an iced coffee in front of me, milk swirling into the dark liquid. It's my usual order here at Holy City Roasters. I'm a coffee fiend—the kind that goes straight from bed to the coffee pot. I love the smell, the taste. The ritual of sitting down with the day's first cup.

But looking down at my coffee, fragrant and ice cold, I'm hit by an unpleasant realization. I don't know what the rules are exactly about drinking coffee when you're pregnant. But I can't imagine any doctor would recommend having a fourth cup of the day, especially at 8 P.M.

I feel short of breath. Like my lungs are gripped in an invisible fist. My eyes burn with tears.

Olivia runs a hand across my back. "Aw, sweetie, talk to us."

"Do you not like the coffee?" Gracie asks, clearly distressed.

I blink, taking a quick breath through my nose, and shake my head. "Coffee looks delicious. I just—" Another breath. Best to just come out with it. "I'm pregnant. Took the tests right before I called you guys."

Eva gasps. Olivia gapes.

A tear slips down my face, catching on my lips.

"But you told me things were quiet on the dating end lately," Gracie says. "That you weren't feeling your regulars."

I tug a hand through my hair. "That is true. But there's this guy I haven't told y'all about."

"Who?" Eva says. "Why haven't you told us?"

I wrap my fingers around my coffee, the condensation cool against my palm. Look down at it. My friends would never judge me.

But I still feel a pang of shame. I've been fucking my boss. Not only that. *Hate* fucking my boss, the two of us exchanging bodily fluids but rarely conversation. We meet, we screw, we smoke a cigarette. Then we go our separate ways.

I'm all for a hot, anonymous tryst. I'm a feminist lit professor with a lady boner for romance, for crying out loud. How could I not be into a woman seeking sexual satisfaction, no matter what that satisfaction looks like?

But now that a baby is involved, the scenario feels different. This is the father of my child we're talking about. Not some smoking hot French guy I fooled around with when I was a nineteen year old foreign exchange student. I feel like I should at least know something, *anything*, about the guy who knocked me up. Not for lack of trying. Whenever I ask about anything non-work related, Greyson stonewalls me.

He completely shuts me down.

So I know next to nothing about him, aside from his preference for Marlboro Lights and penchant for growly rudeness.

"He and I have a very...casual arrangement. I haven't mentioned it to you guys because"—I lift the cup, rotate it, drop it back on the table, careful not to spill the coffee—"we work together, and we don't want anyone to know."

"Wait." I feel the heat of Gracie's stare. "Is this someone you're working with on Luke's barn?"

I look up. Meet her eyes. "It is. Greyson Montgomery."

She gasps again. Louder this time.

No, not louder—it's just Eva gasping, too.

"What?" I ask, shooting her a worried look.

"Nothing. I just, um. I dated his brother, Ford, when we were younger."

"*The* Ford?" I say. "The one you pined after all through your twenties?"

Eva purses her lips and nods. "That's him. Guy was my first everything. Including my first heartbreak."

"Ooompf," Gracie says. "First one stays with you, doesn't it?"

"That one stayed with me for years," Eva replies. She turns back to me. "Anyway. I remember Greyson. A little serious, but a nice guy. He's protective of Ford. Really cute, too."

I scoff. "Nice guy? Eva, Greyson is a complete asshole."

Gracie blinks.

"I didn't know assholes were your kink."

"Me either. Alphaholes are totally not my trope of choice."

Gracie grins at the romance reference. Like me, she's been obsessed with romance lately. Specifically Olivia's yummy historicals.

"Greyson was always straight edge, but he wasn't a jerk," Eva says. "At least from what I can remember. I wonder what happened."

"No clue." I shrug. Swallow. "We were so careful."

Olivia reaches across the table and puts her hand on mine.

"I get that you just found out. But do you have any feelings either way?"

"About keeping it?" I sigh for what feels like the hundredth time. Try to make sense of the swirl of feelings and thoughts inside me. "Honestly, I don't know. I'm considering all my options."

"If I were in your shoes, I'd do the same," Olivia replies. "You remember when I got pregnant my first year in grad school."

"I didn't know that," Gracie says.

"Yup. It was with my boyfriend at the time—my first real boyfriend," she says, nodding at Eva. "We were young. Broke. I ended up not keeping the baby. We just weren't ready to be parents, you know? So I'm glad I had the choice."

I sip my coffee. Let out a breath. "I have to say that now that I'm in this position, I'm relieved the option is there. I mean—" I let out another breath. "Shit, y'all. We were *so careful*. I don't know how this happened. It sucks. Really, really sucks."

"Would you consider adoption?" Eva asks.

"To be honest, I don't think so. I get that it's a great option for some people. But if I'm going to keep the baby, I think—at this point in my life at least—I'd want to be the one to raise him or her."

Olivia reaches over to take my hand. "This is a big decision, Julia. I can't imagine how heavy it must feel to you, but I recognize how hard it is. You know we're your village, right? No matter what you decide, we'll support you one-hundred-percent. I'll hold your hand on the way to the clinic, same as I'll hold your hand while you're screaming for an epidural."

"Always," Gracie says. "No judgement from me."

"If I didn't judge you for your escapades with the French footballer, I'm certainly not going to judge you for this," Eva says with a smile.

"Thank you, guys. Seriously. I don't know much about having a baby, but I do know I can't do it alone."

"If you do decide to go the having-the-baby route, maybe you could try to find a community of moms-to-be," Olivia adds. "I know our yoga studio up on Spring Street offers prenatal classes. Probably a great way to meet other mamas."

A rush of heat behind my eyes.

My nose starts to run.

"Damn it," I say, wiping my eyes with my napkin. "Why do y'all have to be so fucking awesome?"

"Because we love you and we want to see you happy," Gracie replies.

In that moment, I know that no matter what I end up doing, I'll be okay. All because I have these supportive, open-minded, incredibly generous women in my life.

I'm lucky and privileged in more ways than I can count.

And yet I still don't know what the right call is here.

"I recognize that this isn't the end of the world," I say. "Yes, it sucks. But it could be much worse. I guess...I mean, I guess I just really like my life as it is right now. I don't feel like I'm missing anything. Would I like to be in love? Sure. Would I like to have a family? I mean, yes and no. Not with a guy like Greyson, that's for damn sure. I've always wanted kids in a 'maybe someday' kind of way."

Eva dips her head. "All valid points. I've never wanted to be a mother myself. The whole kid thing holds very little appeal to me."

"I can get that. Now that I actually have the chance to do the kid thing, though..." My eyes smart against a fresh wave of tears. "I don't know. I mean, am I ready to give up my freedom? Am I ready to be a single parent?"

Gracie rubs my back. "You have time to think about it. Are you going to tell Greyson?"

"Yeah. As terrible as that conversation is going to be, he deserves to know."

"He might surprise you," Olivia says.

"Doubtful. But I appreciate the thought." I look at Olivia. "By the way—and sorry for the change of subject, but since I'm thinking about it—the barn will definitely be ready in time for the date you guys had in mind. How's the wedding planning coming along?"

Olivia grins. "It's coming. But tonight is about you. You'll keep us updated on where your head's at, right? And you'll call if you need anything?"

"Of course." I manage a tight smile. "I know I keep saying this, but thank you. For understanding. And for not judging me."

Despite my friends' support, my thoughts still whirl on my walk home. I may be a free spirit, but that doesn't mean I'm reckless. French footballer aside, I am pretty intentional about the decisions I make. Especially the big ones. I always thought that if I had a baby—and that was always a big if—it'd be the result of years of careful planning. I'd bring that baby into the stable, loving home my partner and I had worked hard to build.

But maybe that's just it. Building that home requires sacrifice. It requires being tied down.

I'm not sure I ever want to make that kind of sacrifice. My dreams are important to me. I've worked hard to make them come true. How many of those dreams would I have to give up to have this baby?

Then again, how many new dreams would I create if I went the other way and kept him or her? Yeah, I'd be losing a lot. But maybe there's something to gain.

Something I haven't thought of yet.

Chapter Five

JULIA

A trip to the doctor's office the following week confirms the results of my at-home tests.

My OB-GYN sends me on my way with a literal bagful of literature. Breastfeeding and childbirth classes. A page-long list of fish you are and aren't allowed to eat. A pamphlet on options.

My head is spinning.

It's a beautiful fall day, the weather sunny and mild. My amazing TA, Irene, is handling my afternoon class, so I don't have to head back to work. I've always been a big walker; it's where I do some of my best thinking. When I get home, I cue up *My Romp With the Rogue* on my phone—I'm on my second read because I love it so much—pop in my earbuds, and head outside.

Outside Charlotte's bedchamber, Callum was still very much a monster. Growly. Rude. Impatient.

But in it?

In it, the man proved to be an altogether different creature.

They'd been married for weeks now, and he came to her chambers every night. And every night, it all felt thrillingly new.

Even now, buttering her toast the morning after he had her up against a wall, had her bent over her writing desk, and had her once more in the warmth of her bed, her toes curled at the memory of his ministrations.

He took charge, certainly. But he could also be tender. Generous.

Even kind.

It made Charlotte think there was a good man behind the mask.

Which begged the question—why did he hide behind it?

She nearly jumped when he appeared in the doorway. He was in breeches today, topped with a smart waistcoat that accentuated the breadth of his chest and shoulders.

She knew what he'd ask before the words left his mouth. His eagerness for an heir was obvious from the start.

"Any news?"

Charlotte shook her head. "Not yet. I shall inform you of any as soon as I have it myself."

"And your courses?"

Normally, she'd blush at discussing such personal matters with anyone, much less a man. But with Callum, it almost felt...natural.

Easy.

"No sign of them yet."

He fell heavily into the chair across the table from hers and reached for the toast.

"Why are you so eager?" she asked. "For an heir?"

Callum's eyes flicked to meet hers. "It was in the marriage contract. I must have an heir in order to inherit my uncle's land."

"I think there's more to it than that." She straightened, gathering her courage. "Your butler informed me your brother was your only sibling. Your mother died when you were young, and your father spent his life in London, leaving you behind in Scotland. Exactly how lonely were you?"

He went very still. Clouds gathering in his eyes.

"We do not speak of my brother in this house," he replied evenly. "I forbid it."

If only Charlotte were not drawn to forbidden things.

I walk for hours. Up East Bay. Across the Ravenel Bridge and back. Walk through my thoughts, parsing through fears, hopes, histories.

I end up standing in front of a familiar, four-story facade on Church Street in the South of Broad neighborhood.

The house I grew up in during my teenage years.

Daddy and I pored over paint samples for months before deciding on the white-on-white color scheme. Our inspiration had been a house in London's Notting Hill, which we'd photographed on one of our many trips to Europe over the years.

I take out my earbuds. My grief hits me square in the gut, leaving me breathless. I miss him. Every damn day. I was always close with my parents. But Daddy and I had a special bond. He was a well-known architect here in Charleston, and we were both obsessed with design. Specifically European design, and the travel and the history that came with it.

He was the best travel buddy, my biggest cheerleader, and my shoulder to cry on. Losing him was like losing a limb. I knew I'd never move in the world the same way again.

I grip the wrought iron gate guarding the driveway, trying to steady myself. Trying to breathe.

Squirrels dart across the lawn and climb up an old oak tree. The humid, salty smell of the ocean, just down the street, permeates everything.

I swallow the tightness in my throat. Heart racing.

What in the world am I going to do about this baby? This feels adult and scary in a way nothing else ever has. Not going away to college or getting a job or starting my own design business.

This is not at all the direction I imagined my life would take.

Then again, I'm thirty-four. I have the privileges of a great job with decent benefits, a healthy savings account I've worked for years to build, and an amazing support network. I've had plenty of time to experience the world on my own and achieve my goals. If I decide to have this kid, chances are I could provide the kind of life I want for her and for myself, too.

This pregnancy was unplanned. But in many ways, I am not unprepared.

Yes, this isn't how I imagined my experience of motherhood would play out. Namely, I thought I'd be doing this baby thing with a great, sexy, preferably bookish guy who adored me as much as I adored him, and who was committed to being an equal partner in all things. Parenthood included.

And yes, there's a chance Greyson will want to be involved. But even if he is, can I count on him to be that equal partner? How would we co-parent when we can hardly look at each other without engaging in verbal fisticuffs (shout out to historical romance for making that word a regular part of my vocabulary)?

Bottom line: am I ready to take on single parenting? Yes, I have a village that is ready and willing to help out. But at the end of the day, it will just be me and this baby against the world. I won't have a partner to take over diaper duty in the middle of the night after I'm exhausted from a feeding. I don't have a parent to offer advice or just *be* there when I've had it or my nipples are bleeding or I'm out of coffee.

Doing this alone is going to be fucking hard.

The hardest thing I've ever done.

I'm scared.

But I've done enough scary things in my life to know that sometimes being frightened is a good thing. It means you're taking a chance. Doing something that's risky and big. You're diving into life headfirst. Diving into *experience*.

As a woman of appetite—for food and liquor and the occasional cigarette, yes, but also for knowledge, for late nights and literature and *feeling* and family—I am all for experience.

Blinking, I look up at my parents' house. I'm flooded by all the memories this place holds. The big stuff—graduations, birthdays, holidays—and the little ones, too. How Mom would make blueberry muffins from a box on Saturday mornings, making the whole house smell like sugar and butter. Her sitting at the counter with me, hiding her wine in a Solo cup while walking me through my long division homework. Dad playing music in the living room, the three of us dancing to Sir Elton, Springsteen, Melissa Etheridge (he went through a Lilith Fair phase in the late-nineties.)

I *miss* that.

The sense of belonging.

It hits me that maybe this baby is my chance at building a new family. At recreating that belonging, just with someone new.

Someone I created.

It's what Lady Charlotte was implying when she asked Callum why he wanted an heir so badly—that he'd lost his family and wanted to create a new one. That he was lonely, and searching for a sense of belonging.

Taking a deep breath, I turn and start walking again. I walk and I think. I *am* in a place where I can raise this baby how I want to. I could give her a good life in a loving, secure, stable home.

I also have the means, the resources, and the support to (hopefully) enjoy motherhood myself. Again, things that are important to *my* decision making process. I have great insurance and really good doctors. Solid maternity leave at my job. A job that pays me enough to cover quality child care when I go back to work. I've already achieved a lot of what I set out to do in my career. I've traveled, I've had a *great* time. I've gotten to meet incredible people.

I am one lucky bitch with a lot to share. And share it I do, with my students, the charities and causes I support, and my community.

If I chose to, I could share it with a baby, too.

I have no sentimental notions about motherhood. But the more I think about where I'm at and who I've become, the more I'm starting to believe this baby thing could actually be fun. Hard, yes. Exhausting, totally. But how cool would it be to teach her how to read? To love her and learn who she is, what she's passionate about, her likes and dislikes? Travel with her, even?

How cool would it be to take the idea of motherhood and make it my own? Do it my own way, because I can?

I'd be giving up a lot to have this kid.

But the flip side of that equation is that I'd be gaining a lot, too.

A family. The privilege of experiencing the world through a new set of eyes.

Yeah, having a kid without a dedicated partner is not what I thought I'd be doing at this point in my life. It's going to be a struggle to let go of what I'd hoped my path would look like and embrace how things will actually shake out.

There's no telling if this path is any better or worse than others I could have taken.

But that doesn't mean it's not the right path.

That doesn't mean I won't find happiness on it. And who knows, maybe Grey will want to be involved in the baby's life. Maybe he'll actually want to be the super invested co-parent I'm looking for. Both my parents were very involved in my life from the start. They showed up to almost everything: tennis matches, spelling bees, birthday parties. I'd love for my son or daughter to have both parents be involved that way, too.

I'd love for this baby to have a special relationship with his or her father, the way I had a special relationship with mine. It made my life infinitely richer.

In fact, if Greyson does want to be involved—and that's a big if—maybe I should tell him that. I should make that my expectation: that he's as invested in this baby's upbringing as I'll be. Seems only fair. The more upfront I am about what I hope for from him, the easier things will be going forward. I imagine co-parenting is a minefield, even with solid communication. Best to get in the habit of being honest from the start.

If Greyson doesn't want to be involved, well...then I'll deal with it. The baby will have plenty of adoring aunties to make up for not having a daddy.

My heart pops around inside my chest.

I'm still not totally sure about keeping this baby. But I am definitely leaning that way.

One thing I am totally sure about? How fucking dismayed Greyson is going to be when I tell him. I've seen firsthand how a control freak like him responds to unexpected news.

Not well.

Whatever. I'm not responsible for his reaction, same as I'm not responsible for fixing his jerk-off behavior.

That's on him.

Either way, I have to tell him.

Taking a deep breath, I shoot him a text.

Chapter Six

GREYSON

Julia: I need to talk to you. Can you come to my place tonight?

Greyson: What's going on

Greyson: youve never invited me over before

Julia: We need to talk in person.

Greyson: Are you ok?

Greyson: Something happen at the barn

Julia: Everything is fine at the barn. My address is 23 Longitude Lane. It's the apartment above the garage. House with blue shutters. I should be home by 7.

Greyson: Have a ton of research to do. Will be in the office until 8:30 or so

Greyson: I'll be downtown

Greyson: I can come after

Greyson: You sure you're ok?

Julia: 8:30 works.

I know something's up because Julia never gave me a straight answer to my "are you okay" question. I dwell on it more than I should throughout the afternoon.

Is she going to quit? Have I finally pushed her over the edge? I thought we worked decently well together, despite disagreeing on almost everything.

Have we given each other an STD? Not likely, considering we always use condoms. But I guess there's always a chance.

Whatever's going on, I need to know what it is, and I need to know that Julia's okay.

I'm running late from the office—I'm never late to work events, but personal stuff is a different story—and I'm at her door at quarter after nine.

Julia lives on a cute little lane not far from my condo on South Adger's Wharf. Her place is an old carriage house set above a double garage.

I knock on Julia's door with the outside of my fist. I slide my phone back into my pocket, taking care not to crush the pack of cigarettes I have in there too.

I'm about to knock again when the door opens. Julia glances up at me. She's channeling Joni Mitchell tonight in a straw hat and flared jeans with holes in the knees.

She looks drawn. Eyes swollen and a little red, like she's been crying.

My heart dips. I put my hand on the door, opening it wider as I take a step toward her.

"What is it?" I ask, eyes locked on hers.

Her eyes move to my chest. Move back up to my face. She tilts her head. "Come in. We need to talk."

I close the door behind me, heart thumping as I follow Julia inside.

The place is tiny but impeccably decorated. There's a galley kitchen to my left and a living room to the right.

Julia nods at the sofa in the living room. "Please, have a seat."

Sinking into her cushy velvet sofa, I cross my ankle over my knee and hold my hand there. Julia takes a seat in the chair across from me, setting a glass bottle—*Topo Chico, Mexican Sparkling Water*, the label reads—on the glass coffee table between us.

Something about the water makes my gut prickle with ice. Julia strikes me as the type to finish the day with something stronger.

"I'm pregnant," she says, right on cue. "I haven't been with anyone besides you, so...yeah. Baby's yours."

My heart trips to a stop.

For a second my vision contracts.

I'm a partner at a venture capital firm. Before that, I worked in private equity and investment banking. I know stress. Usually I can growl my way through it.

But this? I don't know where the hell to begin with this.

I am careful. I don't make mistakes often. When I do, though—

They're big. Case in point.

How could I be so careless? How could I knock up the employee I should've avoided but slept with instead?

What the fuck what the fuck what the everloving *fuck*?

"Julia," I stammer. Unsure what else to say.

She blinks, looking away. "I thought you should know. Trust me, no one was more shocked than I was when I took those tests. And when the doctor confirmed it..."

Another wave of emotion. The thought of Julia being by herself when she got the news—not once, but twice—makes me irrationally angry.

"You went to the doctor without me?"

"I did," she says. "I wasn't sure what to expect. I sure as hell wasn't ready to deal with your wrath."

The edge of my cigarette pack pokes into my ass. I'm hit by an acute need for nicotine.

"I would've gone with you," I growl. Proving her point, but whatever. "You shouldn't have had to do that alone. I'm sorry."

Her eyebrows pop up. "I'm perfectly capable of dealing with this baby on my own."

I run my hand across the back of my neck. I'm sweating.

"I know you are. No one is more capable than you, Julia. But I would've liked to have gone with you. I'm sorry I wasn't there."

I should apologize for more than that. But my tongue feels like stone in my mouth.

I'm totally out of my depth here. Over the past three years I've built a stone wall around my heart, as much to keep people out as to keep myself inside. The barrier is there for good reason.

Then this happens.

How the fuck am I supposed to keep boundaries clear—keep Julia at arm's length, keep from hurting her—if she's pregnant with my kid?

"I tried as best as I could to be careful," I say. "I swear I would never, ever be careless with you, Julia."

"We weren't planning this. Obviously. But I'm thinking—" She swallows, her expression softening. "I think I'm going to keep it. The baby."

Sweat breaks out everywhere. Along my scalp and spine.

My heart is beating inside my face, threatening to split it open like the skin of a ripe tomato.

I am not against babies in general. My brother has a three year old daughter who's got me wrapped around her little finger. But *having* a baby myself—with Julia—starting a family—

I don't do those things. Not because I don't want them. But because they're not meant for me. I had the fairy tale, and I walked away from it. I'm the bad guy in this story. Not the hero.

Bad guys don't get happy endings.

"It doesn't make sense to me either," she continues, offering me a tight smile. "I'll be honest, I still haven't fully sorted out my reasons. But I just feel this...this tug. This tiny, tiny tug pulling me over to the dark side."

"The dark side?"

She laughs. "Motherhood."

I scoff. Her smile loosens ever so slightly.

"Anyway." She straightens. "I know I just dropped a bomb on you, and I don't need answers right away. I don't expect or need you to be involved in the baby's life. Like I said, I'm totally capable of taking care of him or her on my own."

"Julia, let me stop you—"

"Please," she says, holding up a hand. "Let me finish. I've got plenty of amazing support, financial or otherwise. But if you are interested in being involved, I want to be clear about what my expectations would be. I'm looking for a true partner—a co-parent who'll shoulder a fair share of the responsibility of raising this baby. I ask that you show up and be there for her the same way I will. That you're just as invested in raising her as I am. Both feet or none at all kind of thing. I'm not playing that game where I force you to grow up or show up. I don't need the hassle or disappointment, and neither does this baby."

My hand tightens around the back of my neck. Yeah, I may be scared shitless, but I'm not a deadbeat. It hurts that Julia would ever think I'd leave her to deal with this mess on her own.

If I'm going to be a dad, even if this whole thing is a terrible surprise, I'm going to do it right. I've never done anything halfway in my life. And my own parents are pretty damn amazing role models. I've always wanted to live up to them.

I want to do the right thing here. For the baby. For Julia.

Then again, what is the right thing when you ruin every good thing you touch?

I still have to try. I've worked hard over the past few years to provide for my family.

I'll work harder to provide for this baby.

I go with the most obvious, if most painful, solution.

"I'm in. One hundred percent. Should we—" I clear my throat. "Get married?"

A look of horror crosses Julia's face. "*No.*"

I'm surprised to find I'm offended by her emphatic refusal, even though part of me is also incredibly relieved.

I already fucked up one marriage. The thought of entering another, even for altruistic reasons, makes my skin itch with imaginary hives.

"I'm sorry. That came out wrong," she explains, taking a sip of water. "I just meant that I'm a romantic at heart, and if I ever do get married, I want it to be because I'm crazy in love, not because I got knocked up."

A stab inside my chest. My hand slides from my neck to the offending spot just above my breastbone.

I know all about getting married for the wrong reasons.

"I understand," I say. "I just want you to know that I'm all in, Julia. I take care of my own, and our baby will be no exception."

I always, always put my family first. Especially after what I did to them. I have many sins to atone for.

"Greyson." She looks at me and frowns. "You should really take some time to think about this. The weekend at least. It's a huge decision. And I don't want to get my hopes up if—"

"I don't need time. If you're in, so am I."

Julia's still looking at me. Eyes getting wet again.

"You're going to be a real partner?" she says. "The co-parent I told you I'm looking for?"

"Yes."

She puts a hand on her face. Blinks. "Okay then."

I'm gripped by the wild desire to take that hand in mine. I can't imagine what she's been through over the past week.

But I can't reach for her like that. She's not mine to have. Never was. I can support her, and be there for this kid. But I can't be her *person*. I'll fuck it up. And fucking it up has bigger consequences all of a sudden. I won't just be hurting Julia; I'll be hurting my kid, too.

A kid who didn't ask to be here. I will not put my relationship with him or her at risk.

I clear my throat. "Where does that leave us?"

Julia takes a breath. Lets it out.

"You mean are we still going to fuck in the backseat of your car?" She tilts her head. "I think you'll agree it's probably best if we refrain from the hate sex for the time being."

It's the right call. Even if we didn't end our arrangement, how could it be just sex knowing there's a baby involved?

Doesn't mean I'm not disappointed. Epic sex is hard to come by.

I nod. "Okay. You'll let me know when your next doctor's appointment is? I'd like to be there."

"You don't—"

"I'd like to be there," I repeat. "If you want to go alone, fine. Well. Not fine, but I'll respect your wishes. If you'd let me tag along, however, I would very much like to go with you."

Julia meets my eyes. Hers a little puzzled, like she doesn't quite know what to make of me. "Okay. Okay, yeah, sure. My head is swimming right now. But my next appointment happens to be my first ultrasound. They'll measure the baby and make sure everything's all right. Take some pictures and see exactly how far along I am in my pregnancy."

Her pregnancy.

The words hit me like a ton of bricks. Shit just got real.

We're going to have a baby.

I'm going to be a daddy.

Jesus take the wheel, 'cause I have no fucking idea what I'm doing.

"I never asked when you're due," I say.

"June twenty-third."

A smile tugs at my lips. "That's my mom's birthday."

"Really?" Julia asks, grinning.

It's the first time she's smiled all night—I'm good at making her smile when we're naked, but when we're dressed it's an entirely different story—and for half a second my heart swells.

Don't.

But I do. I let her smile make me feel better. Like an idiot.

"My mom will be thrilled," I say. Which is true. My parents really are awesome, and they'll be over the moon about having another grandbaby. I'm not sure how they'll feel about my relationship, or complete lack thereof, with Julia. But it's too late to go back and change how it all went down now.

"Does your family live here in Charleston?"

"They do," I say. "My parents live in Ansonborough—Wentworth Street—and my brother lives over on Queen, near Harleston Village."

Julia's grin grows wistful. "Must be nice having everyone so close."

"It is. Although sometimes it gets a little intense. We see a decent amount of each other. I work a lot, so that tends to get in the way of family time."

"Always so busy," she says, eyes on my face.

We look at each other for a beat. Then another. Her eyes are still swollen, but they're brighter now than when I first arrived.

My God is she a beautiful girl. I'd really, really like to pull her onto my lap right now and make her feel better the only way I know how. It's been a week since we fucked last—not that I'm counting—and I'm craving her. Her scent and her honesty and her surrender.

I'm always craving this woman.

I spear a hand through my hair instead. Doing my best to ignore the sudden heaviness in my groin. My dick is what got us here in the first place.

Must. Ignore.

Lord Jesus, when are you gonna take this wheel?

"Next appointment. I'll be there. Let me know when it is," I grunt.

"Okay," Julia says, smoothing the fabric of her leggings over her thighs. "It's on my calendar. I'll double check and get back to you."

Those thighs. They were wrapped around me on Wednesday, all smooth skin and strong muscle, Julia's head falling back as I rocked into her tight, hot cunt. My teeth on her nipple, her fingernails in my back, my thumb on her clit.

She was pregnant. We just didn't know it yet.

"I should go," I say, standing abruptly. I need a cigarette. Possible castration as well. This woman makes me regress into a horn-dog teen with blackout level desire, and I need some air if I'm going to stick to our no-hate-sex agreement.

Julia stands, too. Leads me to the door, wrapping her arms around her chest. She winces.

"You okay?" I ask, stopping with my hand on the knob.

"I'm fine. My boobs are just really sore. And my nipples are, like, these spirals of icy death when I get cold."

"Oh. Wow. That sounds...intense." It hits me that I haven't asked how she's feeling. Fuck me, I'm a douchecanoe. "How are you feeling? Aside from the White Walker nipples."

Julia's grin is back, and it is doing things to me.

"You watch *Game of Thrones*?"

"Yes. How are you feeling?"

She lifts a shoulder. "All right. Just this low-grade garbage-y feeling that is a not-so-nice reminder that something is off. No real nausea, although that isn't supposed to peak until week eight or nine. We think I'm only six weeks along, so we'll see. Otherwise, I feel a little bloated. And tired. Really, really tired."

"Anything I can do? Anything you need?"

Another tight smile. "At this point, I think it's just about muscling through."

"If you need anything—"

"I told you. I can take care of myself."

"I know you can. But if you want help, I'm here."

The look in her eyes softens. "All right."

"Okay."

I'm not okay. I'm fucked.

But as one beat passes, then another, our eyes locked, the silence between us swelling with feeling, I forget why I'm setting myself up to fail.

Julia blinks, breaking the spell. I clear my throat and turn the knob. Can't do a hug or even a handshake. I don't trust myself right now.

"Don't forget to let me know when the appointment is," I say, opening the door.

She nods, tucking her hair behind her ear. "I'll text you."

"Goodnight, Julia."

"'Night."

Closing the door behind me, I let out a breath. My cigarettes are burning a hole in my back pocket. I'll go to Ford's. While I don't exactly feel like talking, I definitely don't feel like being alone.

I need some company. Advice. An exorcism if this half chub doesn't go *away* already.

Because I'm a masochist, I glance over my shoulder one last time. My eyes catch on the narrow window beside the door. Julia is still standing in the foyer. Her throat works as she swallows, pulling her hat off her head.

Her blonde waves are wilder than ever.

My heart clenches. She's struggling.

I'm whipping around and reaching for the doorknob before I even know what I'm doing. But then Julia is straightening her shoulders, her chest rising on a deep inhale.

I still want to go to her.

Don't.

I lean my forehead against the door. Mimicking her deep breath as I try to still the herd of galloping horses inside my chest.

An hour ago, I lived my life in black and white. I had a solid grasp of right and wrong. I had control over my world. The people in it.

Now, though, I can't tell up from down.

Balling my hands into fists, I force myself to turn around and leave.

Chapter Seven

GREYSON

I let myself into my brother's house, leaning down to pick up a doll—the scary looking one that pees after she "drinks" her bottle, Bryce's unfortunate favorite—left by the front door. Ford is in the kitchen in sweats and a t-shirt, banging away on a laptop.

"I told you I'd work through the Moore Foods model," I say, tossing the doll into the overflowing toy bin beside the table. "Put it away. Isn't it past your bedtime?"

Ford glances up at me and grins. "Three year olds go to bed at seven. I try to make it to eleven. Besides, I'm better at models than you are."

"Baby go down okay?"

"She's still got that little head cold, so she was cranky. But once she was out, she was dead to the world."

"The antibiotics are working, then."

Ford leans back, crossing his arms. "You know you're going to destroy any shot Bryce has at a healthy, independent adulthood with your helicopter uncle-ing, right?"

"Look, I may not be around all that much, but it's my way of showing I give a fuck—keeping up with how y'all are doing."

Ford's wife Rebecca died from cancer not long after Bryce was born. I immediately stepped up in a way that I could—we agreed that I'd take the helm at Montgomery Partners while Ford worked part-time. I wanted him to be able to grieve and take care of his then-infant daughter without worrying about deadlines or project management or fundraising.

It's an arrangement that we've kept to this day. Ford's been bugging me a bit for more responsibility. But I'm not sure he's ready yet, and I'm happy to cover for him in the meantime. Even if it does mean working eighty or ninety hour weeks.

Work is what I do. It's what I'm good at.

It's how I can give back to the family that's given so much to me.

Working this much means I don't see Bryce as often as I'd like to. But I try to have dinner with her and Ford at least once a week, and I see them at Sunday supper at my parents'.

I'm crazy about that little girl. She's opinionated, stubborn, and a master of looks that kill. Just like me.

I couldn't be prouder.

"As long as I'm still her favorite, I don't care." I hold up my Marlboros and nod at the back patio. "I need to talk to you."

"Everything okay?" he says, raising his eyebrows.

"Not by a long shot."

He gets to his feet with a groan. "I'll get the whiskey."

I'm already on my second cigarette when Ford steps out onto the patio, careful to close the door softly behind him. He's got two tumblers of brown liquor in the fingers of one hand and a baby monitor in the other.

He sets a tumbler on the railing by my elbow, glancing at my cigarette.

"You're going to quit, right?" He takes a sip from his glass. "The cigarettes. Punishing yourself."

I grunt in reply.

"We were happy to let you have your vices at first, but it's been three years, Grey. Don't you think it's time to give up the ghost?"

I draw hungrily on my cigarette and let out a steady stream of smoke. "Nope."

Sighing, Ford leans his elbows on the railing. The city is quiet around us. The autumn bite in the air feels good on my skin.

"Did you see Cameron today?" he asks softly.

My gut contracts. Always does at the mention of my ex-wife's name.

I reach for my whiskey and take a healthy pull. Fire spreads down my throat and through my chest, loosening the tightness there.

"I didn't. But I did find out I got Julia Lassiter pregnant."

Ford drops his whiskey on the railing with a *thump*. His stare burns a hole in the side of my head. I take another drag, feeling dizzy. Did I eat tonight? I try to remember, but everything before *I'm pregnant* is a blur.

"The designer on the Rodgers' Farms project?"

"That's the one."

"Our employee."

"Technically she's Luke Rodgers' employee. But yeah. Same one."

"The woman you're constantly complaining about?"

"Yes."

"The one you're always growling at."

"I growl at a lot of people."

"Not as much as you growl at her." A stunned pause. "Wow. Wow, it actually makes a sick kind of sense. She's the only person, man or woman, I've ever seen go toe to toe with you so often, and so...passionately. Y'all were fucking the whole time, weren't you? There's that saying—the one Mom always uses—that love and hate are two sides of the same coin." He scoffs. "Jesus, how did I not see it sooner?"

Another pull of bourbon. "Baby's due in June. She's keeping it."

My throat suddenly feels tight.

I still can't believe I'm going to be a daddy.

Me. The control freak. The broody asshole.

The marked man.

Ford puts a hand on my arm. He's too smart to say shit like *it's going to be okay*, because he knows better.

Still. The small gesture makes me feel slightly less like dying.

I'm the big brother. I look out for Ford, not the other way around. It's really nice, though, having him here.

"You know I'm going to be a helicopter uncle now too. Just to bust your balls."

I scoff. Tamp out my cigarette in the heavy glass ashtray I brought over the day I left Cameron. Ford gives my arm a squeeze before dropping his hand.

"So are you and Julia, like, together, or...I mean, how are y'all going to work this out?"

I lean my forearms against the railing and dig my thumbs into my eye sockets.

"I don't know," I say quietly. "Ford, I don't know what to do."

Ford lets out a breath. "Been a spell since I heard those words from you, Grey."

"No shit. This is new territory for me. Care to offer any fatherly wisdom?"

"Well, for starters, what are you afraid of? Aside from the obvious holy-shit-I'm-going-to-be-responsible-for-a-human-being thing. Which, don't get me wrong, is a big deal. But I know it's not responsibility that makes Greyson Montgomery piss his pants."

I sigh, feeling a familiar pinch in my neck and shoulders. For so long I've been scary good at pushing aside the guilt and the hurt leftover from my divorce so I can take care of Ford. Bryce. Our business.

Pure, gun-to-my-head survival mode.

It's served me well. But now—

Now I'm not so sure what my next move should be.

"I'm scared of failing again," I say. "Of fucking up. Royally. The way I did with Cameron."

Fucking up any relationship I might have with Julia. Fucking up this fatherhood thing.

"Grey. You fell out of love with someone. It happens."

"I didn't just fall out of love. I destroyed someone's life. Cameron was ready to have kids, for Christ's sake. We had everything."

"And you were miserable. You knew you didn't love her enough, you knew she deserved someone who was crazy about her. So you did what you thought was right. And it was the right call—leaving. Even if it didn't feel like it at the time. She was a nice girl. But she wasn't good for you."

I press my thumbs more firmly against my closed eyes, making bursts of color break out against the backs of my eyelids.

"I'm a quitter, Ford. A liar. I made a promise, and I broke it. People like that don't get another shot."

I hear the ice in his whiskey clink against the glass. "So you think what? Karma is going to swoop in and cut you down if you allow yourself a little happiness? If you give yourself another shot at love?"

"I never said anything about love," I growl. "I'm in lust with Julia. That's it. And yeah. Yeah, what if that's true? What if I get my heart ripped out because I ripped out Cameron's? Or worse, what if the weight of my fuck up lands on the person I want? What if she gets hurt, or the baby does? I swear, Ford, I'm going to wreck myself or wreck her or wreck all three of us. I am the fucking drunk driver of relationships."

Ford lets out a bark of laughter. "Strong metaphor there, Shakespeare. Your mind works in *very* weird ways."

"Fuck you."

"Ever consider that you've already had your heart ripped out? Slowly, over the course of your marriage? You fell out of love with Cameron. Which hurts. But she's not blameless. Same as you're not some trigger happy Tybalt, bound to destroy everything you touch."

"Tybalt? What? Who are you?"

"The guy who paid attention in English class, dickface," Ford replies crisply. "Arguably, *Romeo and Juliet* has no one true bad guy. But if there was, Tybalt would be a strong contender. The point I'm trying to make is maybe you've paid your dues. Maybe you've suffered enough. Hell, you signed the papers years ago, Grey. You've been punishing yourself for longer than that. That's a lot of heaviness to carry around. Ever think it's not fate that's holding you hostage, but *you*? What if you're the one holding the proverbial gun to your head? Not karma. Not destiny. You. You've punished yourself enough. Put the gun down, Grey."

Tugging my thumbs over my eyelids, I straighten, blinking away the blur.

Don't I wish I could put the gun down. Even if I could—even if I could forgive myself and let my past go and let people in—would Julia let *me* in? Do I even want her to?

We're so different.

And it's been so long since I've had any kind of real relationship, platonic or otherwise, with a woman outside of work. Would we be better co-parents as acquaintances rather than friends or fuck buddies? What if friends turns into something more? Our chemistry is hit-of-heroin level insane. Bad for you—so fucking bad—but *so* fucking good.

It's just the *more* that gets me.

I don't want to risk *more* for all the reasons I just told Ford.

But what would I be missing out on if I didn't take that risk? What would I deprive my kid and her mother of by holding back? Would Julia consider more with me? She said point blank she's a romantic at heart.

This is not a romantic start to a relationship, that's for damn sure.

I finish my whiskey in a single gulp.

"Think about it, all right? Forgiving yourself," Ford says, shooting me a meaningful glance.

I grunt in reply. "The baby news stays between us for now."

"Of course. But you know Mom is going to shit a brick when she finds out. She's going to be so excited. And so...surprised."

Scoffing, I look out over Ford's backyard, strewn with Little Tikes everything. I don't have a yard at all. Where's my kid going to play?

I make a mental note to call my realtor, Vanessa. Ask her to put out some feelers for a new place with enough space for a swing set and maybe a soccer net.

I can't provide my kid with married parents. But I am able to provide in other ways. I've got money. Lots of it. Julia asked me to be invested in this baby's upbringing. What better way to do that than raising him or her in a real home with a real backyard and space to grow?

"Because I haven't given Mom and Dad enough surprises," I say.

"Shut up." Ford nudges me. "This is a good surprise. Mom's going to want to meet her, you know. Julia. Like, yesterday."

"I know." I grab my cigarettes and slide them into my back pocket. I'm going to regret that last one tomorrow morning at the gym.

"I imagine this was a shock for Julia, too. You should send her something."

I raise a brow.

"Flowers. Fruit. Something to let her know you're thinking of her. Rebecca had a really shitty time of it during her first trimester. It's hard for you, but it's harder for Julia. Don't forget that."

"Right," I say, nodding. "Okay. Good call. Thanks for listening. And for the whiskey."

"No problem." Ford glances at the baby monitor. "Bryce's gonna be bummed to know Uncle Grey was here and she didn't get to play with you."

"Tell her I'll be by on Friday. Y'all still down for dinner?"

"You don't have to bring dinner."

"I'll try to make it by six, although I won't be able to stay long because I've got an eight o'clock meeting."

"Who schedules an eight o'clock meeting on a Friday night?"

"I do. Only slot I had left for the weekend. Someone's got to pay the bills."

Ford sighs. "You know, I can—"

"I got it. Y'all just text me what y'all want to eat."

"Thank you. And Grey?"

"Yeah?"

"You're going to be a great dad."

The breath catches in my throat. I swallow.

"Thanks," I say.

Even though I don't believe it. Not for one fucking second.

Chapter Eight

JULIA

Julia: You sent me a lemon tree.

Greyson: I did

Greyson: Do you not like it? I thought you could use the lemons. Put them in your topo chico because you can't drink and that sucks

Julia: It does suck. But the lemons make it suck a little less. Thank you.

Greyson: how are you feeling?

Julia: All right. No white walker nipples to report lately, so that's a plus.

Greyson: The night watch salutes you.

Greyson: doctor's appt Tuesday after next, right?

Greyson: have it on my schedule 2 PM

Julia: Yes. I'll send you the address.

Greyson: thanks for letting me tag along

Julia: Thank you for the tree. Very un-dickish of you. Almost sweet. I'm not quite sure what to think of it, to be honest.

Greyson: that makes two of us

Julia: BTW. Your texts are SO unlike you in person. You're such a perfectionist. So intentional about everything. But you fire off texts without a filter. Or a quick spell check.

Greyson: no time for spell check in texts

Greyson: I just send them as I go. more efficient that way as I get hundreds of them a day on top of calls

Greyson: you're also kind of different in texts. You fly by the seat of your pants in life. But your texts are v polished

Julia: It's the lit professor in me. Can't help it. Proper punctuation is kind of a kink of mine.

Greyson: interesting kink

Julia: Not as interesting as yours.

File this under things no one tells you about being pregnant: it's *hard*.

At least that's been my (admittedly limited) experience so far.

Even though it was a surprise, I'm grateful that I was able to get pregnant. I know not everyone is that lucky. But man, I am not enjoying the experience. At all. In fact, I'd go so far as to say it's downright awful.

So much more awful than I thought it'd be. I'm only seven-ish weeks in, but I can already tell this motherhood thing is not for the faint of heart.

Physically, I feel...not great, but not super ill, either. It's like having a perpetual hangover I keep hoping to sleep off but can't.

The exhaustion is crushingly constant. I am a walking zombie during the day, and can barely make it past 7 or 8 P.M. before falling into bed, too tired to even read. And yet I wake up most nights, usually a little past midnight, and I'm unable to go back to sleep. It's horrible.

My nausea has gotten much worse. I always feel like I'm on the verge of losing whatever my last meal was all over the floor. Which is totally awesome when you're in the middle of a lecture in front of thirty five students.

But it's the mental piece of the puzzle that's been especially tough. I've been walking around in a fog. It's like some alien life force has invaded my brain, hijacking my moods and my ability to manage them. I've never experienced depression before, so I didn't even recognize the symptoms until I googled them (the internet has simultaneously become my best friend and worst enemy these days): huge spikes in anxiety so severe it borders on paranoia. Insomnia. Relentless feelings of being overwhelmed and helpless.

Turns out prenatal depression is a real thing, and I definitely have it.

I'm lucky to have a great therapist on speed dial. She's helped me come up with some coping strategies. Regular walks, time with close friends, plenty of rest. I'm taking it one day at a time, crossing my fingers and toes this mental and physical fog clears up in the supposedly magical second trimester. If there's one thing I have heard about pregnancy and babies, it's that no phase lasts forever.

Right now, it's all about getting through to the other side.

The other side of what—this trimester? This pregnancy? All the unknowns in my life?—I couldn't say.

I can say I was not at all prepared for how difficult the experience has been. Isolating, too. I'm waiting to hit that all-important 12 week mark to tell people about the baby, as that's when the chance of miscarriage decreases significantly. Until then, I'm kind of forced to suffer in nauseated silence.

It's Thursday, and my classes don't wrap up until after five. I'm scheduled to have a meeting with Luke and our contractor at Rodgers' Farms this evening—countertops, backsplashes, and plumbing fixtures all went in late last week, and I need to check on progress—but I am beyond wiped. My mood took a nosedive at lunch and never really recovered. And no matter what I munch on, the simmering roil in my stomach won't go away.

I know if I attempt the forty minute drive out to Wadmalaw Island, especially at rush hour, I'll fall asleep at the wheel and/or throw up all over myself.

I may not always be on time, but I never back out last minute. I feel terrible as I call our contractor and Luke to tell them I won't be by. Gracie immediately calls back, asking if I need anything.

"Do you have any experience with mercy killings?" I say. "You know, Old Yeller style?"

I can hear the smile in her voice when she replies. "Hang in there, friend. Luke's been growing a few varieties of mint here on the farm.

I'll put it in my favorite tea blend and drop it off in the morning. Maybe it'll help soothe your stomach."

Just when I think I'm off the hook, my phone starts to ring again.

My gut clenches when I see Greyson Montgomery's name on the screen.

Just my luck. No doubt he was planning to be at tonight's meeting. And no doubt he's going to ream me out for cancelling it.

Just like the dick he is.

A surge of anger moves through me. Yeah, he was sorta-kinda sweet when I told him about the pregnancy. The lemon tree was thoughtful, too. But he's been the same old Greyson at work. Abrupt. Aloof. Growly.

I slide my thumb across the screen, stiffening my spine in preparation for battle.

"This is Julia," I say.

"Hey." His voice is gruff. "How the hell—"

"Don't you *dare*," I say, my throat thickening. I wish I didn't cry when I get angry, but I usually do. My haywire hormones certainly aren't helping. "Don't you dare do this right now. You have no idea how terrible I feel about cancelling the meeting, but this pregnancy is kicking my ass. I can't sleep, so I'm a barely functioning narcoleptic during the day. And the fact that they call it morning sickness is a joke. I have it all day, every day, and I spend most of my time offering to sell my soul to whoever'll take it just so I can keep down what I eat. And did I mention the depression? That's been a fun little cherry on top of this shit sundae. I'm dealing with all of that, plus teaching a full course load while also juggling the Rodgers' Farms project. I am trying my best, Greyson. I really am. But I just don't feel well enough to drive all the way out to the farm tonight. I had no idea I'd be this sick or this tired. But I rescheduled the meeting with Ken and Luke for first thing Monday morning, and I had Gracie send me some pictures of the progress to make sure there were no glaring issues that needed to be addressed. I have it under control. Just like I always do. So back the fuck off."

A pause.

Hot, rage-y tears leak out of my eyes left and right.

"I was calling to ask how the hell you're feeling," he says at last. "I know you wouldn't cancel a meeting unless something was seriously wrong. I called because I'm worried about you, Julia."

My stomach dips. Hard.

Hard enough for me to jump to my feet and scurry to the sink, afraid I'm going to puke.

Greyson called not to be a dick, but to check in on me?

To make sure I'm okay?

The idea makes my eyes fill with tears all over again.

A different kind.

"Why didn't you tell me?" he continues. "About the depression? And the sickness? I had no fucking idea."

It's my turn to pause.

"Because. You haven't asked. And because we decided we'd be co-parents. We said nothing about being friends. Or confidants. Honestly, I didn't think you'd care."

He growls, but this one is different. Anguished, almost.

"Of course I care. I..."

I blink.

"Where are you now?" he asks, letting out a breath.

I blink again. "What?"

"Where are you?"

"I'm at home. Why?"

"Have you eaten?"

Another stomach dip.

"I haven't," I say carefully.

My eyes catch on the cute little lemon tree on the counter beside the sink.

"Would dinner make you feel worse or better right now?"

My eyes move to my narrow pantry door. I was planning on saltines slathered in Skippy—chunky, not smooth—for dinner.

Real food would probably be better.

Yeah. Much better.

"Better. I think."

"I'll be there in an hour. Craving anything in particular?"

My heart thumps. What the hell is happening?

Greyson and I have never eaten a meal together.

Hell, we've never had a real conversation. I guess we had half of one the other night about my pregnancy. But we've never had an in-depth talk, much less over dinner.

Which, up until now, seemed totally normal. Preferable, even.

But now that line is blurring all of a sudden. And I can't tell how I feel about it. Too stuck in the clusterfuck of all these other emotions to untangle the single thread of this one.

Help.

Does he really want to bring me dinner?

"Do you really want to bring me dinner?"

"I do. I've never seen anyone sell their soul before. Is it usually the devil who bids the highest? Or, I don't know, the ghost of David Bowie or something?"

A bark of laughter escapes my lips. I'm so startled by it—by this sense of humor I've never seen in him before—that for a second I can't breathe.

"Usually the devil," I hear myself replying. "But you already knew that."

Greyson chuckles. This deep, chocolatey smooth sound that I feel in my nipples. But instead of hurting, they...tingle. Pleasantly.

"Are you implying I'm a Satanist?" he asks.

"Oh, yeah. Yeah, absolutely."

Another chuckle. "You wouldn't be the first. I'll bring the food."

"And I'll bring the exorcist. Maybe Bowie, too, just because. By the way, RIP to that guy. He's so missed. Also—I could really go for some grits right now. Cheesy, creamy, bad-for-you grits."

"Noted. Anything else?"

I think on that for a minute. Notice the tightness in my chest and in the skin on my face has loosened a bit. Tears are drying up, too.

Now I'm just hungry.

"Surprise me," I say.

We hang up, and I spend the next hour wondering if I should change into something that isn't my oldest, stretchiest, grossest pair of yoga pants and "I like big books and I cannot lie" sweatshirt.

I decide against it. I have nothing to prove to Greyson. Just because he was cute for all of twenty seconds doesn't mean he's a nice, stand-up guy. The kind worth putting real clothes on for.

While I wait for him, I fire off some emails. I've started to look into my maternity leave—how long I have, what I'll get paid, when I'll be going back to work—so I set up a few meetings with people at the college to figure it all out. Six months to go in my pregnancy, and already the work of being a mom has started.

I regret staying in my yoga pants when, exactly an hour later, I open the door to find a scrumptiously dressed man standing on my stoop, a paper shopping bag in one hand and a plastic bag in the other.

My heart hiccups as I drink him in. Trim waist emphasized by a brown belt. A crisp white dress shirt, unbuttoned at the neck. Sleeves rolled up to his elbows, revealing enormous forearms the size of waffle bats—the fat ones used by my friends to beat up their kid siblings when we were little—and a Rolex. Gold this time. Worth more than my undergraduate education if I had to guess.

Greyson's eyes meet mine. Even in the dim twilight, their color is striking. Forward. Bold. Just like the man they belong to.

The scent of his aftershave, smoke and something else, fills my head.

He is *enormous*. Broad enough to fill the entire doorway.

I put a hand on the jamb to steady myself.

For half a heartbeat, his gaze moves over my body. A muscle in his jaw twitches. The look in his eyes when he glances back up—it's hard. Heated. Like he's pissed off. A handsome Hulk about to blow.

Do my yoga pants really offend him that much?

My spine stiffens again. Nipples harden to points. Okay, that hurts now.

If he's going to be a jerk again—

"I got you the best grits in town. And a double cut pork chop." He holds up a brown paper bag. "Made sure it's well done. Eli bitched about it, but whatever. Google told me pregnant women are only supposed to eat well done meat."

I can only stare at him.

He went to The Pearl. Elijah Jackson's restaurant. Arguably the best in town. Best grits for sure, considering they're milled by Luke and cooked by Eli.

The Pearl also happens to be the hardest reservation to get in Charleston. They book months in advance. And as far as I know, they don't do takeout.

Except, apparently, for Greyson Montgomery.

He got me grits. And made sure my pork chop was well done.

I'm clinging to the jamb for dear life.

"You okay?" He looks over my shoulder. "Exorcism go wrong? David Bowie not show?"

A smile tugs at my mouth despite the riot of *things* going on inside my torso. My head.

"I was waiting for you." I step aside. "Come in."

Chapter Nine

GREYSON

Do not look at her ass.

Don't.

Yoga pants, sweet Jesus—

"You can set the food on the table." Julia nods at the round table beside the kitchen. Pretty and impeccably styled, just like the rest of the place. "Can I get you something to drink? Wine? Cocktail?"

"I have the beverages taken care of." I pluck two bottles of Topo Chico from a plastic bag and hold them up. "Just need a bottle opener."

Her eyes move from the bottles to me and back again. She hesitates. For a horrible second, I think she's going to cry.

See? I am not good at this nice thing.

But then Julia is blinking, clearing her throat as she opens a drawer and tosses a heavy brass corkscrew my way.

"You remembered," she says.

I catch it. Let out a silent sigh of relief. Pop one bottle, then the other.

"The carbonation help with your nausea?"

"Little bit, yeah. Plus it gets kinda boring drinking plain water all day, so it's nice to change it up. Although that stuff"—she nods at the bottles—"is hard to find."

"I know. Had to go to a few spots before I found it at a bodega up in Elliotborough of all places," I say, bringing the bottle to my mouth.

Julia raises a brow. "Wow. You really go the extra mile for the women you knock up."

My lips twitch against the mouth of the bottle. She's always been sharp. But I didn't know she could be funny, too.

"Least I can do."

"What a gentleman."

"But I thought I was a Satanist?"

"That, too. They're not mutually exclusive concepts, you know. Being a gentleman and a devil worshipper."

"Or just a devil."

"Right, in your case."

I take a sip of the Topo Chico. I prefer flavors simple. Unadulterated. Why I drink my bourbon neat and never fuck with mixers.

The sparkling water is very simple but very good. The carbonation is different. More subtle than what I'm used to.

"This is pretty delicious," I say. "Refreshing."

She glances at me over her shoulder as she opens a cabinet. Pulls a face, like she isn't quite sure what to make of me.

To be honest, I'm not sure what to make of me either. I agreed to co-parent. Nothing more. Which, in my mind, meant I could keep Julia at arm's length while still showing up for the baby. I could be a good dad without getting emotionally involved with my kid's mother.

But then Julia broke down on the phone. Ford warned me she'd be going through a rough patch during the first trimester. But being the idiot member of the male species I am, I had no concept of just how rough it'd be for her until she laid it all out in explicit terms.

I felt like such a shithead in that moment. A stupid, helpless shithead.

I do not like feeling helpless. Control is my drug. I'm a do-er. A man of action and competence.

So I offered to bring Julia dinner. I couldn't *not* offer to help her feel better, even just for a little while. I may be heartless, but I'm not neglectful. The Satanist accusations notwithstanding. I also have a rare night free of calls, meetings, or emails.

Doesn't hurt I love to eat.

Mom still talks about what a happy baby I was as long as I was fed. She adored what a good eater I was. And still am. No one cleans up her chicken and dumplings like me.

Well. Bryce is giving me a run for my money these days. God she's cute.

Turning back to the cabinet, Julia reaches for some plates. Her shirt rides up, revealing a slice of smooth, pale belly.

My skin prickles to life.

Don't.

I came here to comfort Julia. Not to yank those fucking pants down and make her come.

Would coming make her feel better, I wonder?

I shove the thought from my head and busy myself with the food. Eli packaged everything in brown paper containers, and I open them one by one to see what's inside.

Julia's pork chop. My flank steak. Eli's pimento cheese with house made seed crackers. Sides of collards and grits—the "bad for you kind" that Eli is famous for, made with plenty of stock, salt and half and half.

Julia's stomach rumbles audibly as she sets plates and silverware on the table.

She hands me a napkin. A real one, white cloth, monogrammed. Looks like some kind of heirloom.

"Smells *so* good," she says.

I grab a chair and pull it out. "Sit. I'll fix you a plate."

She hesitates. Gives me that funny look again.

"What?"

"You're being nice."

"And?"

"You're not nice. Ever. To anyone."

I manage a smirk, even as something in my chest contracts. "Doesn't mean I can't feed a woman who's had the day from hell. Sit."

She looks at me for another beat, eyes narrowed as they bounce between mine.

My face warms. A familiar tightness gathering in my groin at her nearness.

She smells good. Always has. She never let me kiss her mouth, so I'd always focus on her neck and chest. The scent of her skin there—equal parts sweet and sexy—drove me fucking wild.

Still does, if my heavy cock is any indication.

Do.

Not.

Jesus, I want to though.

Just when I'm about to fling myself out the nearest window, Julia slides into the chair. I tuck it underneath the table.

"Oh!" she says, reaching for her phone. "Before I forget."

A second later, the opening beats of "Under Pressure" fill the kitchen.

"Just in case Satan doesn't show," she says, flashing me a grin.

My heart skips a beat. I look away. Focus on the food.

"I always thought this was a Queen song," I say as I fix her a full plate.

"The guys in Queen and Bowie wrote it together. And then obviously Bowie performs it with them, too."

"I take it you're a Bowie fan, then."

"Oh yeah. I love to dance. And David Bowie's music is compulsively danceable, you know?"

I wouldn't, actually. I haven't danced in I don't know how long.

I also haven't listened to music over dinner. Unless you count the theme song from "Paw Patrol"—Bryce demands that show is on day and night over at Ford's place.

I haven't sat *down* to dinner with someone who wasn't an investor or potential partner in forever. We have Sunday supper at my parents' house, and I eat with Bryce and Ford every so often. But other than that, I usually eat dinner out with work people or in front of my laptop at the office, or at the kitchen counter at home. Shove food in my face while I catch up on emails or research.

It's not glamorous. And it gets boring. But it's a great way to get shit done.

"Thank you." Julia looks up at me as I set her plate in front of her. Her eyes are serious. "For doing this. Bringing dinner. Totally unexpected, but I really appreciate it."

I settle into the seat across from hers and fix myself a plate of steak and collards. I try to ignore the rush of satisfaction I feel knowing I made her day better.

"I'm sorry you're feeling so shitty," I say, slicing into the steak.

"My doctor warned me all this stuff would peak around eight or nine weeks. But nothing can really prepare you for the reality of just how sucky it can get sometimes." She dips the tines of her fork in the grits and takes a bite. "Especially when you're used to being in charge of your life. Like your moods and your ability to get stuff done. I like to be busy, but this baby is kind of forcing me to slow down. Which I'm sure can be a good thing. But right now, it just feels kind of depressing, to be honest. Doesn't help that I can't really tell anyone that I'm pregnant yet. You're going through some pretty heavy shit, but you can't say anything to anyone about it. I've had to turn down a bunch of invites. The second my friends and colleagues see me not drinking, they'll know something's up. I'm too tired to go out anyway. When I am done for the day, I am *done*. It all combines to create this kind of shit storm of self-imposed isolation and endless nausea. I'm just not enjoying the things I usually love."

"Like?"

"Arguing with you, for one thing."

I scoff. She's egging me on, and I like it.

She's also being real. Honest. Holding nothing back, not even the tough stuff. The vulnerable stuff.

I like that. Like always, I'm drawn to it. Not to her hurt. But to her authenticity. Her bravery in admitting things are less than perfect. In my world—the one I used to inhabit, anyway—you don't see that all too often.

"I'm pretty good at asshole," I say.

"The best. You really think you should be so proud of that, though?"

I lift a shoulder. "Probably not."

Julia takes another bite, this time of collards. "I usually love my job —well, both my jobs. At C of C, I adore my students and my colleagues. I'm good at what I do. But these days, teaching feels like a chore. I'm even struggling with my romance class, which has always been my favorite."

"A class on romance?" I sip my water. "That sounds cool."

Julia tilts her head. She won't stop looking at me like this—like she's never seen me before.

She picks up her water, eyes still trained on mine as she drains her glass.

"It is cool. Really cool. I've taught it for three semesters now, and it's become one of the most popular classes in College of Charleston's catalogue. Olivia teaches a creative writing class on romance too, focusing primarily on craft. Together we're creating this romance-based curriculum that's the first of its kind. I'm really proud of it. But being on campus recently has felt like a drag. Same with design, and reading, and walking. Basically I hate everything right now except TV and food."

She watches as I refill her glass. Nudge the container of crackers and pimento cheese her way.

"So eat," I say.

Julia doesn't hesitate. She slathers a seed cracker with pimento cheese and pops it into her mouth. Chewing, her expression goes soft, and she makes this noise.

A moan. A sigh. A moan-y sigh.

The kind she'd make when I'd play with her pussy. Splaying her lips wide with my fingers. Rolling my thumb over her clit, gentle but insistent, her hips curling in time to my strokes.

My cock twitches. Does she *know* she's making those noises as she eats?

Does she *know* she's making me summon Satan and David Bowie and whoever else will listen because I'm on the verge of tackling her? Taking her right here on this table?

Where the fuck is that exorcist when you need him?

I clear my throat. "You're a very...vocal eater."

Julia grins, turning to her pork chop. "When I like something, you'll know it. Am I making you uncomfortable?"

"No." I meet her gaze. "Maybe."

She grins, her blue eyes lighting up with mischief.

Chapter Ten

GREYSON

It's the first time I've seen Julia's eyes come alive like this since she told me she was pregnant.

Makes me light up too. My chest lights up with satisfaction, even as the heaviness in my groin continues to demand attention.

I look away. Eyes catching on the bookshelf behind Julia. I didn't really pay much attention to her place last time I was here. Too distracted by the news that I'd knocked her up, most likely in the back of my Yukon.

The apartment is tiny, less than a thousand square feet I'd say, and most of the furniture she's got is diminutive in scale. This bookcase, however, is massive. Looks roughed up, antique. It's painted bright white, and the towering shelves are artfully crowded with stuff. Books, mostly. Hardbacks—I have to squint to see the authors—Betty Friedan and Virginia Woolf, shoulder to shoulder with a sizable collection of paperback romances. Pages yellowed. Spines creased.

They're styled in such a way that each shelf almost looks like an art exhibit. Picture frames, plates, and small, antique looking canvases completing the look.

"You really do like your romance," I say.

"Love it," she replies. "Romance novels are many things to me.

They challenge me. Make me more open minded. But right now, they're comfort reads. So I amend my statement. I hate everything except TV, food, and historicals. Olivia's historicals in particular."

I notice the same guy—older, with a nose and eyes that match Julia's—is in a lot of the pictures. The two of them in front of the Acropolis in Athens. On a wide, glossy porch that overlooks the Battery here in town. One where Julia is in a Harry Potter get-up, black robes and all, smiling wide beside what looks to be Hogwarts castle. The man is with her. Beaming with pride.

"My dad." Julia turns around to look at the pictures, resting her forearm on the back of her chair. She sighs. "He was pretty fucking awesome. Amazing architect and even better father."

"Was?"

She meets my eyes from the corner of hers. "Yeah. He passed away a year ago. Miss him like crazy, if you can't tell by this, like, Princess Di style shrine I have set up to him. I miss her like crazy too. But my obsession with the royals is neither here nor there." She motions to the Hogwarts picture. "I really wish my dad was here. For a lot of reasons. But I could really use his advice on this whole parenthood situation right now. I mean, I have a great group of friends who have been nothing but supportive. Family is different, though."

My chest tightens. I can't imagine how badly I'd be wigging out about the baby if I didn't have Ford to go to for advice, or to my parents for moral support.

Don't get me wrong, I'm still wigging out. But I'd be an absolute fucking mess without my family.

"I'm sorry, Julia. I had no idea. Do you not have any other family around?"

"Not really. My mom died a couple years back. I don't have any siblings, and my cousins live kind of all over the place."

"That's tough," I say, and I mean it. Not only is Julia sick as a dog. She also has no family to go to. No parents to help her, no siblings to share the exciting news with.

She's got a full life. That much is obvious. Jobs, friends, travel. But to not have any family—family she was clearly really close to—

I honestly can't imagine.

"This is so good, by the way," she says, taking another bite of pork chop. "What about you? I know you said your family lives close, but are you actually close with them?"

I nod, swallowing a bite of steak. "I am. I bitch about them sometimes, but I really did luck out. They're great."

Julia smiles. The kind that makes the skin around her eyes crinkle. "The gentleman Satanist loves his family? I almost don't believe it."

"They're the only thing that's kept me going since—" I clear my throat for what feels like the hundredth time. We are *so* not going there right now. Or ever. "Suffice it to say I'd be much growlier without them."

Julia's brows go up. "That's saying something. Any growlier and you'd be a werewolf. Not the sexy *Twilight* kind, either."

"Please." I furrow my brow in mock consternation. "I'd make the best werewolf. And the sexiest."

"Because you'd make biting peoples' heads off look good?"

"Because I'd make a great bad guy. I am one in real life."

Julia turns back to face me. Her gaze moves over the food on the table before landing on mine. She looks at me for a full beat. Eyes narrowed with a question I do not want to answer.

Sweat breaks out along the back of my collar.

"You're not all bad." Her voice is kind. "Just mostly."

"Bad enough," I say gruffly.

I get back to my plate. Wolf down (pun intended) what's left of my collards and finish off my steak.

"You done?" she asks.

I stand, reaching for her plate. "I'll clean up."

"I got it."

"Don't make me growl, Julia. Sit."

Julia smiles and stands, gently removing her plate from my hands. "Growl all you want. Cleaning up was always my job. How about you clear the table and I do the dishes?"

"You sure you're up to it?"

"After that meal? Absolutely. If Elijah's grits and pimiento cheese don't revive you, then you're past saving."

Julia gets to work at the sink while I refill the take-out bag with our empty boxes. Gathering our silverware and glasses, I turn to the kitchen to see Julia shimmying her hips. Little, barely noticeable movements that are perfectly in time to the beat of the song that's playing —"Rebel Rebel."

An anthem for Julia if there ever was one.

For half a heartbeat I just stand there. Pure creeper style. Transfixed by the easy sway of her pert little ass. She's murmuring the words now, scrubbing and shimmying and generally being cute as fuck.

My thoughts swirl and shift as I watch her. She's had a shitty time of it. The morning sickness, the depression. Never mind the lingering shock of an unexpected pregnancy. Her dad died, she has no family around, and she's struggling to find joy in the stuff she's usually very passionate about.

But she's still singing.

Still dancing to Bowie like a bomb didn't take out life as she knew it.

There's a lesson here. The one about dancing in the rain or despite the rain or some shit like that.

But beyond the country song platitudes—her dancing makes me feel something.

Turned on, yeah. That's a fucking given.

But there's something else. Something I can't put my finger on.

Maybe it's just feeling anything at all that's got me sidling up beside her. Wanting to put my hands beside hers on the lip of the sink and melt my cock into the sweet curve of her ass, even though I shouldn't.

Wanting to *stay*. Dance. Fuck. Feed her.

I hate the thought of her being alone.

And it's not lost on me that I didn't think once about work while I've been here.

I didn't think about my past, either.

I was here. Fully, sometimes painfully, present.

Julia calling me to account, as usual. Calling me on my bullshit without even knowing it.

And yeah. Now that I've caught a glimpse of who Julia is, beyond the designer who loves to bust budgets and my balls, I admit I'm curious.

Really fucking curious about who she is. What she likes.

Where she comes from. That picture of her at Hogwarts—did she go to school at Oxford? Cambridge?

And what about the travel? Who does she jet around the world with now that her dad is gone?

What are her favorite places to visit? Where would she like to go?

What about historical romance does she find so comforting?

Did she get her love of design from her dad?

Underwear—does she wear it with those yoga pants? Or does she go commando?

I blink. Can't remember the last time a woman made me curious like this.

It's dangerous.

Jesus, I really am going to turn into a werewolf if I don't get out of here. Right now.

I nudge her with my hip and set everything I'm carrying in the sink. "I got the rest."

I don't realize how close I'm standing until she looks up, our gazes locking. My stomach takes a nosedive.

I'm continually struck by how pretty she is. Face flushed from the heat of the water running from the faucet, wisps of her hair escaping the messy knot at the crown of her head.

Blue eyes bright. Happy.

Did I really do that?

I shove the idea from my head. Makes me feel too warm and squishy inside.

I do not do warm, and I especially don't do squishy. Unless Bryce is in the room. Then all bets are off.

"You know that in romance, villains usually don't help out. They definitely don't do dishes."

Fuck, I'm smiling.

I'm gripped by the wild thought that I'd just have to lean down to kiss her. On the mouth this time. Tilt my head and go in for the kill.

"What do they usually do?"

"Break hearts."

And just like that, the spell is shattered. Reality crashing through the happy haze of the moment.

Bound to happen anyway. Doing one woman one favor doesn't erase the very bad things I've done to others.

I finish the dishes in silence. When the dishwasher is loaded and the table wiped down, Julia leads me to the front door.

"Thanks again for dinner," she says. "I really enjoyed it."

I manage a tight smile in reply. Shove my hands in my pockets. I know I need to keep my distance. But there is no way in hell I'm letting this woman deal with this pregnancy alone now that I know how difficult it's been.

"Let's check in with each other more often, okay?" I say. "I won't bother you too much, but I do want to know how you're doing."

She looks at me. I look back.

"Okay," she says.

"And you come to me if you need anything, all right? Even if it's just a resupply of Topo Chico."

"Got it."

"I want you to mean that."

"I do. I'll keep in touch."

She's still looking at me.

I'm still looking at her.

Get. The fuck. Out of here.

But my feet won't move.

The space between Julia and I thrums. Tightens, somehow, despite the bubble of *feels* expanding inside my torso.

Before I know what she's doing, Julia's going up on her tiptoes and curling her arms around my neck.

I stay very still, trying my damndest to ignore the fireworks exploding in my groin, my chest, my head.

She feels so good against me.

So damn good. Soft and vulnerable and *warm*.

"This pregnancy thing is hard. And very heavy," she murmurs against my shoulder. "But you've made it feel lighter for a little while. Which helps. More than you know. Thank you, Greyson."

Carefully—*care*fully, one or both of us will break if I move too fast, or squeeze too hard—I curl my arms around her waist. Close my eyes as I let myself hold her.

Just for a minute, I tell myself.

Just for right now.

Her hair tickles my nose. I resist the urge to inhale a deep lungful of her. Scent and sweetness.

My body electrifies at the feel of hers.

I *like* this.

This, whatever this is. The satisfaction of knowing I did a good thing?

The knowledge that she's trusting me—touching me—making me feel alive in a way I haven't in a long, long time?

"Some of the best things in life are the ones you have to work hardest for," I say. "Maybe this baby is one of them."

I let her go, even though it kills me.

The cigarette I smoke on the ride home does nothing to calm me down.

I don't think anything will when it comes to Julia.

Chapter Eleven

JULIA

Greyson: midday check-in

Greyson: Go.

Julia: Is this a thing now? You checked in this morning.

Greyson: And you were feeling like shit post-coffee. Any better?

Julia: Actually, yes. Starting to feel better on the whole. My Bumpin' app tells me my symptoms could start to abate now that I'm inching toward the second trimester. Still have a few weeks to go though.

Greyson: Praise David Bowie

Greyson: just downloaded the app. It thinks I'm the one who's pregnant. I'm 8 weeks and two days, and I may be starting to show.

Julia: Nausea? Tender breasts?

Greyson: Oh yeah. I honestly don't know how you've been doing this for so long.

Julia: Totally sucks. Not going to sugar coat that.

Greyson: Don't. I like your honesty.

Greyson: So your dad was an architect. Did you learn design from him?

Julia: You're being nice again.

Greyson: Amuse me

Julia: Yes. He was a big fan of preservation. His specialty was restoring historic homes. You have him to thank for my appreciation of timeless design with a twist.

Greyson: Your expensive taste you mean

Julia: Don't tell me you're not obsessed with how Rodgers' Farms is turning out. I see that twinkle of appreciation in your eye when we're out there.

Greyson: Julia. It's beautiful. but you don't need me to tell you that

Julia: I don't. Still nice to hear though. Are werewolves too bashful to give praise in person?

Greyson: Baby steps.

Greyson: Where should I pick you up tomorrow for our doctor's appointment?

Julia: I can drive.

Greyson: So can I. Let me hep

Greyson: *help

Julia: I'll be at my office on campus. 23 Coming Street. Yellow building that's leaning to the side. Can't miss it.

Greyson: always thought it was funny how all the sorority houses are on Coming Street.

Julia: The irony right? The only time I came in college was with my vibrator. See you at 2.

I'm starting to have good days again.

Don't get me wrong, the bad days are still there. The exhaustion is real, as is the anxiety. But the depression that's plagued me for weeks has started to lift. I'll get whole hours of energy and clarity, the fog that's clouded my brain thinning just enough for me to get decent work done.

Today is a good day. Even my students notice I have some pep in my step during class and office hours. It's so nice to feel even a little bit like myself again that I get excited.

Or maybe it's the fact that I get to (hopefully) see the baby today that's got my heart beating a little faster. I've read a lot about my first ultrasound. They'll measure the baby to determine exactly how far along I am.

They'll also measure its heartbeat, which is a very good indicator of how healthy the fetus is. At this stage, a healthy heartbeat means I'll likely carry this baby to term. But a sluggish one, coupled with a baby that measures smaller than expected, could mean bad news.

I'm nervous. But more excited. I cling to that excitement like a drowning woman clinging to a life preserver she's just been tossed. The uncertainty and the anxiety about everything have been relentless lately. It's nice to feel good about things for a change.

Nice, and confusing, if I'm being honest. I (clearly) have very mixed feelings about impending motherhood.

I love the idea of starting my own family. But I hate the way I feel, physically and mentally.

I'm excited to teach my son or daughter all the things my parents taught me—the things I *wish* they'd taught me, too. But I would kill for a perfect margarita on the rocks. Salt, silver tequila, serious deliciousness.

I miss uninterrupted sleep. I get up at least once a night to pee now.

I miss feeling sexy.

I love waking up refreshed and dried out. No hangover, no alcohol or cigarettes giving me a day-after headache.

I miss being master of my thoughts. My emotions. My body.

The alarm on my phone goes off at 1:55 P.M. I finish the email I'm working on, make a few notes in my planner, and pack up to go.

Then I wait.

And wait.

2:05. 2:12. 2:22.

My appointment is in less than ten minutes. The drive to my doctor's office takes twenty.

We're going to be late.

Really late.

I shoot Greyson a text, but get no response. I try calling him too. He doesn't pick up.

Just when I start to panic—and get pissed off—I hear the familiar growl of an engine outside. Irene, my TA, leans back to look out the window.

"Who is *that*?" she asks, leaning back a little farther.

I grab my phone off my desk. "Blue Yukon?"

"Yup. Guy behind the wheel is—" She lets out a low whistle. "God. Literally a god."

I grin. "As in Jesus?"

"As in Achilles. The one played quite memorably by Brad Pitt."

Scoffing, I rise to my feet.

"You have the essays?" I ask.

Irene blinks. Turns back to her desk and sets her hand on a neat stack of papers. "On it. I'll type up my thoughts. I'll also enter the participation grades for Rom 101 and send out an email about next week's office hours. Anything else?"

"You're the best. I'd also love some ideas on topics for Rom 101's exam paper. I'm thinking something to do with endings—happily ever afters—and what we expect from them as readers." I slide the straps of my tote bag over my shoulder. "I'll have my phone if you need me. Otherwise, see you in the morning."

Irene nods, a small smile playing at her lips.

"Just out of curiosity—does Achilles out there belong to you?"

My pulse skips a beat. "No. No, he doesn't. Why?"

"No reason. You're just kind of...red."

I put a hand to my face. My skin is hot.

Well, shit. Because I'm not feeling discombobulated enough over running late to the ultrasound. Now Greyson Montgomery has to revert me into a blushing teenager with a crush.

Granted, it's a tiny crush. I blame the lemon tree and the surprisingly self-aware Satanist jokes he made. Grits didn't hurt, either.

Neither do the cutesy texts.

Who knew the guy had a soft side? Makes me wonder where he's been hiding it all this time.

Why he's been hiding it. The lit professor in me—the romance enthusiast, too—hungers for the story.

There's definitely a story here, that I know for sure.

I also know the guy *never* runs late for business meetings. But he's almost half an hour late for our first doctor's appointment together.

Our baby's first ultrasound.

Greyson's eyes follow me through the windshield as I make my way down the sidewalk.

My face is on fucking fire. I'm feeling a million things, too many, too much, all at once.

I run my fingers through my hair, releasing it from behind my ears. Hoping it'll cover the worst of the inferno.

Greyson is finishing up a call as I climb inside the truck.

"Agreed about inventory"—he cuts me a look and mouths *sorry* —"yep, yep, we'll do the classics in addition to some picks that are off the beaten path...yep...hey, John, I hate to do this, but I really have to go."

I buckle my seat belt. Greyson guides the truck into traffic.

"Right. Sounds good. Okay. Thanks." He hangs up and tosses his phone onto the dashboard. Blows out a breath. "Sorry. So sorry I'm late. Got stuck at lunch with one of our biggest investors. Then I got stuck on that fucking call for an hour. We're partnering with a local sommelier to open a champagne bar in NoMo, and the whole thing is turning out to be the biggest pain in the ass ever."

I look at the clock on the dash. Look at him. "You're half an hour late, Greyson."

"I know, I know, and I'm really fucking sorry." He brings his brows together. "Julia, I mean that. It won't happen again."

"It never happens for work-related things, does it? You being late."

He adjusts his grip on the wheel. "I'm trying here, Julia. This juggle is new to me."

"It's new to me too," I say, remembering how cool he was about me cancelling that meeting with our contractor the other night. "But this a big appointment. I've been looking forward to it all week. I'm going to be really upset if we have to reschedule because we're late."

"I'll be upset, too. Look." He accelerates the truck. "I'm putting the pedal to the metal. I'll bribe the doctor if I have to so she'll see us. We'll get these pictures taken, come hell or high water. I promise."

I arch a brow. "And you don't make promises you can't keep."

He cuts me a look. "Exactly. We'll make it, Julia."

Letting out a breath, I fall back in my seat.

"Fine. Just try to be on time next time, okay?"

"Of course." He glances at my massive work tote, stopping at a light. "Got everything you need?"

"I think so."

I turn to set the bag in the backseat, but Greyson lifts it out of my hands and sets it back there himself. The fabric of his button down stretches across his massive chest as he twists. I can see his nipple, hard enough to poke through his undershirt.

My mouth waters. The stress over being late all but forgotten. He looks so good today.

So good. Crisp button up—this one is light blue, making his eyes really pop. Rolled up sleeves, square jaw, full lips.

A dimple in his chin I've never noticed before.

I *miss* that. The nipples. The poking.

Focus. I have to focus. Not on nipples but on prenatal appointment stuff.

"Still feeling good?" he asks, turning back around. "You said you were 'pretty fucking fabulous' this morning."

"Pretty good, yeah. Just lots of ups and downs lately. One minute, I'm feeling good. The next I feel like shit—yesterday my back was killing me. One minute I'm totally convinced that keeping this baby is the right decision. The next, not so much." I swallow. "It's a lot to handle. But you seem to be handling it okay. The baby. Minus the whole being-thirty-minutes-late-to-our-first-ultrasound thing."

He cuts me another look. Brows furrowed just enough to make the slanted creases between them appear.

"What?" I ask.

He looked at me this way when he came over for dinner. Like he doesn't know what to make of me.

"You're honest to a fault, aren't you?"

"Try to be. I already told you—I really can't stand people who are full of shit."

He turns, focusing his attention on the road.

His hand moves as he tightens his grip on the wheel.

"I didn't realize how many of those people there were in the world," he replies gruffly. "My world."

"Kind of shocking, isn't it? Not only the amount of bullshit-y people, but also the people who *buy* their own bullshit. Like they genuinely believe the lies they tell the world and themselves about how perfect their lives are."

"Yes!" he says. "Exactly. It blows my mind. Like appearances are the most important thing. Warping your entire existence to fit that perfect mold."

I arch a brow. "Sounds like you have some personal experience with that mold."

A shadow moves over his features, dampening the excitement of seconds before.

"It's easy for me to feel certain. About the baby, I mean," he says, and I fight a sense of whiplash at the sudden change of subject. I struck a nerve. I want to know why. "You're the one who's pregnant. This baby is affecting you a lot more than it's affecting me. I don't feel like ass all the time. I don't have to give up booze and cigarettes. It's unfair. If I could be pregnant for you, I would."

I scoff. "You'd really be a werewolf then. Biting everyone's heads off because you'd want a cigarette so bad."

"I'd end up in jail."

"Oh, yeah, no question about that."

One side of his mouth curls into a smile so handsome I feel it inside my skin.

"You're handling this with much more grace than I ever would, that's for damn sure," he says.

"Grace? Please. I bitch and moan constantly. I'm still waiting on that 'glow' all pregnant women are supposed to get. And I've offered my soul to David Bowie more times than I can count in exchange for everything from a very large glass of wine to a good night's sleep. A paragon of happy motherhood I am not."

He's looking at me again. Like that.

Like he has no clue what I am. But whatever it is, he kind of adores it.

Adores me, just for telling my messy, often nonsensical truth.

"Good thing you've got a Satanist to help you through."

I laugh. The tickly, happy kind of laugh that runs up and down my sides and lands in the center of my being.

"Satan owes you a solid, huh?"

"Many favors, yeah. Happy to call a few in on your behalf."

It's my turn to look at him. The square, solid, masculine lines of his profile.

Feeling rises up inside me.

"What if it's not okay?" I say quietly. "The ultrasound. The baby. My depression. What if something's really wrong?"

His eyes meet mine. "Then we'll deal with it. You and me and David Bowie."

I smile. The words *you and me* sticking inside my head.

Maybe this isn't where I thought I'd end up.

But right now, it doesn't feel half bad.

Chapter Twelve

GREYSON

Venture capital makes for strange bedfellows. I've courted baristas-turned-entrepreneurs. Farmers intent to sell their grits, milled from heirloom varieties of corn, to the retail market.

I've fielded proposals from foul-mouth chefs tatted up to within an inch of their life and surgeons seeking a second life as restaurateurs. I do business with Harvard grads, hardscrabble fishermen, chemists-cum-distillers with a talent for making the best gin this side of the Atlantic.

But I never thought I'd find myself hanging on every word a chatty ultrasound tech in heart-spattered scrubs utters as she squirts a lube-like substance onto Julia's belly.

It's surreal.

And it happens so fast. One second, the tech is flicking the lights off and directing our attention to a TV screen on the far wall.

The next, the inside of Julia's uterus is on that screen and my heart is pounding so hard my head throbs in time to its beat.

A small black space appears on the screen. Inside that space is a tiny, *tiny* baby-shaped thing.

"Looks like there's just one sac," the tech says, pressing the wand a little more firmly against Julia's belly. "No twins this time."

"Thank God," Julia says. Words tight, like she's holding her breath.

I lean forward in my chair. "You all right?"

Julia nods, making the paper on the exam table crinkle. "I'm good."

"Let's measure this little peanut"—a few more keystrokes—"yep, yep, eight weeks and five days. Puts your due date a few days earlier, but since you're still within a week, we'll leave it at June twenty-third for the time being. See that?" The tech points to a moving bit in the baby's center. "It's your baby's heartbeat. We can listen..."

She hits a few keys.

Then: *swoosh swoosh swoosh*.

The baby's heartbeat is loud enough to drown out my own.

I feel a sudden, searing pressure behind my eyes.

"Look at that," the tech is saying. She bangs a few more keys, and the sound disappears. "Heartbeat is 173 beats per minute. Perfect. Peanut is lookin' real good, y'all."

I look at Julia. A single tear slips quietly down her temple.

She's smiling.

She looks at me. Eyes all soft and earnest and so beautiful *I'm* suddenly the one who's struggling to breathe. She reaches out and grabs my hand, giving it a quick squeeze. Hers feels small and warm in mine.

Warmth that I feel moving up my arm into my chest. I sniffle, blinking hard.

Julia's smile gets bigger.

"Looks like we won't need David Bowie. At least for the time being," she says.

"That's a relief," I reply. Still blinking, because these goddamn tears won't clear up.

"You good?" she asks.

"Yeah." I look away and swallow. "How about Charlie Brown or Lucy?"

"What?"

"The Peanuts. You know, the cartoons? What if we nicknamed our baby Charlie or Lucy?"

She's still smiling. "I like that. Charlie Brown."

I don't want to think about the last time I cried. But I think it's safe to acknowledge that this kind of crying feels different. Better.

I can't remember the last time something good happened outside of work. For me. In my personal life, I mean.

Granted, I haven't allowed good things to happen, because that's how people get hurt.

Why then, is this good thing going down right now?

Why do I feel this good—why do I get to be with a woman who *makes* me feel this good—when I fucked up so bad?

The cynic inside me can't help but wonder when the other shoe is going to drop.

But for the first time in a long time, I want to let myself have this moment. Feel it. The relief and the happiness and the hope.

I want to feel alive, fully. Julia's kind of alive. The kind that makes you dance to eighties music while washing dishes.

Because it feels so. Damn. Good.

But there's no way I can forgive myself that easily. I can't just decide I'm done with the guilt. The shame. I have to earn forgiveness. And honestly, my crimes are such that I'll be working to balance the karmic scales forever.

That's what happens when you destroy a perfectly good person's perfect life.

Julia and I are led to another exam room, where we meet with her doctor. We ask a million questions; the doctor assures Julia her symptoms should start to abate once she hits her second trimester in a couple weeks. She tells Julia to keep an eye on her depression and notify the office immediately if it worsens or she has thoughts of hurting herself. We set up our next appointment—12 week ultrasound—which I immediately mark on my Google calendar with the note *DO NOT BE LATE!!!!!!!*

I'm still lost in my thoughts when I hold the office door open for Julia. I step out into the gloom of the late afternoon behind her. Typical of Charleston in November, the air has a slight bite to it. Crispness finally overpowering the humidity that's cloaked the city since May like a wet blanket.

We walk side by side, her elbow brushing mine.

"I really am sorry I was late," I say. "But I told you we'd get those pictures taken."

She grins. Eyes on her feet. "It's all right. I'm glad we were both there to see it. The ultrasound, I mean. How cool was that heartbeat?"

"The coolest," I say, and I mean it.

"So." She looks up, squinting against the gloom. "What are you up to tonight?"

"Tonight?" I blink. "Not much. I have a couple site visits to do this afternoon, a phone call with an architect, and then I was going to finish up some work at home. Go to bed early."

She grins. "Your Friday night sounds almost as exciting as mine. Such party animals, you and me."

"Hashtag adulting sucks. Why do you ask?"

Julia lifts a shoulder, gliding her hands into the pockets of her jacket. "I feel like we should celebrate all this good news. Charlie Brown's alive. So am I. You and I haven't stabbed each other yet. Probably our biggest win to date. Not to mention the Rodgers' Farms project is wrapping up, and we rocked the shit out of that thing."

I'm grinning, too, as I slow my steps. Meet her eyes.

I should not.

Should not give in to the temptation of basking in this woman's sunshine a minute longer than I have to. It's dangerous, this *want*.

But what am I supposed to do? Let her go home to her empty house by herself? Yeah, I'm sure she's got friends to call. Gracie. Luke. Olivia.

But this is *my* baby. This is *our* good news to celebrate.

I also like the idea of having someone to cook for. I miss it. Opening a bottle of wine and making a fucking mess of my kitchen.

"Why don't you come over for dinner?" Julia continues. "My treat this time. I don't cook, but I'm kind of the best at DoorDash, so..."

"I cook," I reply, making a mental note to call my mom after I drop Julia off. "Come over to my place. Supposed to be shitty weather tonight—we can eat and maybe watch a movie or something."

Julia runs the tip of her tongue along her bottom lip.

I bite back a groan. Lord, that lip. What I would give to sink my teeth into it. Taste it for the first time.

Stop. It.

"That sounds nice. Really nice. But you have to know that this pregnant woman doesn't Netflix and chill. Like, *chill* chill."

"Please." Stopping, I spread my legs. Cross my arms. "That shit's for amateurs. I don't 'chill.' I'd never ask you to 'hang out.' I'll fix you a real meal, pour you a shot glass of really good wine, and put on a movie you pick."

Her blue eyes dance. "You don't fuck around, do you, Greyson?"

"Not when it comes to the women I knock up."

She laughs. The sound making butterflies take flight inside my torso.

Fu-uuuck. Fuck.

Should not.

But Lord help me, I'm in it now.

"All right," she says. "That sounds great. What can I bring?"

"Just your stretchy pants."

"Stretchy pants?"

"Yeah. Stretchy pants time is my favorite time. Bring yours. And the ultrasound pictures." I nod at the folder Julia holds in the crook of her arm. "I'd like to make some copies on my printer."

"Done." Her eyes rove over my body. "No offense. But I'm surprised you own stretchy pants. Hell, I'm surprised you own any pants that aren't perfectly tailored, custom made slacks."

My lips twitch. "You noticed my pants."

"I've stroked many things of yours. I'm sorry to say your ego will never be one of them."

I laugh. Flutters erupting inside me.

Fuck these butterflies for life.

I've missed them.

My mom picks up on the first ring when I call her as I dash from one meeting to the next. I haven't told her about Julia or the baby yet—timing hasn't felt right—but that doesn't mean she's not excited to hear from me.

"Grey," she says, and I can hear the smile in her voice. "Hey, baby. How you doing?"

Not okay. Excited. Relieved.

Terrified.

Yeah, I'd say mostly terrified.

"I'm all right. What about you? Sorry to be a bother."

"You're never a bother. Everything all right?"

"Everything's fine." I clear my throat. "That chicken and rice recipe you make. You know, with the sausage and onions and celery and everything? Tell me about it. I've made it before, but it's been a while."

"Chicken Bog. Your grandmother's recipe," Mom replies. "It's a keeper. Lots of work, but that's never stopped you. Having some company over this weekend? Someone special, maybe?"

My heart clenches. Mom sounds hopeful.

Guarded.

But hopeful nonetheless.

Unlike Ford, my parents have never explicitly encouraged me to start dating again. They've never been pushy. Never forced an agenda on me. One of the five thousand things I love and admire about them.

I know they want me to be happy again. And even though they don't say it, I can tell they'd love more grandchildren.

That, I can help with. The happiness bit—

Not so much.

"A friend. Julia." I take a sharp breath. I don't know why I just shared her name. It's almost like I *want* my mother to ask me about her. "She hasn't—uh—been feeling so great, so I thought I'd make her some comfort food. Your specialty."

Mom pauses. I can see her in my head: eyes and smile lighting up with curiosity.

"Bless your heart. That's very sweet of you. I can't remember the last time you had a *friend* over for dinner."

I swallow. Hard. "So, the meat. I remember you said to have the butcher cut up a whole fryer chicken—split the breasts so the pieces are all the same size and cook evenly."

"This Julia—do y'all work together? How did y'all meet?"

"Yes, at work. And it's andouille sausage, right? I'll go borrow some from Elijah. Maybe he's got some homemade stock I can get in on, too."

"I've got a couple quarts in my freezer with your name on them. Has Ford met Julia yet?"

Oh, Jesus. This was a stupid idea. The last thing I want is to get Mom's hopes up. I crushed her before. I won't do it again.

But Lordy, do I want to talk to her about Julia. Tell her how she's got me in knots. That she's interesting and accomplished and likes to dance. How she makes *me* want to dance.

I do not dance. Not to Bowie. Not to anyone or any song.

I miss it, though. Having fun. Letting go. Taking chances that don't involve balance sheets or business plans.

"He's worked with her, too, yeah," I say.

"Well I'm happy for you, Grey. You deserve some excitement and happiness in your life. Is Julia from Charleston?"

"Mom," I groan. "She's just a friend, all right? And as far as happiness and excitement are concerned—"

"You deserve them, just like everybody else. You work hard, baby. You're a good brother and a good son. A good boss, if the tiniest bit demanding. Let yourself have some fun. It's long overdue."

I let out a breath, feeling a slight thickening in my throat.

Sometimes I wish my family wasn't so awesome. The knowledge that I disappointed them would be easier to swallow. But instead, they readily forgive me for things I don't know if I can forgive myself for. And offer me homemade chicken stock to boot.

How the fuck am I supposed to turn that down?

What if I accept Mom's stock and her forgiveness too?

I still don't feel like I deserve either. But now, out of the blue, I want it. The forgiveness. The happiness and excitement.

I want to put this guilt down. I just don't know if I can. Carrying it has become second nature. It's my why, my how. My life.

Who am I if I'm not the workhorse? What do I do if I'm not punishing myself?

Am I really allowed to just...I don't know, let this go and be free? Julia's kind of free.

Am I the one who gets to decide?

If not me, who?

If not now, when?

I don't have answers. But I do have dinner to make. Wine to pick and pour.

So I finish my meetings, swing by Mom's house for instructions and stock and grab some andouille from Elijah. Pick up the rest of what I need at the grocery store.

I take a quick smoke break on my balcony before the rain starts. And then I put on my stretchy pants, roll up my sleeves, and get to fixing Julia dinner.

Chapter Thirteen

JULIA

Back at home, my mood dips after the high of the appointment wears off. I'm learning this is the new normal as I hit the end of my first trimester and inch toward my second. Just when you think you've turned a corner, your body screams "psych!" and you're back in the throes of first trimester trauma: a vicious bout of nausea, depression, or fatigue.

Right now, I'm feeling all three. So on my walk over to Greyson's, I put in my earbuds and listen to *My Romp With the Rogue*. It's the third time I'm listening to the book. Nothing like some broody-hero-castle sex to lift one's spirits.

Charlotte climaxed with a soft shout, her fingers curling into his bare chest. Her sex pulsed around him, making him shout, too.

Looking down at him, she bit her lip and rolled her hips. Milking him to his own completion despite being nearly boneless with hers.

He slid his hands up her sides. Caressed her skin, her breasts. Her back. Saying with his hands what he couldn't with his words.

At last she collapsed on top of him, sweaty and warm, and he felt his heart thump soundly in his chest.

"How," she panted, "does this keep getting better?"

He brushed the hair back from her face and met her eyes.

Because you're unafraid, *he wanted to say.*

You're not afraid to tell your truth.

Would she be afraid of his truth, he wondered?

"Have you not heard?" he said instead. "We Scots excel at many things. But we truly are the best at this."

She shook with laughter, cuffing his shoulder. "What about me? Am I not the best at it, too?"

His wife was so unafraid in taking her pleasure.

In her curiosity.

She was brave where others—strong men, men of title and stature—had cowered.

She was open with him, and trusting with him, when he kept her shut out of his life. Except in here, in the comfort of her bed.

He owed her more than that.

"You are," he said softly. And then, after a beat: "You should know I killed my brother in cold blood."

Turns out Greyson's townhouse is only a few blocks from my place. Go figure we had all that sex out on Wadmalaw at Luke's barn or in parking lots around town when we lived less than a five minute walk from each other.

Bottle of bourbon tucked under one arm—along with cigarettes and condoms, I noticed he always had a bottle of brown liquor in his glove box—and the folder with Charlie Brown's ultrasound pictures tucked under the other, I head his way a little after seven.

He lives on South Adger's Wharf, a cobblestone street that runs alongside Charleston Harbor.

It takes a lot to charm a seasoned Charleston resident like myself. But this street?

This is about as charming and romantic as the city gets.

Slowing my steps, I almost twist an ankle on the uneven cobbles as I gawk at my surroundings. This part of town is *old*. I can tell by the weathered brick facades of the homes I pass, original iron earthquake bolts dotting their walls. It's a little known fact that Charleston sits on a fault line. Homes on the peninsula were constructed with bolts running through the walls that could be loosened when an earthquake struck, allowing the walls to move rather than crumble.

The loamy smells of salt and marsh hang heavy in the air here. Weathered metal hitching posts, once used to tie up horses, stand attention just outside the front doors I pass.

The street curves. Glancing down at the address Greyson texted me, I look up to find it in front of me.

I take in the brick exterior of a two-story townhouse. It's the largest on the block by far, facing the water. The uneven brickwork and creeping vines are juxtaposed by modern steel windows. Gas lamps flicker beside the black front door, which is tucked beneath a second story balcony.

For several heartbeats I just stand there and stare. Stray raindrops catching on my hair, my shoulders.

I don't know what I was expecting Greyson's home to look like. This place is sleek and sexy, yeah. Like any bachelor pad worth its salt would be. It's in an exclusive—and expensive—part of town.

But it's got this beauty—this romanticism—that takes me totally off guard. Huge pots of purple flowers sit on either side of the front door. They line the balcony above my head, too. There's a sleek brass knocker on the door itself. Custom made, from what I can tell.

The place is immaculately maintained. Thoughtfully restored.

Daddy would love it. This is exactly his wheelhouse: a thoughtful restoration where history and modernity meet.

Grief, sharp and swift, slices through my chest.

I draw a quick breath, blinking hard. For a second I contemplate turning around. Shooting Greyson a text to say I'm not feeling up to dinner. I want to lick my wounds alone. Maybe take a bath and go to bed by eight like the winner I am. This weird mood just won't quit.

But then the front door is opening, and Greyson appears, leaning one massive shoulder against the jamb. He must've been waiting for me. Watching.

His eyes lock on mine. They are an arresting shade of blue against the early evening gloom.

Literally arresting. My heart's not beating anymore.

Greyson doesn't smile, but those eyes of his do when they take in my outfit. I went with my *nice* yoga pants this time and C of C hoodie.

"I approve of your stretchy pants choice," he says. He crosses his arms, making the muscles in his biceps bulge against his shirt.

I run my eyes up and down the thick, broad outline of his body. I've never, *ever* felt weak in the knees. But right now, taking in Greyson's off-white henley and the *tight* navy sweats that hang low on his hips, my left knee literally gives out.

"Hate yours," I manage.

His lips twitch. He steps aside. "I can tell. Come in."

Stepping into his foyer, I hold out the folder.

"For you," I say. Then I nod at the bourbon in the crook of my elbow. "And this, obviously, is for Charlie Brown."

"Kid after my own heart. Eight weeks and she already has a taste for the good stuff."

"You have no *idea* what I'd do for a good Old Fashioned right now."

Greyson tilts his head. "I've got something better."

I follow him down the hall. Notice the picture frames on top of a chest of drawers we pass. There's a baby in two of them, along with Ford and what I can only assume are other members of their family.

During the interactions I've had with Ford, he's always mentioned his daughter. I wonder what kind of relationship Greyson has with his niece.

Glancing back up at him—the strong lines of his shoulders and back, the alarmingly satisfying way they press against the cozy fabric of his shirt—I wonder again what his story is. I'd had him pegged as a one-dimensional egomaniac. The typical greed-is-good, emotionally stunted corporate hack.

It's becoming clear he's more complex than that.

I like complex men. Same as I like complex characters in fiction.

My hunger to know more about him is a pang that won't go away.

Speaking of hunger. The smell of something buttery and warm makes my stomach grumble as we head down the hall.

It's a homey smell. A comforting one. Growing up, my mom cooked dinner almost every night. The yummy smell would hit me all the way upstairs in my bedroom, where I'd be doing homework or chatting with my friends on AOL instant messenger on the off chance I could hijack our phone line for dial-up internet.

When was the last time someone cooked a meal for me?

Yeah, Greyson and I are wearing pants with elastic waistbands. But this—him cooking, the two of us sharing a meal that doesn't come in takeout boxes—feels extraordinarily special.

Vaguely I wonder where Charlie Brown will sleep when he or she arrives. I imagine we'll need two cribs, right? One at my place. One here, at Greyson's.

The idea of seeing bottles and blankets and bouncy seats in his gorgeous home makes me smile.

My weird mood, which had already begun to dissipate, clears altogether. Replaced by a kind of buzzy-soft excitement.

I just have this feeling about tonight. A good feeling.

The hall opens up into an enormous kitchen with exposed brick walls and soaring ceilings. My gaze roves appreciatively over the quartzite-topped island, the antique wooden beams on the ceiling, the cabinets that are just the right shade of off-black.

It's not my style—too big, too masculine, too industrial—but I can appreciate the craftsmanship and careful design that went into it.

Go figure. Greyson is all about budgets and timelines at work. But at home, it's obvious he's got real taste. Or, at the very least, enough money to *buy* real taste.

He sets the bourbon on the island.

"Your house is beautiful," I say. "Also. Whatever you're making smells amazing."

"My grandmother's chicken and rice," he says, pouring red wine from a fancy looking decanter into two glasses: a wine glass and, as promised, a shot glass. "She called it Chicken Bog, that name is kind of unfortunate, so we go with chicken and rice. Best comfort food there is. Seemed right for a cold, rainy night."

I take the shot glass he holds out to me, swallowing the lump that's suddenly formed in my throat.

I don't cook. But I do know about chicken and rice. It's a classic low country dish that's been around as long as anyone can remember. You simmer a bunch of veggies, rice, and chicken together in a huge pot. Sounds simple, but if you do it right, it actually requires a lot of effort. As evidenced by the countertop beside the range: it's littered with cutting boards, measuring cups, the crispy skins of onions.

Greyson put real work into this. And thought. And care.

It's his *grandmother's recipe.*

Also, he poured me wine. Granted, a teeny tiny bit of it. Two sips at most. But he's not being judge-y about me having some, and I appreciate that. So damn much.

In his own way, Grey is being supportive. Being there for me. And look how much better I feel. I need to take Olivia's advice and go to that prenatal yoga class already. Build a support system there, too.

Greyson taps his glass against mine. "Cheers, Julia. I'm really glad everything went well today."

"Me too. Thanks again for having me. And for knocking me up, I guess. Who would've thought we'd make such an A-plus fetus?"

He laughs. "Not me, that's for damn sure."

His eyes stay on mine as we sip the wine.

"Wow," I say, smacking my lips. "That's good."

"Better than an Old Fashioned?"

I grin. "Yeah. You were right. I'm not typically a red person, but this is delicious."

"Are you just saying that because it's the first alcohol you've had in two months?"

My turn to laugh. God I like it when he gets flirty.

"Probably. Either way, it's still delicious."

"Because you can only have a little bit of it, I wanted to pour the best. I'm picky when it comes to blends, but this Pinot Noir one is exceptional. Made by a small winemaker in Napa Valley."

The lump in my throat returns. Wrong that I'm insanely touched he opened a really good bottle of wine just for me? Even though I can only have half an ounce of the stuff?

"Of *course* you're a wine snob," I tease. Because if I don't make a stab at some humor I'm worried I'll start to tear up.

"It's the Satanist in me. Even Lucifer appreciates good grapes. Here." He pulls out a stool at the island. "Sit. Dinner is almost ready. Can I get you some water? Topo Chico? I grabbed some the other day. You got me addicted to the stuff."

I sit, the soft parts of my chest swelling.

"That would be great, thanks."

He sets a bottle in front of me, then gets to work at the range. Greyson is usually so tightly wound. But here, in his kitchen, he's... relaxed, almost. Doesn't hurry, moving from the fridge to a drawer to a bowl on the counter with measured, easy movements. Whisking oil into the bowl, he takes his time, telling me how his mom taught him to make salad dressing from scratch as he whisks and whisks.

The muscles in his forearm popping in the most erotic way imaginable.

Watching him is hypnotizing. And fun. Who knew Greyson Montgomery was capable of enjoying himself? His obvious ease and excitement is infectious. I could sit here and watch him forever. I never in a million years would've guessed he'd be so good at making me feel comfortable and at home. Least of all in the vast expanse of his bachelor pad.

But that's exactly how I feel. *At home*. The savory-starch scent of a homemade meal in the oven warming the kitchen. Good wine in hand. Cozy clothes. The delicious enigma of a man I have all evening to contemplate and ogle.

Rain outside. Warm inside.

Again. Not where I expected to end up. Not in a million years.

But if I'm being honest? I'm not sure there's anywhere else I'd rather be right now.

Which scares me.

And also makes me feel happier than I have in a long, long time.

Chapter Fourteen

JULIA

Greyson lifts an enormous pot out of the oven and sets it on the range. The delicious smell of home-cooked goodness intensifies.

I can't help but check out his butt in those tight joggers.

I really like him in fitted pants. *Really* like him.

"Let me help," I say, standing.

He shoots me a look over his shoulder. "I got this—sit. Do you prefer breast, thigh, or drumstick?"

"Breast, please."

"Gotta ask, is it too early for boob innuendos?"

I grin. "Never."

"Good. Because I have a real appreciation for the breasts. So tender."

"Satisfying."

"Big. A nice handful."

I hold up my cupped hand, pretending to weigh one. "Bet yours are gorgeous."

"Not as gorgeous as yours."

Wrong that I'm smiling and blushing and preening at his terrible tit joke?

"You noticed."

"I've stroked many things of yours," he shoots my line back at me, grinning. "But I'm sorry to say your ego ain't gonna be one of 'em, sweetheart."

I bite my lip.

My God, this guy is Christian Grey-ing me. The meal, the muscles, the dirty mouth.

I like it when he calls me sweetheart.

The memory hits me out of nowhere. Greyson yanking down the neck of my dress. Leaning in and taking my nipple in his mouth, sucking it to a hard, hot point through the transparent fabric of my bra.

Arousal spikes through my center.

I never let him kiss my mouth. Felt too intimate for the kind of sex we had. But he sure as hell kissed me everywhere else. The heat of his mouth against my skin—

Makes me shiver, even now.

"You okay?" Greyson's brow is furrowed as he sets a plate in front of me. "Is it too cold in here?"

The food smells so good.

He looks *so damn good.*

I am suddenly so, so turned on. By his sweats and his sweetness.

"Fine," I say. "I'm fine."

On fire, but fine.

He sits on the stool beside me, and we dig in.

Immediately flavor explodes in my mouth. The buttery-ness of the rice against the smoky-sweet flavor of the sausage is insane. Chicken is perfectly done, salty and juicy. Veggies are melt-in-your mouth amazing. Even the salad, simple baby greens lightly dressed in Greyson's white balsamic vinaigrette, is restaurant quality.

It's delicious and satisfying in a way I can't quite describe.

"You're doing it again," he says.

"Doing what?"

His gaze slips to my mouth. "Making noises while you eat."

"I can't help it. This is fucking insane, Greyson. Like, the best thing I've eaten since I found out I was pregnant."

He scoffs, shoveling a huge forkful of rice into his mouth. "I wouldn't go that far. But thank you."

Thunder rumbles overhead.

"Seriously." I nudge him with my elbow. "You're clearly good at this—cooking."

"You sound surprised."

"Does it make me sound like a jerk if I am? I always took you for the kind of guy who lived off raw kale and the souls of innocent children."

He shoots me a look, sipping his wine. "I mean, yeah, I devour plenty of that stuff, too. But I do like to cook. It's actually what spurred my decision to get into the hospitality industry."

I pull back. "Really?"

I'd always assumed Greyson did what he did for the money. The prestige. The excuse to wear thousand dollar suits.

But it's apparent that I'm quickly becoming the poster child for that adage—the one about assuming making an ass out of you and me.

"Really. I started my career in investment banking. Knew it wasn't for me, so I went back to business school. Ended up working at a venture capital firm in Silicon Valley after I graduated, which was cool. But it was focused on tech, an industry I wasn't crazy about. And I always knew I wanted to end up back here in Charleston at some point. Be close to my family and everything. I also knew I loved food. Eating it, mostly, but making it, too. Talking about it, sharing it, doing interesting stuff with it. Those things I *am* crazy about. So I saved my pennies, worked on building a small stable of investors, and eventually took the leap with Ford to found the firm."

My heart skips a beat.

So Greyson loves food and family.

Two things I never would've guessed. Although the pieces are starting to click together now. Him working with his brother. The pictures of his niece in the hall. His grandmother's recipe.

Maybe that explains his dedication—often extreme and *very* often annoying—to his work.

Maybe it's about family rather than fortune.

And that kind of changes everything, doesn't it? Who he is.

How I feel about him.

I'm attracted to this man. Have been since we met. But now I'm really, really intrigued by him, too.

I want to know more. Maybe because we're starting a family together—well, our version of it, anyway—and I am drawn to this idea that he's a family man at heart.

Because I'm not sure *I'm* that kind of person?

Because I don't have a family of my own anymore?

"You're full of surprises." I use the edge of my fork to cut my chicken. I feel like he could do the same to my heart right now. They're both fall-off-the-bone tender. "Tell me more. About you."

"What do you want to know?"

"Let's start with an easy one. Favorite color."

He looks at me. Eyes searching mine for a beat.

"Blue. You?"

"Purple. Favorite travel destination."

"Anywhere with good food. Current favorite is Nashville. Honorable mention for New Orleans and Asheville. Guess I have a thing for the 'villes these days. But I have a feeling your favorite spot is more far-flung than my picks."

"It is." I nod. "I love London for the literary history, but Paris will always have my heart. What's your favorite book?"

"Probably the *Lord of the Rings* trilogy. Or *The Name of the Wind* by Patrick Rothfuss."

Rain is pelting against the windows now. The storm made it dark outside earlier than usual; I can see our reflection in the panes.

I raise a brow. "You're a fantasy guy."

"I am. Don't have a ton of time to read for pleasure anymore, but when I do, yeah. It's Potter or George R.R. Martin. Some horror, too. Big Stephen King fan." He sets down his fork and puts a hand on his belly. "Whew."

Nodding at his plate, I ask, "Are you gonna finish that?"

He grins. Nudges the plate toward me, his fingers brushing mine.

"All yours, Julia." He watches, lips curled into that handsome as hell grin, as I clear his plate. "What about you? What's your favorite romance?"

"Way too hard to pick."

"If you had to. Gun to your head."

I chew thoughtfully for a moment. "I love super feel-y romance. Books that give you that delicious ache in your chest, you know? For a historical—I'd say *Private Arrangements* by Sherry Thomas. So, so great. As far as contemporary, I'd say my current favorite is *Landslide* by Kathryn Nolan. Or *The Kiss Quotient* by Helen Hoang. Then there's Kennedy Ryan's stuff. It's pretty damn incredible—I teach her books a lot in my classes. Tessa Bailey's cop romances slay me in the best way. Oh! To go back to historicals, I adore Elizabeth Hoyt—she writes slinky, feely sex like no one else—and you know, our very own Olivia is working her way up the ranks, too. *My Enemy the Earl* will be a perennial favorite of mine. I love how that book explored themes of self-determination and choosing authenticity over expectation. Powerful stuff."

Greyson is still looking at me. But now his grin is in his eyes, too. Gives his expression this wistfulness. This...

Adoration.

My stomach dips.

"What?" I say, turning back to my food.

"Nothing." From the corner of my eye I see him shake his head. "No, wait, it's not nothing. Julia, you light up the whole fucking room when you talk about shit you're passionate about. I've—I don't know if I've ever seen anything like it."

I swallow a bite of chicken. Swallow again.

"The same way you lit up when I gave you free reign to talk tits?"

He erupts with laughter. A big, deep belly laugh that tickles me to the point that I start to laugh, too.

"I'm only human, sweetheart."

I put my hand on his chest. For half a heartbeat I consider grabbing his shirt and pulling him to me and kissing him.

I give him a playful shove instead.

Before I can pull back, he grabs my wrist. My body leaps at the contact, pulsing with awareness that gathers between my legs.

"I mean it," he says. "You know who you are, Julia. And you're not afraid to *be* who you are. To take chances, even after you've been through hell. I admire that."

I look at him. Heart thumping.

Lightning flashes through the windows. More thunder, louder this time.

"This afternoon on the way to the doctor's office—you said something about how many bullshit-y people there are in your world. Ever consider the idea that those aren't your people?"

"I think I'd considered it. But I hadn't taken the idea seriously." He draws his thumb gently over the inside of my wrist. Once, twice. Making the throb inside my skin grow tenfold. "Not until now, anyway."

There's a universe inside that reply. A novel's worth of scenes, stories, answers.

I want him to *tell me that story*. More, even, than I want him to touch me like this all over. Softly, intently, knowledgeably.

"Tell me what you mean by that," I say.

But before I can ask him to, he's dropping my hand and gathering up our empty plates. Both of which are, coincidentally, in front of me.

I blame Charlie Brown. Even though he/she is only the size of a raspberry right now, when my appetite is back, it's back in a big way.

"Why don't you make yourself comfortable on the couch?" He nods at the sleek sectional on the other side of the room. "Have you picked a movie you want to watch? I can get pretty much anything On Demand or through Amazon."

I push back my stool and stand. Lordy, I'm full. In the best way.

"I told you, Greyson, I do the dishes."

"I got it. Go sit."

"You sit. This meal must've taken you hours to prepare. My turn to do the work."

"You're not gonna let this one go, are you?"

I pull the sleeves of my hoodie up to my elbows. "Nope."

"Fine. How about we clean up together then?"

"Last time I'm letting you help."

Chapter Fifteen

GREYSON

The lights flicker just as we sit down.

"Good Lord." Julia glances over her shoulder at the windows above the sink. "Getting nasty out there, isn't it?"

I turn on the TV. "Let's hope the electricity stays on long enough to finish a movie. Whatcha thinking?"

She looks at me, blue eyes alive with mischief.

Julia's felt like shit. She's had an exhausting week, same as me. But she's still burning with energy. This liveliness that throws my own cold, dead heart into depressing relief.

My house is buzzing with her warmth. Same as my blood.

Probably explains why I almost kissed her. By some miracle I was able to curb that impulse at the last minute. But it'd been close.

Too close.

"Can't decide if I want sweet or salty."

"Sweet or salty?"

"Yeah. Sweet, like *Father of the Bride.* Or salty, like episodes of *The Sopranos*. I was going to suggest *Twilight*, but then I assumed your inner werewolf fangirl has seen that one a hundred times, so..."

I smile. I love how she holds no punches. There's no beating around the bush with this girl. No bullshitting. She's straightforward about who she is and what she wants, and I fucking like that. A lot.

"Team Jacob for life. Your pick."

"Go figure, I'm team Edward. No wonder we never got along. How about *The Sopranos*?"

"I could go for some Tony and Carm," I reply, pulling up the OnDemand portal.

"Isn't Carmela kind of the best?"

A boom of thunder rattles the windowpanes. Sounds close. The storm must be right over us.

Immediately my mind goes places it shouldn't. What if it lasts all night? What if it's too dangerous for Julia to walk home?

What if she stays and we touch and we flirt and we end up naked?

"Kind of? She is *the* best. There are so many great characters on this show, but I have to say that she's my hands down—"

I nearly jump when the electricity blinks out with an audible *zap*.

"Uh oh," Julia says.

The sudden arrival of near-complete darkness is discombobulating. I blink once, twice, waiting for my eyes to adjust to the sea of blackness we're swimming in.

Wrong that my first thought is *oh shit I hope this doesn't mean Julia's going to leave*?

I'm not done yet. Not done feeding her—I have two pints of Jeni's ice cream in the freezer. Sweet cream biscuits and peach jam and Savannah buttermint.

I'm not done talking and laughing and just being with her.

I'm voracious for this woman in every way imaginable.

In ways I have no right to be.

I should take this as an opportunity to politely but firmly suggest our evening is over. I haven't had too much wine to drive; I could easily take her home and call it a night.

But I can't. I haven't had this much fun—felt this good—in years.

My eyes start to adjust, shapes and silhouettes coming into view. I find Julia's eyes. They glimmer in the dark. A sparkler that's just been lit, emitting its first flashes of light.

"Do you have any candles?" she says, rising. "A flashlight maybe? I think my phone is somewhere on the counter..."

I dig my phone out of my pocket and turn on the flashlight. "I got it. I'll go find some candles and grab my iPad—I think I have a few episodes of *Game of Thrones* on it if you'd like to watch that?"

She blinks. Furrows her brow.

Then she smiles. "Okay. Yeah. Sounds great."

"Cool. I'll be right back."

Ten minutes later, Julia is lighting the motley assortment of candles I found underneath my sink while I scoop the ice cream into bowls. iPad tucked beneath my arm, I hand her a bowl and settle on the couch beside her.

Our knees brush as she crosses her legs pretzel style. My cock leaps.

I nearly bite off my tongue trying to keep it in check.

Can*not* sport wood. Not now. Don't want to scare her. Give her the wrong idea.

But Lord, how good does the wrong idea sound right now?

I shove the thought from my head and attempt to ignore the throaty noises Julia makes as she eats her ice cream while I cue up *Game of Thrones* on my iPad.

I try to prop it up as best as I can on the coffee table in front of us.

"Yes!" Julia says around a mouthful of ice cream. "It's been so long since I watched the first season. I love how we get to see all the families together—the Starks in particular—before basically everyone dies."

"You know"—finger poised above the play button, I glance at her over my shoulder—"all your movie and TV show picks are about family. Creating it. Losing it. Loving it, even when it's made up of a bunch of murderous Italians or sparkly vampires."

Julia's face is lit by the glow of the screen. Her spoon halts midway between her bowl and mouth. She looks at me for a beat. Looks down at the spoon. Then she slides it into her mouth. Slowly pulls it back out again, a sliver of pink tongue making an appearance as she licks at the corner of her mouth.

She swallows.

I scream. Silently. As the head of my cock glides up the seam of my sweats.

Shit no stop.

"Haven't thought about it that way," she says, looking down at her bowl. "But you're right. Now that I'm thinking about it, too, everything I've read or watched over the past year kind of is about family in a way. I guess...well. I really miss mine."

"I'm sorry. I know I've said that fifteen times already, but I mean it." I look at her. A day ago—hell, even just this afternoon—I don't think I would've been comfortable talking to her about this stuff.

But now it seems wrong not to. Maybe because I'm inspired by Julia's way of cutting through bullshit to get to marrow. I'm inspired and frankly awed by her willingness to give this part of herself up and be vulnerable. I *want more*. Which probably makes me an asshole, considering I've given her nothing beyond headaches at work and a surprise fetus.

"I honestly can't imagine how much it fucking sucks to lose your parents."

Her eyes are getting wet.

"It does suck. I think about them a lot anyway. But now that this whole thing is going on," she says, making a circling motion in front of her belly, "my grief has hit a new low. I think all the time about how much they would've loved being grandparents. How proud they'd be. The joy of telling them this news—even though I got knocked up by a Satanist—Greyson, it would've been awesome. I'd give anything to see their faces when I told them about Charlie Brown and how healthy he is. My mom would go crazy buying all that smocked baby shit for him. She really, really loved kids. Dad would already be building this, like, post-modern swing set in their backyard. They're missing this, *I'm* missing that part of this. I want so badly for it to be different sometimes...it's hard."

Tears clump on her eyelashes. She lets her spoon fall into her bowl with a *clank*. I sit back so that we're eye to eye on the couch. Candlelight flickers across her hair. The curve of her cheek.

My heart is pounding, and I don't know why.

"I don't know what it's like to lose a parent," I say. "But I do know how it feels to want so badly for something to have gone differently. It haunts you. It hurts."

"It does." Julia turns her head a little to look at me. "You know that's part of the reason why I chose to keep this baby—because I lost my family, and this is a way of creating a new one. It won't be the same, obviously, but maybe it's not supposed to be. Maybe this is my chance to make lemonade."

"When life hands you lemons," I say with a tight grin because I can't fucking breathe. "Right."

"I'd actually prefer to use those lemons as a twist in an ice cold martini. But I guess lemonade is the next best thing when you're pregnant."

Can't help it. I reach up and catch a tear with my thumb. I'm gripped by the desire to take her face in my hand. Hold her and kiss her and tell her, without having to say a thing, how much I admire her.

You're devastating.

You're stupid gorgeous.

You're brave in all the best ways, and you're making me want to be brave again, too.

Which is dangerous.

So fucking dangerous. I'm going to hurt one or both of us. All three of us.

But I still find myself leaning into the conversation anyway. Like I have nothing to lose.

Like I deserve another chance.

"Takes courage," I say. "To put yourself out there again with this baby after losing so much. I'm in awe. How? Why?"

Her eyes bounce between mine. "Because I have to. What's the alternative? Staying down? Living small and scared? Yeah, it takes balls to get back up after you've had your ass handed to you. When you've lost the people who matter most to you. But the people whose lives and careers I admire are the ones who kept trying. Who fucked up or fell short or lost again and again but still got up *one more time*. Maybe I've read too much fiction, but I've found that it's usually that last ditch effort that turns things around. If it doesn't, at least you go down trying, you know? At least you did the brave thing. The *right* thing."

"But what if you didn't do the right thing? What if you did something really fucking terrible?"

She looks at me. Waits for me to explain.

When I don't, she continues.

"You learn from it. You take it as a lesson and try to do right the next time around. Just because you're a villain in one story doesn't mean you can't be a hero in another. I happen to like characters with complicated pasts. Nuance is a big turn on."

When was the last time I spoke so honestly to someone?

When was the last time someone spoke so honestly to me?

It's terrifying.

It's the fucking tits.

"You saying bad guys turn you on?"

"I'm saying guys who sometimes do bad things for good reasons get me wet. Humanity in all its messy, imperfect glory is sexy AF."

I laugh. What a peach this woman is. Cracking dirty jokes in the middle of crying.

Also. Deep down, I knew ending my marriage was the right move. But it all felt so horrible—my ex's heartbreak, my family's too, the emotional and financial fallout—that the bad kind of overshadowed the good.

When is breaking someone's heart *ever* not a bad thing?

When your reasons are good.

Somewhere in the back of my mind, at some point during my divorce, I'd considered that concept. Turned it over in my head and heart, ultimately discarding it because it meant I could absolve myself of guilt, and I wasn't ready to do that yet.

What if I'm never ready?

What if I'm ready now?

"You learn all that from romance?" I ask.

"Sure as hell did," she says proudly. "It's a genre that's criminally underrated."

"I believe it."

"So are you going to tell me about this bad thing you did? Or are you going to politely ignore me like you did in there"—she tilts her head toward the kitchen—"and hit play on the Starks?"

I look at her, running my tongue along the inside edge of my front teeth.

I feel close. Close to ready.

But that's not ready enough. This is years of emotional weight I'm trying to shed. Years of fucked up thinking and living.

I lean forward and hit play. I half expect Julia to call me out. Call me a coward.

I deserve it.

But instead she settles into the couch and picks up her spoon.

Her shoulder touches mine. I don't move. Neither does she.

We watch Ned Stark's life unravel in companionable silence. And even though part of me feels riled up inside, another part feels calm and contented and quiet.

I could get used to Julia's brand of Netflix and chill.

Chapter Sixteen

GREYSON

Halfway through episode two, Julia's head lolls and falls lightly on my shoulder.

My heart skips a beat. Body warms.

I look down and see that she's asleep. Eyes closed, chest rising and falling in an easy, slow rhythm. She feels warm and solid against me.

There are few places Julia and I haven't touched each other. I've had fingers and tongue all over her body. She's had me in her mouth, between her legs, between her tits.

But we've never had contact like this. Flirty, soft, fun touching that's making those butterflies in my stomach take flight.

She's trusting me. Me, the wolf.

This smart, brave woman thinks I'm worthy of her trust, despite knowing the strength of my bite.

Is it fucked up that that fills me? To the brim?

I want to wrap her in my arms and fall asleep with her right here on the couch. But she's exhausted, for one thing, and probably is in desperate need of a good night's sleep in a real bed.

For another, I don't trust myself not to wake her up and fuck her five ways to Sunday.

That can't happen. For a lot of reasons.

A new one that wasn't there before. I like Julia. *Like* her. What if I show her my dark side—what if I tell her the truth about what I did—and she hates me for it? Judges me? I don't want to lose her.

What if she sees the real me and runs?

So I reach for the iPad, careful not to move her, and turn it off. I slip one arm under her torso, the other underneath her knees. Bending my legs so I don't lift with my back, I stand, cradling her against my chest.

Julia makes a noise, eyes fluttering open.

"Shit, did I fall asleep? I'm sorry. I'll go home. Wait, Greyson, are you—"

"Carrying you up to my bed? Yes."

Her lips curl into a sly, sleepy little smile. "Are you going to have your way with me? How villainous."

"Nah. Thought I'd play the hero tonight and let you have your rest. I'll sleep down here."

Julia lifts a brow. "See? Villain in one story, hero in another."

"Don't tempt me," I grunt, climbing the stairs. "If you knew what is going through my mind right now, you wouldn't be saying that."

"Heroes are allowed to have dirty minds." She loops her arms around my neck, resting her head against my chest. "I actually prefer them that way."

Sweet baby Jesus.

As if I couldn't want this woman more.

"Help yourself to anything you need," I say as I carefully maneuver Julia into my bedroom. "Bathroom's right in there, and I've got plenty of clothes in the closet if you'd like to change. Usually I enforce a strict no-clothes policy in my bed, but I'll make an exception tonight. If you get hungry, just come get me and I'll whip something up for you. There's plenty of leftovers, and I've got some Greek yogurt in the fridge, too. I was reading that pregnant women should have some protein in their snacks, so..."

But Julia is asleep again, arms falling from around my neck.

I tuck her in, careful not to wake her. Grin when she lets out a contented sigh as I pull the covers up to her chin. I turn the heat down at night, so I don't want her getting cold.

I want to climb into bed with her. God, do I want that. But I have no illusions about what will go down if that happens. Plus, I don't want her waking up in the middle of the night next to a dude she doesn't remember falling asleep with.

So I leave the hall light on and head back downstairs.

The rain's let up a bit. I grab a cigarette and step outside onto the balcony, making sure to shut the door firmly behind me. Don't want any second hand smoke getting into the house with Julia inside.

Outside, the air is chilly but humid. Charleston in late autumn and winter.

I light the cigarette and take a big inhale. I wait for the usual release that comes—the fleeting lightness—as I slowly exhale, tilting my head up to the sky.

But it doesn't come.

Furrowing my brow, I take another drag.

The realization hits me on the third inhale.

The lightness doesn't come because it's already there.

In my head and my chest. My limbs. My mood.

I don't need nicotine to make me feel better because I already do.

I already feel warm and fuzzy. Julia is upstairs. Charlie Brown, too. Both of them safe and warm under my roof. I fed Julia, I made her laugh. I lit her up and drew her out. Drew parts of myself out in the process.

Is this what happy feels like? It's been so long.

But these butterflies—they just won't quit.

Part of me wants to smoke the rest of this cigarette. No question I'm 100% addicted, and my body craves the nicotine. But another part—a part I don't recognize—wants to see if I have the willpower to put it out. Right now.

Exactly how deep am I in here?

How much power do I really have to choose what happens next?

Julia's making me want something other than *hurt*.

But do I really believe I can heal? Do I really think I deserve to?

Just because you're a villain in one story doesn't mean you can't be a hero in another.

I take one last drag. Sneak another. My hand shakes as I stub it out.

But I do it. I put the fucking thing out.

I duck back inside before I change my mind.

Julia

I wake up in a bed that's not mine.

The sheets are silky cool. Cotton percale, Egyptian if I had to guess.

And the pillow smells like bergamot.

It smells like Greyson.

A rush of heat floods my core. I blink open my eyes and suck in a breath. I'm swimming in the middle of an enormous bed, the covers tucked tightly around me.

I'm a burrito. In Greyson Montgomery's bed.

Last night comes back to me in a rush. The sonogram, *The Sopranos*, Greyson's grandmother's chicken and rice and a half shot of Pinot.

My God, that *chicken*. And that *rice*.

And the way he looked in those tight joggers and tighter henley.

I remember him carrying me up the stairs, Callum-the-angry-Scot style. The way he held me was so careful. Grip firm but touch gentle.

He made me feel safe.

Never in a million years would I have thought I'd feel safe with this man. Egomaniac boss. Instigator of fights. Slayer of vaginas.

But here I am. Tucked sweetly into his clean, cavernous bed. Still full from the amazing meal he made from scratch to celebrate Charlie Brown's first ultrasound.

My stomach flips when I think about Greyson sleeping next to me. We didn't have sex—that much I know—but maybe we slept together. Literally. For the first time ever.

I turn my head. Feel a pinch of disappointment when I see the other half of the king bed is neatly made. Where did he sleep, I wonder? Sofa? Guest bedroom?

Why didn't he sleep with me? The shock of waking up next to him is almost too delicious to contemplate.

An ache fills me.

I miss the smell of his skin and the weight of his body. The feel of his mouth on my neck. The things he'd do with those big, knowledgeable hands of his.

I'm so drawn to his confidence.

Last night, that confidence faltered when we were talking about taking risks and second chances. But I'm drawn to that, too—the crack in his facade, the glimpse of real human vulnerability.

As much as I want to know what his story is, he's got to be ready to tell it.

I'll wait patiently in the meantime.

My heart stumbles around my chest as I pad to the bathroom, already punch drunk at the prospect of seeing a scruffy, sleep-rumpled Greyson first thing in the morning.

I find him passed out cold on the sofa downstairs. He's got one arm bent behind his head. Snoring softly.

I smile and pull the thin blanket a little higher over his chest. He may run hot—his skin was always scalding to the touch—but it's freezing in here.

The scent of last night's meal lingers in the air. My stomach grumbles. I glance at the kitchen. I may not cook, but I know some people who do.

I wonder how Greyson takes his coffee. Does he even drink it?

Only one way to find out.

Half an hour later, there's a soft knock at the front door.

Gracie stands on the stoop, a tray of coffees in one hand and a paper bag in the other.

"So y'all needed some nourishment after working up an appetite last night, huh?" she says with a grin, holding out the goodies. "This should do the trick. Two bacon-egg-and-cheeses on Marie's croissants. I threw in a pumpkin scone, too. Good for that quick sugar energy if y'all, I don't know, decide to go for another round or whatever."

I press a kiss to her cheek, and pass her a few bills as she hands me the coffees and food. "I already told you that this sleepover is as innocent as it gets. Please note my hoodie and pregnancy pooch. But thank you for bringing all this over. Greyson made dinner last night, so I figured breakfast was the least I can do."

"Are y'all, like, 'hanging out' now?" she says, bending her fingers in air quotes.

"No." I play with the lid on my iced coffee. "Maybe. I don't know. I think...Grace, I think have a little crush on him. More than a crush."

She arches a brow. "Didn't see that one coming."

"Me neither. I feel like I'm in the Twilight Zone. He was so awful for so long. But now that I'm getting to know him—"

"He's actually turning out to be a good guy?"

I scoff. "I wouldn't say good. Interesting, maybe. Layered. Complex. A little fucked up."

"You're in *trouble*," Gracie says, still grinning.

I look down at the coffee. Let out a sigh. "Yeah."

"Chin up." She puts her hand on my arm. "You're only tied to this guy for the rest of your life. You've got plenty of time to figure out how you feel about him."

I laugh. "Thanks again for the impromptu delivery service."

"Anytime. And don't forget brunch tomorrow! The girls and I want to talk about your shower."

"My shower?"

"You knew we'd want to throw you a baby shower. I know it's early, but let's at least pick a date and get you going on your registry, all right?"

I feel a familiar swelling in my throat. "Thank y'all. Really. I couldn't do this without you."

"It's an honor to be part of your village." She gives my arm a squeeze. "This sweet baby is gonna get a lot of love. See y'all later. And say hi to Greyson for me and Luke!"

I close the door and take a breath. I'm smiling and tearing up all at once.

The moment I found out I was pregnant, things were looking pretty grim. I felt like shit, I was having a baby with a guy I did not like, and I felt very, very alone.

But now, in the space of a couple months, all that has changed. I didn't think I'd ever feel this full or this...hopeful, I guess, ever again.

I'm starting to see glimmers of the magic of parenthood everyone talks about.

I'm starting to get excited about this baby.

About being a mom.

"Jesus, Julia, I was worried you left."

My stomach dips so hard and so suddenly at the sleep-roughed sound of Greyson's voice, I nearly drop our coffees.

I spin around to find him standing in the hall a few paces from me. Barefoot. Dark hair everywhere. Blue eyes trained on mine as he runs a hand over his stubble.

My.

Fucking.

God.

Desire, hot and sudden, catches between my legs. Stays there, pulsing.

"My bed was empty," he continues, crossing his arms over the barrel of his chest. "Couldn't find you anywhere. Thought maybe I'd scared you off."

"Lucky for you, I don't scare easy," I manage. "Even when you're being your growly Satanist self."

His eyes do that thing where they light up. Smile. He nods at the goodies in my hands.

"What'd ya get?"

"Breakfast. From Holy City Roasters. Wasn't sure how you took your coffee, so I went with black."

"Like my soul?"

I grin. "Exactly."

"Lucky for you, that's actually how I like it. C'mon." He tilts his head toward the kitchen. "Let's eat."

Chapter Seventeen

JULIA

"So I was thinking," Greyson says, licking a stray bit of melted cheese from the tip of his first finger.

"What were you thinking?"

I sip my coffee. God that's good. Before I got pregnant, I was the first person in line at Gracie's coffee shop when it opened at six A.M. Hands down, her cold brew is the best I've ever had. I order a small these days instead of my usual large, but I'm grateful I didn't have to give it up altogether. I would really be a zombie without my daily dose of caffeine.

"Now that we know everything is looking good with Charlie Brown, I'd like to tell my parents."

I look at him. Pale morning sunlight streams through the kitchen windows and catches on his stubble, turning the ends to gold.

"Okay," I reply.

Greyson meets my gaze. "Would you like to do it with me? My mom is making Sunday supper tomorrow. Come."

A familiar heat prickles to life behind my eyes. I blink, hard, my lips working their way into a smile.

This means something. Greyson opening up his family to me.

Greyson opening up at all.

"Last night you were talking about what a bummer it is that you don't get the chance to share the news with your parents," he says. "I want you to have a chance with mine. I want you to meet them, Julia."

I'm biting my lip again, Anastasia Steele style.

I'm overwhelmed. All this goodness. Greyson's scruff and this coffee and his kindness.

Kindness that is turning me on something fierce right now.

"I'd love to."

He grins, and I swear to God the sun burns through the windows even brighter.

"I have to warn you." He takes a bite of his sandwich. "My family is great, but the energy and the attention can get overwhelming."

"I'm okay with that."

"You say that now, Julia, but you haven't met my mother. Ever since Bryce—Ford's daughter—was born, Mom's been dying for more grandchildren. There will be screaming. And about fifty thousand questions, most of which will be very personal and/or totally inappropriate."

Laughing, I finish my sandwich. Before I'm done wiping my hands on my napkin, Greyson is breaking the pumpkin scone in two and placing half on my wedge of tin foil.

Why?

Why does this simple gesture make me feel like I'm about to smile or cry or both?

"What?" he says in reply to the look I give him. "Charlie Brown likes sweets. So does his mom. Y'all inhaled that ice cream last night."

"It was Jeni's," I stammer.

"So good, right?"

"The best."

"I only get the best for you and Charlie."

I'm still looking at him. He's still looking at me.

I can smell the toothpaste on his breath.

My heart is beating loud and strong inside my chest.

I can't.

Jesus, I can't hold it in. My desire for him. The joy I feel just breathing the same air, being in the same room.

I *can't*. Wasn't I just giving a speech to Greyson about living bravely? About putting yourself out there, even when you're scared?

Lord am I scared. But every bone in my body is screaming *do it*. Take the chance.

Find out if he tastes as delicious as he looks.

Tiny tremors erupt just inside my skin as I lean forward. Greyson watches me. Forehead not exactly furrowed, but I can just make out the two lines between his eyebrows.

My heart is beating so. Hard.

I curl my hand around his chin, pressing my thumb into the sweet little indent there.

And then, before I can chicken out, I close my eyes. He draws a breath.

I tilt my head and press my lips to his.

His mouth is warm and *soft*. Full. My nose brushes against the scruff on his cheek. I smell his bergamot aftershave. A hint of cigarette smoke.

Smoke I feel rising up inside my body as desire burns me alive. My pussy throbs. Lips tingle.

Please, I silently beg. *Kiss me back. Kiss me with the need I saw in your eyes last night.*

The need I felt in his touch.

Then again, maybe I imagined it.

Because he pulls back suddenly, breaking the kiss. His eyes dart between mine, wild and fiery.

Fuck.

Fuck fuck fuck. I pissed him off. I crossed a line.

I drop my hand, putting it on my stomach like I can catch it before it falls too fast, too far.

Oh, God, how stupid—

"Julia," he growls. Brows curving upward, softening his expression.

"I'm sorry. That was completely—I don't—I'm so embarra—"

But then Greyson is taking my face in his hands and bending his neck and capturing my mouth with his. His lips slant over mine, open and slick. He pulls at me, drawing me up to meet him as his tongue licks slowly into my mouth.

He growls again when my tongue meets his. This desperate animal sound that makes my nipples pebble. He deepens the kiss. Hard and hungry. Like he's been starving for this.

For me.

My hands reach for him, fingers tangling in the soft fabric of his shirt. He feels impossibly solid here. Warm and big.

The desire between my legs becomes acute.

He turns his head, nose brushing mine. Never breaking the kiss, just moving knowledgeably and confidently through it. His scruff chafes my skin; I'm definitely going to have some beard burn going on after this.

Not that I mind. I don't care if my skin turns to sandpaper. This kiss—

I just.

No words.

I surrender to the force of Greyson's gravitational pull. He's rising to his feet, he's taking me with him, my body's melting into his as I loop my arms around his neck and curl into his warmth.

What an idiot I was not to let this man kiss me. Because he can *kiss*. Maybe I'm just starved for sex or human contact or both. But fireworks are going off behind my closed eyelids in celebration of just how juicy and good his mouth feels against mine.

Who the fuck *is* this man? The asshole, the cook, the secret Satanist sweetheart?

I glide my fingers into the hair at the nape of his neck. His hands trail down my sides, thumbs dipping into the waistband of my pants.

Desire, sharp, slices through my core. I'm feeling weak in the knees again.

I roll my hips into his pelvis. He groans. He's hard. As desperate for me as I am for him by the feel of it.

I give his hair a tug.

Plucking at my bottom lip, he says, "My bed. I'm enforcing the no-clothes policy this time."

"Please," I pant. "Please God yes."

This man knows what he wants.

He wants me.

Following him up the stairs, I marvel in the feeling of knowing what I want, too.

For the first time in a long time, I feel certain.

I feel right.

I feel like myself. Caffeinated. Curious. Sexy.

And that's kind of the best feeling of all, isn't it?

The second we enter his bedroom, Greyson is tugging his shirt over his head. For a whole heartbeat, I get a marvelous view of his bare back. Broad shoulders that narrow to a slender waist. Muscles bunching under smooth skin that's smattered with freckles.

I decide that backs are a criminally underrated part of the male physique.

Reaching out, I trail my finger down the furrow of his spine. Lingering one beat, then another, just above the curve of his ass.

He's got *such* a nice ass.

Not like I ever had much chance to explore his body. Our encounters were always quick and to the point. Dirty, yes. Creative? Sometimes. But we never lingered. Now that I'm thinking about it, I wonder if I've ever been fully naked with Greyson before. One—or both—of us usually left some clothing on in the interest of expediency.

I hope that's not the case today.

Turning his head, Greyson looks at me over his shoulder. Eyes landing on my hoodie.

"What the fuck did I say about my no-clothes policy?"

A shiver darts up my spine. He's being growly and impatient—the villain, the werewolf—and I love it. I grab the hem of my hoodie and stride in front of him, yanking it over my head as I make for the bed.

Before I can get there, Greyson grabs me by the hand and pulls me against him. My back to his front. I suck in a breath at the delicious sensation of skin on skin.

He leans down to press a kiss to my neck, nicking me with his teeth as he hooks a finger into my bra clasp at my back. He uses his thumb to guide the clasp free, and pushes the straps of my bra over my shoulders.

It falls to the ground.

My nipples are simultaneously a little sore and screaming for attention. I reach behind me and dig my fingers into his hair again, arching a little so he takes the hint.

His palms smooth over the sides of my torso just underneath my underarms toward my front.

Gently—with a softness that takes me off guard—he cups my breasts, carefully kneading them in his palms.

Electricity spreads throughout my skin. My eyes flutter shut.

One thing that's always struck me about Greyson is how hard he grabs things. Opportunity. Timing. The world's balls.

But right now, he's achingly tender. Taking my tits in his hands and gathering their weight in his palms, like he's touching light.

The divine for the first time.

"This okay?" he murmurs, lips brushing my ear. "I know you said you were sore."

I fist his hair in reply. "This—so good."

He leans down and kisses my neck, sending bolts of heat straight to my clit. I moan. His hands move to my yoga pants, and then he's tugging them over my hips.

I step out of them, one leg at a time. I'm naked. Unprepared. I usually get regular waxes, but that went out the window with my positive pregnancy test. Couldn't fathom getting my pubic hairs ripped out while in the throes of morning, noon, and night sickness.

My body has changed, too. My nipples have gotten bigger and darker. I'm not showing yet, but my stomach is distended. Like I just ate the person-sized burrito I was this morning.

But right now, I don't give a fuck. I'm turned on and I'm doing this.

I'm sexy just as I am.

A fact Greyson confirms when I turn around to face him. His eyes rake shamelessly over my body, making goosebumps break out on my skin.

"Baby, you look—"

He reaches out. Puts a hand on my belly and shakes his head.

"What?"

His eyes lock on mine. "Beautiful."

Cannot. Even.

I grab the tie at the waistband of his sweats. Give it a tug, releasing the knot. The waistband sags just the tiniest bit, revealing a vein that snakes down his groin and an arrow of dark pubic hair.

My pussy *sings*.

Licking my lips, I pull his sweats down a little more. Just enough to bare his cock. It juts obscenely—unabashedly—from between his hips.

Man's got a gorgeous dick. Not huge, not little, just right. It stands straight up, the shaft smooth, save for the two veins that line the underside. The head is pink and perfectly round.

I wrap my hand around him, reveling in the feel of his skin. Hot. Tight. It's been so long since I touched him like this.

I've missed it.

He hisses when I draw my thumb over the head. I look up and meet his gaze. Give him a slow, easy pull, working the skin over his shaft.

His eyes are hooded. He leans down and kisses my mouth, gliding a hand onto my face.

"So good," he repeats against my lips. "So good, baby."

He moans when I pull a little harder, tightening my grip. I slip a finger lower, giving his balls a caress. His hips buck. He bites my bottom lip.

"Nu-huh," he growls. "You come first. Like always."

My heart dips. And then he's lifting me by the backs of my thighs, his dick pressing against my belly as he takes one, two steps and sets me lightly on the bed.

I fall onto my back, my knees parting. Greyson's eyes catch on my pussy as he steps out of his sweats.

His nostrils flare.

I want him there. So badly.

At first, that's what I think he's going to give me. He climbs over me, covering me with his big, broad body. Trailing his mouth over my knees, my belly, stopping to gently suck on a nipple before kissing my chest and neck. My legs fall completely open, and he settles between them, bracketing my head with his elbows.

The hair on his thighs brushes against my legs. The thrill of having him completely—completely naked, no boundaries, no rules—is indescribably sweet.

He nudges my nose with his and kisses me. Deep.

He's kissing me nonstop. Like he can't get enough.

Like he's got a lot of time to make up for.

Never breaking the kiss, Greyson rests his weight on one arm and reaches between us with the other. He grabs my knee and guides it to his hip, spreading me wider.

My blood leaps when I realize what's coming next.

His hand sweeps down my leg toward my hip. He lifts his body, and glides his palm over my pussy, pressing the heel into my clit.

"Greyson," I moan, the crown of my head dragging across the duvet as I arch against him, clawing at his chest.

"My God you're soft," he replies roughly. "Ready."

"Are you gonna make me beg?"

He smirks. "Only if you want me to."

He removes his palm, and glides a finger up the length of my slit, back to front. Circles my clit, which makes me want to scream. Dips inside, which makes me want his cock.

Pressure.

Enough of all this pressure. I need relief.

Just when I really am about to beg him to put on a condom—yeah, I'm pregnant, but we haven't talked about STDs—and put himself inside me, he starts working his way back down my body. Mouth all over my skin as he hooks my left leg over his shoulder, then my right.

"Oh, yes," I breathe, putting a hand on his head.

It's between my legs now. His eyes meet mine. He watches my expression as he opens his mouth and presses his tongue to my pussy. I see stars when he toys with my clit, my hips starting to roll.

He places his hands on the insides of my thighs.

"Put your feet on my shoulders," he says. "I want all of you. Wide open."

I do as he tells me, spreading myself farther, and he does not hesitate. He eats me out with erotic patience and intention, and I feel a familiar tightening, a maddening stretch that warns of a massive orgasm yet to come. His fingers play with my pussy while his tongue dips inside me, around me. While he gently nicks my clit with his teeth, giving it a quick, devastating suck before moving to explore other parts.

That's what he's doing. Exploring me. Taking his time.

Literally savoring me, letting out these rude little grunts.

"Now you're doing it," I pant.

"Doing what?"

"Making noises while you eat."

His eyes are on mine. They're dancing.

"Sweetheart"—he presses a kiss to the inside of my thigh—"you have no idea how much I missed this. Missed *you*."

My stomach dips as my impending orgasm spirals higher.

"I've missed you too," I reply, gently slicing my fingers through his hair. "The growly boss. Your body. Your tongue, more specifically."

He laughs, my pussy vibrating at the sound.

He laps at me with the flat of his tongue, and my head falls back on the bed. This feels *so damn good*. High thread count sheets at my back. Naked as the day I was born. Greyson's head between my legs, stoking me higher and higher toward my first orgasm in months.

It's not even nine in the morning yet.

Too early to say this just might be the best day ever?

He takes my clit between his lips at the same moment he sinks two fingers inside me. My eyes squeeze shut as my legs begin to shake.

"Grey," I manage, back arching.

"I like it when you call me that. Say it again when you come."

He's kissing my pussy now, stroking and pulling and sucking. My God, the sucking, it's soft and it hurts and I want—

I need—

I reach down and pluck at one nipple, then the other.

My orgasm rips through me, the release so powerful it flirts with the line between pleasure and pain. I buck against his face, but he doesn't stop, slipping his hands onto my ass cheeks and holding me steady as I come.

My legs are shaking and my pussy is contracting and I'm chanting his name over and over again. Waves of sensation roll through me, knocking down every defense, every warning, every fear.

I've read somewhere that pregnant women have increased blood flow to the genital area.

Maybe that explains why this orgasm is to die for. It's the existential kind. The kind you remember. That makes you grateful to be alive.

It's that damn good.

It's happening with Grey.

When I'm finally able to catch my breath, I open my eyes. He's looking at me, expression all soft and sweet, and my heart goes soft, too.

Lord above, I'm in deep, and I'm not even sure how I got here.

All I know is I want more.

"I'm impressed," he says, voice husky. "I've made you come before. But never quite like that."

I give his hair a tug. "Get up here."

"Yes, ma'am."

I grin as he climbs over me, placing his palms on either side of my head.

"This is a fun little role reversal," I say, gliding a hand up his chest. He's got a nice smattering of dark wiry hair here that stands out against his pale skin.

Grey ducks down and kisses me. I taste myself on his mouth.

It turns me on all over again.

"Julia," he says, taking my bottom lip between his teeth, "you've always been the boss. You've always had the power."

Now it's my heart that's dipping. Our lashes tangle as he tilts his head and kisses me more deeply. A hungry kiss. One I'm starting to know well.

"That's not true."

He pulls back. Searches my eyes.

"Think about it, sweetheart. When have I ever not been at your mercy?"

"Uh. The Rodgers' Farms project, for starters."

He shakes his head. "Maybe I won a battle here and there. But you won the war. Honestly, it was over before it even began. You had me under your spell from the beginning. I was enthralled by you from the start. You had the better ideas. The better vision. And you had the better of me."

I swallow, hard. Running my fingers down his arm. The muscles there harden and bunch as I move.

"Then why were you always such a dick? Why'd you fight me at every turn?"

He sighs. A sigh he catches with a small grunt.

"I'm sorry."

I look at him. "I know. And I appreciate the apology. But I think it's fair to say you owe me a real explanation. I admit I've been fighting this sense of whiplash—how you went from the prick in the power suit to the softie charmer who makes dinner and also makes me come so hard I forget my own name."

"I know, Julia. I'm trying. I'm trying." He looks at me for a beat. He's got this pleading look in his eyes.

He's asking me for time. Patience.

He's opening up to me. Slowly, yes. But he's still moving forward. And maybe for someone as locked up and uptight as he is, that counts as real progress.

Also. It's not like we don't have time. Like Gracie said, I've got the rest of my life, literally, to get to know this man. This baby isn't going anywhere, and neither are we.

"Keep trying." I reach for him, wrapping my hand around his hard length. A flare of heat erupts in his gaze. "In the meantime, lemme make you feel as good as I do right now."

Chapter Eighteen

GREYSON

I just might be in love with this woman.

Granted, my rational mind probably isn't working with Julia's hand wrapped around my dick.

But she's giving me time. Giving me the space I need to gather myself. Gather my courage and my thoughts.

I am not a patient man. Especially not with myself.

The fact that Julia is being patient with me makes me want to change that.

She's making me want to change everything.

Which is a scary fucking prospect.

A groan erupts in my chest when Julia gives me a tight tug. I'm so hard right now I'm the size of a goddamn tree trunk. Making her come like that—seeing her surrender to me, to sensation—was the sexiest thing I have ever, *ever* seen.

The taste of her cunt is all over me.

I'm going to come in three seconds if I'm not careful.

Julia twists her wrist as she tugs, curling her palm over my head before moving back down.

Just how I like it.

Closing my eyes, I draw a sharp breath through my nose. My arms shake a little.

"Grey, baby, lay down," she says, her accent thickening. She gives my cock a squeeze. "Let me take care of this."

I love it when she calls me these things. Grey. Baby.

Shiiiiiit this is happening fast.

Who am I kidding? It's been happening all along.

And I'm too far gone to stop now.

Ducking my head to kiss Julia one last time, I roll over onto my back, the mattress dipping beneath my weight.

She props herself up on her elbow beside me. Then it's her turn to climb over me. Her mouth is on my chest, lingering on my nipple before heading south. Her hair, a wild blond halo, is everywhere, tickling my skin as she moves.

My cock throbs as she gets closer. And closer.

Tucking an arm behind my head, I prop myself up so I can watch.

Julia giving head is a sight to behold. I'm not gonna last long, so I want to make the most of every moment.

Straddling my thighs, she shoots me a look.

Leans down, the hardened points of her tits brushing my thighs.

Kisses me, running her tongue along the crown of my dick.

Too. *Much*. My. *God*—

Parting her lips—parting her knees, sinking lower—she swallows my head into the soft heat of her mouth. Careful not to get me with her teeth.

My balls tighten. I bite down on the inside of my cheek. Reach for her, holding back her hair so it's out of her face and I can get a better look.

"*Julia*." It comes out as a moan. A plea.

I am at her mercy. Vulnerable and open and needy.

She's wrecked me.

I'm fucking *wrecked*.

She takes me all the way to the back of her throat in reply. One smooth, steady motion.

Can't help it. I jack my hips. She pulls back.

Immediately I sit up, terrified I've, like, suffocated her or something.

"Julia. Baby. You don't—"

She puts the flat of her palm to my chest and pushes me back. Hard. My blood spikes. Cock throbs inside the warmth of her mouth.

I bite back a smile.

This is a game I like.

This is a question I know the answer to.

"See?" I say, gently pushing her hair out of the way. "See who has the power here?"

My cock in her mouth, she looks up. A wicked gleam in her eye.

Oh, yeah.

Yeah, she gets it.

She bobs down. At the same moment I lift my hips and thrust up.

Julia gags. I feel her soft palate contracting around my head. I go still.

But then she burrows down again. More.

She wants more.

I don't know up from down.

She takes me deep and then I thrust deeper. She's caressing my thigh, my fingers are tangled in her hair and pulling. She moans, the wrist on her other hand working as she tugs at the base of my dick.

Every time she bobs down, I can see the long, lean lines of her back. She's strong. Beautiful. Completely naked and completely at my mercy.

Same as I'm at hers.

"I'm five fucking seconds from coming," I grunt. "If you don't stop now, I'm doing it in your mouth."

That's never happened before. I always finished in a napkin or condom. Too eager—too stupid—too rushed—to do it any other way.

Now that we're actually taking our time, and doing this right, I want to change that.

Julia's eyes flash with heat when they meet mine one last time. And then she sucks. Curls her tongue around my head when she pulls back, then goes deep.

"You want that, don't you?" I say, fisting her hair in my hand.

She sucks harder.

"Swallow," I pant. "All of it."

And then I come.

I come so hard I roar, a sound I've never made before.

Julia keeps sucking, swallowing my hot pulses of cum. My whole *being* pulses in time to my release.

When I'm done, she carefully pulls back. Eyes on mine the whole time.

Reaching down, I run my thumb over her swollen lips.

No trace of cum. She did exactly as I told her. And from the look of it, she enjoyed it, too.

She smiles. This lewd, dirty, amazing little smile.

I take her by the arm and pull her up to me. Kiss her mouth, her neck, her tits.

Kissing her is just as fucking sweet as I thought it'd be. No surprise she's passionate. Soft. Willing to try new things.

"I wish we could do this all day," I say, drawing her up into a deep, warm kiss. The kind that has her rising to meet my strokes, that sweet tongue of hers tangling playfully with mine.

I can taste myself in her mouth. But I also taste her. That knowledge—how she tastes, how she moves, what she likes in a kiss—feels more intimate than our backseat screwing ever did.

We kiss until I'm dizzy. Then I curl her body into mine. The little spoon to my big one.

"Why can't we? Do this all day, I mean?" she murmurs.

"I'm booked solid from ten onward. Meetings, two site visits, and then dinner and drinks with a potential investor."

Julia lets out a breath through her nose.

"Wow. You really do work a fuck ton."

"Well, yeah. When you own your own company, there's no such thing as work-life balance. A lot of people are trusting me with a lot of their hard earned money. I can't fall down on them. Same as I can't fall down on my family." I slide my hand to her belly. "I've got mouths to feed."

"I bring home the bacon, too," she replies. "I don't need you to feed me or Charlie Brown. Although we definitely don't mind it when you cook."

"You have, what, five jobs? Three careers? Work is your life, too."

She laughs. "Greyson—"

"Grey. I like it when you call me Grey."

"All right, Grey. I have one job, and a side gig I do every so often because I'm obsessed with design and it helps me feel connected to my dad. I love my work, but it's not my life. My friends are my life. My books. I travel. Walk. I love antiquing. Music. Dancing I *really* love. Experiences are important to me. I need to do stuff and see stuff to stay inspired—which means getting away from my laptop on a regular basis."

I keep my lips in her hair. Inhale the scent of her shampoo.

"It shows. You're pretty damn inspiring yourself."

"Speaking of getting away from my laptop—I've started looking into maternity leave. When I'd take it. How much I'd take. I've met with my department head and the HR team at C of C to figure out how to make it all work. Have you given any thought to the time you'll take off when the baby comes?"

My heart clenches. To be honest, I have no idea how I'm going to take any time at all off. I haven't been on vacation in years. Never take a sick day. I'm always in the office because I have to be. Maybe Julia and I can, I don't know, hire some help. My parents are retired, and I know they'll be around and willing to help out.

"We'll figure it out," I say, burying my face in the crook of her neck. "God you smell good."

"That's not very comforting—the 'we'll just figure it out' part. I'd like to have a real plan."

"Trust me on this. I always come through, don't I?"

She takes a breath. Lets it out. "Except when you're late for doctor's appointments."

"Hey, we still made it, didn't we? I'll get better, Julia."

"You sure about that?"

"I'm sure."

Another breath. Another sigh out.

Then she arches her back, the curve of her ass pressing into my groin. My dick responds immediately.

"All right."

Lord, this woman is turning me into a monster. An insatiable, hot-blooded, horny monster.

What I would give to spend the day naked with her. Fuck her fifteen times and make her come fifteen more. Every way I could imagine. Me on top, her on top. From behind. In the shower. On the kitchen counter. I'd fuck her 'til we were both too sore or hungry to keep going. Then I'd make her food—pimiento cheese sandwiches, maybe, on fluffy rolls from Gracie's bakery—and we'd watch an episode or two of *The Sopranos* before running back up to bed again.

My God, do I want that. Can't remember the last time I spent a Saturday just dicking around. Having fun.

But I want to take care of my family more. Now, more than ever, it's important that I keep a steady hand and dedicate myself to my work. I'm a provider. It's what I do.

It's who I am.

"So what is it I'm inspiring you to do, exactly?" she says, her voice an octave lower as she reaches back and glides her fingers through my hair.

Damn it I love when she does that.

"You're killing me, sweetheart," I groan. "I don't know how late dinner will go tonight, and I won't keep you waiting. But what if you come over tomorrow night? After dinner? My mom usually serves supper on the earlier side. I'll pick you up at five. Can't let you walk into the line of fire alone."

Julia turns to face me. Lips pulled into a grin that touches her eyes.

"Sounds perfect. And Grey?"

"Yeah?"

"Can you wear tight pants again? I liked how those stretchy pants looked on you. Maybe you have, I don't know, a pair of jeans or something that are just as...fitted."

I lean in and tilt my head and kiss her. Long and soft.

"I'll see what I can do."

Her taste lingers on my mouth the rest of the afternoon.

Between meetings—in addition to having coffee with a couple potential clients, I meet with my realtor to go over some options she put together for a new house—I manage to squeeze in an appointment with my brother at Brumley's, our favorite tailor. The place is a Charleston institution. Located at the very end of King Street, the city's bustling shopping district, it's been around since my dad was having his first suits made back in the seventies. Ford and I have been customers for as long as I can remember.

Ford is picking up a couple suits he'd ordered, and I'm having a new tuxedo made for Eli and Olivia's wedding (Eli's restaurant was one of my very first projects, and he and I have become close.) Recycling the one I wore for my own wedding seemed like bad luck. Plus I want to do something a little different this time around, style wise, after hearing Julia's thoughts on my sweatpants.

Ford holds Bryce in his lap while I step onto a podium in front of a three-way mirror. Rollins, the same tailor I've been going to for years, gets to work on fixing the pants I'm trying on.

I catch Bryce's eye in the mirror. Wink at her.

She blinks both her eyes and smiles. She hasn't quite figured out the one-eye wink yet.

"Whatcha watching?" I say, nodding at the iPad in her lap.

"It's your favorite," she replies with a giggle.

"Oh yeah? What's my favorite? I forget."

"Tiana, silly! Because you love New Orleans."

Be still my beating heart. She says New Orleans with an accent now. *Nawlins.*

We've taught her well.

Ford laughs.

"That is one of Uncle Grey's favorite places." He meets my eyes in the mirror. "He loves the food. And the casino."

"What's a casino?"

"A place where grown-ups go to do...math," I reply, lips twitching.

Ford cocks a brow. "So that's what we're calling it now. Math."

"Hey. I've always been good with numbers."

"Among other things."

"So." I clear my throat. "Julia's coming to Sunday supper tomorrow."

Ford's eyes pop. Mouth curls into a disbelieving grin.

"Lawdy, you've done it now."

"Lawdy," Bryce repeats, not looking up from her iPad.

"How does this look?" Rollins glances up at me as he gives my pants leg a small tug.

I narrow my eyes. "Little tighter."

"You sure?" He gives me a look in the mirror. "This is already a much...er, *riskier* look than what we usually do."

"I'm down to try something different," I say, carefully adjusting the lapels of my jacket so I don't smudge Rollin's chalk marks. "Do you think we could make a satin lapel work here? Maybe in black?"

Rollins and Ford just stare at me for a beat.

Sweat breaks out along my collar.

"What?"

"Nothing," Rollins replies. "You just haven't changed the cut or the color of your suits in..."

"Years," Ford says.

"Ages."

"Since you were born," my brother continues. "I swear you came out of the womb wearing a navy blue Brioni suit."

Ford's eyes are narrowed now. He knows something's up. But what am I supposed to tell him? *Hey, Julia liked my sweatpants so much she tore them off me this morning and gave me the best head of my life. Not only that, she's making me want to take chances and try new things. I think I'm falling for her, and even though I know I should keep my distance I'm going to get more tight pants made because...*

Because I want to look good for her.

Because I want to turn her into the lust-crazed reprobate that I am.

Because I think I'm ready for a change.

"What is going on with you?" Ford says, eyes narrowed.

"What do you mean?"

"The tight pants," he says, nodding at the garment in question. "Inviting Julia to supper. That big goofy grin."

"I'm not grinning."

"You were when you walked in here. Last time I saw you do that was 2015. I like this look on you. The grin, not the pants. What are you trying to be, a stripper? Rollins, we should just put velcro in the seams so Grey can rip them off while doing pelvic thrusts."

I shoot him a look in the mirror. "You're an A-S-S."

"I know what that spells," Bryce says. "Candy."

Ford presses a noisy kiss to her cheek. "You're such a smarty pants." He looks back up at me. "So c'mon, Patrick Swayze. Show us your moves."

"Please," I reply, biting back a smile. "You and I both know I'm more of a Chris Farley in that scenario."

Rollins' shoulders shake with repressed laughter as he pins my pants a little tighter. "Not in these pants you're not. They will definitely split right open if you try to dance."

"Maybe that's what he's going for," Ford says, laughing.

"Go get you some, boy," Rollins adds. "We all need to blow off a little steam now and again."

We finish up by selecting a satin bow tie and cummerbund to match the lapels on my new tux. As I head outside with Ford and Bryce, I admit I'm a little nervous about how this new look will actually shake out.

What if I end up looking like, I don't know, a member of One Direction or something? Harry Styles can rock skinny pants, but I am not in my twenties, nor am I a rockstar.

I'm also twice his size. What if I look like an overgrown Jonas Brother stuffed into a black satin sausage casing?

And does it even matter if Julia digs it?

I buckle Bryce into her car seat while Ford folds up the stroller and puts it in his trunk. Giving the baby one last kiss, I tell her I'll see her tomorrow and leave the door open a crack so she'll get some air.

I turn to see Ford standing on the sidewalk. Hands on his hips, eyes on my face.

"You're more than just 'in lust' with Julia, aren't you?" he says with a smile.

Crossing my arms, I let out a breath.

"I am. Yes."

"Fucking finally! I'm happy for you. Honestly. But tell me, Shakespeare—what happened to being the drunk driver of love?"

"I still feel that way. I mean—I'm still scared of hurting her. Getting hurt. I'm very much aware that there's more than just our feelings on the line here. I told Julia I would be an equal partner in this parenting thing, and I mean to keep that promise."

"I'm glad to hear you say that," Ford says. "But you *are* aware you're going to have to make some big changes in your life to make that happen, right?"

"I'll make it work. Always do." I wave him away. "If I fuck up the romantic piece of this puzzle—really, any piece—I get how real the consequences would be for the baby. But as much as I want to be careful, I also want to put myself out there a little more. Julia—she's so different from anyone I've been with, Ford. Even though she's scared, too, she's still taking chances, you know? She's *real.* Totally fearless. And I find that really fucking inspiring."

Ford's got this gleam in his eyes now. Before I know what he's doing he's wrapping me in a bear hug, pounding me on the back.

"Damn that's beautiful."

"Thanks," I say. "Although I will admit—*that* I'm not so confident about. Being able to open up, to let her in. In a meaningful, lasting way. I don't know if I can trust myself. Or the universe. What if it comes back to bite me in the ass?"

Ford pulls away and looks me in the eye. "Worth it. You've got to see by now that you're hurting people—yourself included—by holding back like you've been."

"I do," I say, nodding. "I see that now. Or I'm starting to, anyway."

He claps me on the shoulder. "Deep down, I think you know you're not the bad guy. You can trust yourself, Grey. You do it all the time in our work, and look where it's gotten us."

"I'll try."

He grins. "That's all I ask."

"I have a favor to ask you, actually."

"Whatever you need."

"Help me play defense for Julia tomorrow at supper? You know, if

Mom and Dad are holding her hostage? It's just been so long since either of us brought someone home, I'm worried they'll go overboard."

"I'd be happy to help. On one condition. As part of this new you"—he motions to me—"can you try to quit smoking, too? Get the gum or the patch or whatever. It's long past time, Grey."

I take a breath. Let it out. Ford holds my gaze all the while. A challenge.

"Deal," I say.

On my way to my next meeting, I make a pit stop at a drugstore and buy a pack of nicotine patches. I even manage to refrain from buying a pack of cigarettes. Guess I'm committed.

Although I admit my heart falls as I read the instructions on the box.

This is going to suck. Hard.

But like I told Julia, some of the best things in life are the ones you have to work hardest for. And I'm willing to work my balls off for her and our baby. I also want to be alive to see that baby grow up.

So I slap a patch onto my arm. Growling the whole time.

It's not a cigarette. But it gives me enough of a nicotine buzz to get through the rest of my day.

Chapter Nineteen

JULIA

Greyson: Hey

Greyson: I know its late

Greyson: dinner took longer than expected. New investor who really likes what we're doing..

Greyson: anyway I'm not asking you to come over because thatt feels too much like a booty call at 12am

Greyson: but I'm thinking about you

Greyson: I am little drunk and want a cigarette so bad but I'm tryin not to have one did I tell you im starting the patch

Greyson: I'd love to get you naked and fuck you twice

Greyson: and then tell you in person how much I like you

Greyson: and how you're making me want to be different

Greyson: because you're different in the best way

Greyson: so much yourself

Greyson: true real

Greyson: no bullshit

Greyson: and your ass in those yoga pants [peach emoji]

Greyson: my emoji use is strictly iconic

Greyson: ironic

Greyson: okay I'll stop now because Im hard I need to take care of it this is is getting I'm sorry

Greyson: night Julia?.

On Sunday morning, I meet Eva, who's in town again, Olivia, and Gracie at Tipsy Taco. It's a low-key spot in the up-and-coming North Morrison area of Charleston that serves some of the best Mexican in town in a funky atmosphere.

Since it's sunny and sorta-kinda warm, we grab a picnic table next to a pair of heaters on the enormous outdoor patio.

"Want a sip?" Olivia says, holding out her Bloody Maria (a bloody mary made with tequila instead of vodka) when she catches me eyeing it.

I manage a tight grin. "I'm good, thanks. Just order a second one and drink it for me. Hell, have the bartender make it a double so you can really taste the tequila. I love it when a cocktail puts some hair on your chest."

"Still missing your liquor?" Eva asks with a smile.

"You have no idea," I reply, picking up my menu. "Although, I have to admit it felt really nice waking up this morning fresh as a daisy. I miss drinking, but I don't miss the hangovers."

I don't mention that masturbating to Greyson's adorable drunk texts contributed to this morning's freshness. When I woke up to eighteen texts from him, I thought for sure someone either died and/or Luke Rodgers' barn burned down.

It was a pleasant surprise to find a sweet little confessional instead. I was flattered—and turned on—by the fact that he was thinking about me. And I'm happy for him that he's trying to quit smoking. Personally, I was always more of a social smoker than anything. Every once in a while I'll crave a cigarette. But it's one of the few things I'm glad I had to go cold turkey on once I found out I was pregnant.

Makes me feel all warm and fuzzy inside to think we're both trying to clean up our acts for Charlie Brown.

Greyson really is trying.

"Feeling better, then?" Gracie asks.

"Much. I'm turning that corner into my second trimester, and I can definitely tell the difference. I'm starting to have more good days than bad—nausea isn't as constant, and the fatigue isn't nearly as crushing as it's been."

Eva eyes me over her menu. "Well, you look great."

"Yeah," Olivia says. "You look happy."

"Thanks. I'm finally starting to feel like myself again, which I'm super grateful for. I will never, ever take for granted having the energy to get through the day without wanting to die and/or cry. Feeling good is a gift."

Gracie arches a brow. "Anyone in particular helping you feel that good?"

"Hey," I shoot back, grinning for real now. "I am perfectly capable of feeling myself on my own, thank you very much."

"I know. But having someone who participates in you feeling yourself is icing on the cake."

"Before we get into feeling ourselves while feeling up other people, can we talk baby business for a minute?" Olivia pulls a notebook out of her bag and uncaps a felt-tip pen. "I know it's early. But I want to make sure we're fully prepared for baby Lassiter-Montgomery's arrival when the day comes."

My grin broadens into a smile, even as I feel a familiar lump forming in my throat. I was just saying how I can finally make it through the day without crying. But I wasn't counting happy tears in that tally.

"Y'all are too sweet. You don't have to do anything, really."

"Of course we do," Eva says, grabbing my hand and giving it a squeeze. "We're your village, and we take that duty seriously. I'm going to be the best auntie ever."

"No way," Gracie says. "I'm going to be the favorite aunt. I already know what he or she will call me. 'Auntie GiGi.'"

Olivia laughs. "That's ridiculous, and I love it. Can I be Big O? I feel like she'll really appreciate the pun when she gets older."

"Considering your profession, I think it's perfect," I reply.

"Eli says it's a little too on the nose, but whatever." Olivia looks down at her notebook.

"Wedding coming along?" I ask.

She nods. "We're ready. I think."

"Excited?" Eva asks.

"We are, yeah," Olivia replies with a smile. "Honestly, I'm just excited to spend the rest of my life with Elijah. As cheesy as that sounds."

"Doesn't sound cheesy. Sounds delightful. Even though he is my brother, and he can be a huge pain in the ass," Gracie says.

Olivia laughs. "So back to baby business. Eva's volunteered to put together a meal schedule."

"Meals? For what?"

"For when the baby arrives," Eva says, like it's the most obvious thing ever. "I made a Google doc where people can sign up to bring you dinner the first few weeks after you give birth. Fair warning, I already took half the slots, so...yeah. Hope you like smoked meat."

"Meat's my favorite," I say with a sly grin.

She wags her brows. "Yeah it is."

Our waitress drops off the chips and queso we ordered earlier. The four of us attack it like it's the first food we've seen in weeks.

"I figure instead of meals I'll provide however many gallons of coffee you need to get through the day, plus all the sweet snacks you can handle," Gracie says as she pops a chip into her mouth.

I blink hard, grateful for the distraction of trying to get as much queso on my chip as possible without breaking it in half.

"Thank you guys. Really."

"And Gracie is heading up the shower, although we would all like to help host it," Olivia says.

"I'm thinking we could do it at Holy City Roasters," Gracie replies, beaming. "Maybe in May before it gets too hot? We could have it out on the patio. Eli's already volunteered to cater it, and of course I'll provide the beverages and dessert. I just hope we'll have enough room. Between you and Greyson, y'all know half this city."

My vision's gone blurry. I can hardly breathe around the swelling in my throat. My friends' excitement about this baby is palpable. Infectious. And their generosity and dedication and *kindness* is downright overwhelming.

I guess I wasn't expecting it because I haven't been feeling especially excited about this whole baby thing myself. I've been too sick, too depressed to see the light at the end of the tunnel.

But now I am feeling twinges of excitement. I can just glimpse that light.

It's kind of...lovely.

Crushingly lovely.

I've never dreamed about my wedding. I didn't have a vision for how many kids I'd have or the family I'd create. I've been to dozens of bridal and baby showers, and while I don't hate them, I definitely never wondered when it would be *my* turn.

But now it is my turn. And I'm realizing that it isn't about the presents or the parties. It's about celebrating a milestone with the people you love. The people who love and support you.

There is so much love at this table right now my heart is bursting.

"Let's also pick a date to put together your registry," Olivia is saying, turning a page in her notebook. "I've asked some of my friends who have young kids for their input, and they gave me some great suggestions. Figured we could use those as a good jumping off point. How do you guys feel about a field trip to Hello Baby? There's one out in West Ashley. Oh! And are you going to find out the gender?"

"You know," I say, squeezing my eyes shut. "I haven't actually thought about that."

"Wait, Julia...Julia, are you okay?"

I *am* crying. All of a sudden.

Hard.

Snotty, sobby, happy crying.

"I love y'all so much," I say. "Seriously, I'm overwhelmed, and I know I'm always crying when we're together, but I was not expecting all this."

"What?" Gracie hands me an extra napkin. "You really think we'd let you have dickhead Greyson Montgomery's baby on your own?"

"He is a dickhead," I say, wiping my nose. "He's also really great and has a really nice penis."

Olivia laughs. "Wow. I wasn't expecting to hear that. Although I had a feeling something was going on between you guys. Something more than just sex, anyway."

"Really?" I sniffle.

"Yeah. For all his growliness and general abrasiveness, Greyson's actually been pretty great to Elijah over the years. He was one of Eli's first investors. This was before people knew who Elijah Jackson was—before The Pearl was even open. But Greyson took a real risk and believed in this chef nobody had really heard of. In fact, it was when Greyson backed Eli that things really started to turn around for him. The Montgomery Partners name has real weight behind it in this town—people trust Greyson and Ford, and when they put their money behind something, people take notice. When The Jam closed"—this was Eli's second restaurant, which never did well despite the success of The Pearl, his first restaurant—"Greyson still stuck by Eli, even though he could've easily tucked tail and run. He did a hard thing, a *good* thing, without having to. He's a stand-up guy, Julia. And because you're you, and you take no crap, and you see through people's bullshit, I knew you'd eventually discover that about him."

Because my heart wasn't swollen enough.

It feels enormous now. Filling my entire chest cavity, squeezing my lungs so that it's difficult to breathe.

"This is not how I pictured my life ending up," I say. "That I'd be thirty-four and single and knocked up by a guy like Greyson Montgomery. I'm still struggling to come to terms with how off-course it is from where I thought my story would be. But the further along I get in my pregnancy, the better I feel, physically and mentally, and the more I get to know Greyson...I mean, it doesn't seem half bad. Sometimes it actually seems pretty damn great. Which I was not expecting. At all."

Olivia grins. "Trust me. I know all about your story taking a hard left when all your life you've been making carefully timed rights."

"Yes!" I say, reaching for the chips. "I liked the path I was on. I liked my life just fine. And then this happened."

"Who's to say you won't like this new path just as much? I never thought I'd end up with my brother's best friend," Gracie adds. "I didn't think Luke was really my type, and I definitely didn't think he'd ever be into me. So even though I had this, like, raging crush on him, I never in a million years thought we'd end up together."

Eva smiles. "And now y'all are so damn cute together it's kind of disgusting. I mean that in the best way."

"Thanks," Gracie says, grinning. "But yeah. Looking back on it, I was glad I got pushed off course. I'm glad I didn't get what I thought I wanted, because it didn't make me very happy. But what I ended up getting with Luke? That *does* make me happy. In ways I never could've imagined."

Olivia nods. "Exactly. Sometimes the best thing that can happen to us is not getting what we want. Because there's something better in store for us. Something we don't see coming."

"Something that will actually fulfill us," I say. "You really think I can be happy with Grey?"

Eva's lips twitch. "You're calling him Grey now? Sounds serious."

My body warms at the memory at the gravel in his voice when he said *I like it when you call me Grey*.

I felt more alive in his bed than I have in months. Alive and sexy and *light*.

"It feels serious," I admit. "I spent the night at his place on Friday. I was telling him how much I wish I could tell my parents about the baby. And he invited me to his parents' to tell them. I'm going over there for dinner tonight."

Eva draws back. "Holy shit. That's actually really sweet."

"Right? I was shocked," I say. "But I'm excited. To meet his family, obviously. But also to find out where he comes from. Maybe get a few clues as to why he is...you know, the way he is. He's been slowly opening up to me, but I haven't gotten the full story."

"I know he got divorced a few years back," Gracie says. "Greyson is a very private person, so he's never explicitly mentioned it to me. But I bet that has something to do with his growling."

My pulse skips a beat. I had no idea Greyson was married. I've had a few friends go through divorces, and it's pretty horrible for all parties involved.

I remember that sliver of vulnerability I saw in him the other night. I thought it was at odds with his intensity. But maybe I was wrong.

He's intensely focused at work. Intensely involved, down to the last detail.

Makes sense that he'd feel things intensely, too.

My pulse skips another beat at the thought of him hurting. The thought of him being *wounded.*

Or was he the one who did the wounding?

"Maybe," I say absently, glancing at Eva's margarita. "I just want him to let me in."

"If he's as crazy about you as it sounds like he is, then he will," Olivia says. "It took me a good bit to let Elijah in. I didn't want anyone to get hurt, you know? So maybe Greyson taking things slow is his way of protecting you."

Shit, I'm going to cry again.

I shove a chip into my mouth. Chew. Swallow.

If Greyson is protecting me—

If he's holding back on my behalf—

If he *gives that much of a fuck*—

The idea is making me ache. The kind of ache I feel when I read an especially juicy romance novel.

Eva nudges me with her elbow. "You all right there, killer?"

"No. Nope. I'm—y'all, I'm so overwhelmed. In the best way? Kind of?"

"Want to talk about penises instead?" Gracie pops another chip into her mouth. "You said Greyson's got a nice one."

"That's as much info as y'all are getting," I say, laughing. "If you need more penis in your life, read one of Olivia's books."

Chapter Twenty

JULIA

There's a prenatal class later that afternoon at the yoga studio Olivia recommended. Stuffed to the brim with lady love and shrimp tacos, I decide to give it a shot.

I just barely fit into my stretchiest pair of workout tights. My sports bra strains over my ever-growing breasts. I feel chunky and unwieldy. But I am determined to make it to class nonetheless.

So I drive to the studio and rent a mat. The dude at the front desk directs me to studio C, all the way at the back of the building.

I put my shoes and purse in a locker and tuck my mat under my arm. The smell of incense tickles my nostrils as I head down the hall, painted orange and decorated with posters advertising various classes and yoga-related trips.

I pass studios A and B on the way. Through the frosted glass doors, I can see there are classes going on in each one. They're packed.

Makes me think there's a real community at this studio. Or maybe that's just me hoping there's a lot going on here. Don't get me wrong, I have an amazing support system in my life right now. But I don't have a lot of mom friends.

I don't know anyone who's going through what I am right now.

It would be really, really nice to have some people to commiserate with.

I pause in the threshold of studio C when I see the twenty or so pregnant women inside. They come in all shapes and sizes, same as their bellies. Some are heavily pregnant, their inverted bellybuttons poking sweetly through their tank tops. Others, like me, aren't showing much at all.

Everyone is chatting. The room buzzes with energy.

I feel equal parts intimidated and...relieved, maybe?

The teacher, an Asian woman with a sleeve of flower tattoos, greets me warmly, beckoning me into the room. She holds a plastic model of a pelvis in one hand and extends the other to me.

"I'm Katie," she says. "Welcome to class. I don't recognize your face. Is this your first time in the studio?"

I don't know why, but my voice shakes a little when I introduce myself. Which in a way delights me, as I'm used to addressing rooms full of people. I'm out of my comfort zone here.

Not a bad thing.

I grab one of the few remaining spots toward the front of the room. Katie sets me up with "props", as she calls them. Two foam blocks, a bolster, and a blanket.

To start class, she has us go around and introduce ourselves.

"Tell us how far along you are, if you know the gender, and how you're feeling. Please, don't be shy with details. We love to overshare in this class!"

I feel a swell of—of I don't know what as the women around me introduce themselves. They talk about a lot of the things I've been feeling. The exhaustion, the *strangeness* of the whole experience.

But more than that, I notice how they talk about it all like it's perfectly normal. Perfectly normal to be pregnant, and perfectly normal to be in love with it or not. The introductions run the gamut from a black woman named Hallie who's had trouble sleeping to a tall woman with blue hair named Fiona, smiling as she tells us this is her fourth baby and that she'd do it all over again because she loves giving birth so much.

Relief.

That's what I feel. A huge, overwhelming sense of relief.

I'm not alone. And I'm not making a mistake by having a baby, and I'm not any less of a woman or a mother for having the feelings I do.

"I'm Julia," I say when it's my turn. "I'm just shy of nine weeks. This is my first baby, and we don't know the gender yet." *We*. Me and Greyson. Sounds weird to say that. Weird and wonderful, too. "I'm feeling...all right. To be honest, the first trimester has been rough."

The room erupts in sympathetic murmurs.

"Mine *sucked*," Hallie says, nodding. "I felt sick the whole time. Not throwing up sick. Just awful sick."

"Same here. That first trimester is all about getting through. Trust me when I say it gets better," another woman adds as she cradles her cantaloupe-sized bump.

I feel like the room is wrapping me in a big old hug.

"Thanks." I swallow. "I'm starting to see glimmers of the light. I've been having some low back pain—I sit a lot at work—but otherwise, just fighting some residual nausea."

"We'll be addressing that low back pain a lot throughout class," Katie says. "It's a very common problem throughout pregnancy."

We move through a series of slow, deep poses that feel fucking amazing. I haven't felt well enough to really exercise all that much, save for a long-ish walk here and there. But it's nice to feel my body blinking awake. Stretching long-neglected muscles. Using my arms and my legs to just move through the flow, breathing deeply as I go.

I suck at almost everything. I have to glance at my neighbors to see what Katie means by cat and cow poses, and I can barely hold downward dog—a "resting pose"—for more than four seconds before my legs start to shake.

But no one seems to give a fuck. Most of us are tired, and slow, and we have aches in places we never knew existed. This isn't about perfecting poses, or breaking a sweat (although I am definitely getting clammy.)

It's about being kind to ourselves and our bodies. Acknowledging the hard work they're doing while we attempt to go about life as usual.

I know I keep saying this, but I feel it here more than ever—I feel like myself as I jump rope my hips, stretch them out in something called pigeon pose. Totally present. Not wanting to fast forward because I want to die. Not wanting to rewind to remember my parents, or the life I had before I got pregnant.

I just move between Lauren, 36 weeks, on my left, and Jordan, 22 weeks, on my right.

Jordan knocks her water bottle over in the middle of class, spilling it all over her mat. I hand her my towel and she thanks me, smiling. Not long after, when we're stretching our elbows away from each other by reaching down our backs, Jordan hands me her strap when I can't make my fingers touch.

It's a simple gesture. Small. But it fills me with this sense of warmth —faith and gratitude, too.

Faith that I'm going to be all right.

Gratitude that I'm not in this alone.

As I move, I can't help but think that my body feels tender and strange. Mine, but not.

Just like my mind.

Letting my thoughts continue to wander as I breathe in and out through my nose, I think about how pregnancy is constantly giving me all the feels. Bad ones. Good ones. It's emotional and sensory overload.

It's life, turned all the way up.

And just like most things in life, it's not all good, and it's not all bad, either. The experience falls somewhere in between. The grey where black and white overlap.

A lot of narratives about pregnancy and motherhood would have us think otherwise—that it's pure magic, that it's happiness and butterflies, that it's all good, all the time.

Without knowing it, I felt like shit about myself because that's not how my experience has been so far. It's been a struggle.

Being in this room has shown me that I am not alone in that struggle.

And I think *that* is magic.

By the time class is over and we're cooling off in shavasana, or dead man's pose, I'm kicking myself for not coming to a prenatal class sooner. This was awesome. And much needed.

"Be sure to join the studio's prenatal Facebook group," Katie says as she collects our blocks. "It's a great way to meet other mamas and stay in touch with each other."

I make a mental note to do just that when I get home.

I introduce myself to everyone I pass on the way out and even manage to chat up Fiona and snag Hallie's number. I don't know much about this whole motherhood thing, but I have an inkling that finding good mom friends is going to be hard. I'm not about to let this opportunity slip through my fingers.

Leaving the studio, I'm walking on clouds. I feel light. At ease.

Comforted, knowing I'm okay, and normal, and just fine, just as I am. No matter what I'm feeling or thinking at that particular moment.

Knowing my body is still there and so am I. Buried somewhere beneath all that first trimester awfulness.

Chapter Twenty-One

JULIA

I admit to being one of those people who thought yoga wasn't a "real" workout. But I'm already sore by the time I get home, and I end up passing out cold on my sofa for two hours because I'm so spent.

Class soothed me, but my hand still shakes a little as I lock my door and head down to the driveway later that evening.

I'm nervous about meeting Grey's family. And excited.

And *nervous*.

The engine of his Yukon throbs in the driveway. A low, threatening sound.

His eyes follow me through the windshield. Like always.

He's got one hand on the wheel. Like always.

He lifts two fingers in greeting. I climb inside the car.

But unlike always, he leans across the center console and kisses my mouth. Scruff catching on my skin.

He smells clean. Like body wash. Hair is still wet and neatly combed. He must've just gotten out of the shower.

My eyes flutter shut. Desire flooding the space between my skin and bones, gathering in my core.

I'm acutely aware of how close his body is to mine. An awareness that's new. Delicious.

I open my eyes. As delicious as he looks in jeans and a blue v-neck sweater.

I'm really liking these weekend versions of Greyson.

"How are you feeling?" he asks.

I meet his eyes. Jesus, were they always so piercing?

"I took a prenatal yoga class this afternoon that I absolutely loved. So that made me feel great."

He grins. "Awesome. I'm glad you gave it a try."

"But right now, I admit I'm a little nervous."

About meeting your family.

About how much I want you.

He reaches over and puts a hand on my thigh, just above my knee. Gives me a small squeeze that's both reassuring and wildly arousing.

"If you can handle the Starks, you can handle my family. They're going to love you. What's that?" He nods at my hands.

"My favorite Chardonnay," I reply, holding up one hand. I hold up the other. "And a signed copy of my current favorite read—Olivia's *My Romp With the Rogue*. I'm on my third read of it. I've kind of taken it upon myself to be her one-woman marketing team here in town, so I'm always passing along copies of her books. I figure your mom might appreciate it. Maybe your dad, too."

Grey's lips twitch. "Are you suggesting *My Romp With the Rogue* is going to have my mom waking up my dad in the middle of the night to have a romp of their own?"

"Yup," I say, grinning.

"First of all, ew. Second—the sex scenes are that good, huh?"

"They're that good."

"As good as ours are?"

The question hangs in the air between us for one beat. Another.

I'm grinning. He's grinning.

Feeling blooms inside my chest. Along with the heady longing pumping through my veins, it's a lethal combination.

"Jury's still out," I say at last. "Think I'm going to need to experience a few more before I decide."

"That can be arranged."

He slides his hand up my thigh. Growls when his pinkie flirts with the inner seam of my jeans.

"You're hot," he says. "You feel hot right here."

"No shit. You smell so good—Grey, you *look* so good—I'm surprised I haven't melted into a puddle yet."

He growls again.

"Fu-*uck,* Julia." He pulls back his hand and spears it through his hair. Takes a noisy breath through his nose, lets it out as he cuts me a glance. "Dinner will be two hours, tops. We can make it 'til then, right? I want you, baby. So bad. Right now. But once I start touching you I know I'm not gonna be able to stop."

I resist the urge to squirm.

"We can make it. I think."

Greyson puts the car in drive. "Brunch. Talk to me about how brunch with the girls was before I break the zipper of my fucking fly."

"Brunch." I clear my throat, giving my most stretchy pair of jeans a tug. "Right. The girls want to throw me a baby shower, which means I should probably put together a registry. I'd like your help with that. Researching what we need. Picking it all out."

"I'm in. Name the date and time."

"Thinking we can start researching now. Pick everything out when we—fingers crossed—make it to the second trimester."

He nods. "Sounds like a plan. Could be fun, too. I imagine it will really start to feel real then."

Looking away, I fight a grin. Not quite sure why I fight it, exactly. Maybe because I don't want to count my chickens before they're hatched. But the idea of browsing the aisles of Hello Baby with Greyson by my side is kind of really, *really* appealing.

When I first got pregnant and decided to keep the baby, I assumed I'd be doing that stuff without a partner. Without Grey.

Fills me with happy tingles to know I will have a partner, and that Greyson and I will tackle that task together. Seems a lot less daunting —and, if I'm being honest, a lot more exciting—now that I'll have his help.

His parents live in an elegant brick townhouse on a quiet, leafy street in Ansonborough, one of Charleston's oldest and prettiest neighborhoods. Climbing the curved staircase to the second floor entrance, Grey's palm on the small of my back, I notice how the light in the windows glows warmly against the approaching darkness.

A spark of excitement catches in my chest. I'm getting that good feeling again—the one I got on Friday night when I went over to Grey's house for the first time.

We stop at the door. Grey turns to look at me.

"I'm glad you came, Julia."

"Me too," I say.

He opens the door and holds it, nodding for me to step in first.

"Helloooo," he calls.

A woman appears in a doorway straight ahead of us. She's wearing a snazzy pair of tortoiseshell glasses and a roll-neck cream sweater and matching jeans.

She's also wearing an enormous smile, her eyes lighting up when they land on me.

"Welcome, y'all! I'm so glad you could make it. Grey, baby, give your mama some sugar, would you?"

She pulls Grey into a hug. There's no awkwardness. No hesitation. There's a warmth and a familiarity about their embrace that makes me melt a little.

This is not the coldhearted Greyson Montgomery I met at the barn how many months back.

His mom has the same Southern drawl that Grey does. A little thicker, little slower. There's something about her mannerisms, her gentle, easy warmth, that almost reminds me of a Southern Meryl Streep.

"Mom, I'd like you to meet Julia Lassiter," he says when they pull back, turning to me. "Please don't scare her off."

Tucking the chardonnay into the crook of my arm, I hold out my hand. "Mrs. Montgomery, it's a pleasure to meet you. Thank you so much—"

"Honey, please call me Eliza. And don't be silly, you're getting a hug," she says. And then she pulls me into her arms. "We are so *very* glad you could join us tonight."

I meet Grey's eyes over Eliza's shoulder. He's smiling.

So am I.

"Very glad indeed! Hey y'all!"

We turn at the sound of another voice in the doorway, and I nearly start. The handsome man standing there looks *exactly* like Greyson, just with a few more wrinkles and salt and pepper hair. But the blue eyes, square jaw, and dimpled chin are the same.

Jesus, those genes are strong. I can't help but wonder whether Charlie Brown—if he's a boy—will inherit them.

Something about the idea makes my heart skip a beat.

"I'm Greyson senior, but everyone calls me Monty," he says, extending a hand.

I turn to Grey. "So you're a junior?"

"I'm actually a third," he says, glancing at his dad. "Dad here is the junior."

Monty claps his hands and rubs them together. "What can I get you to drink, Julia?"

Eliza's eyes drift to my chardonnay. "Some white wine? I've already got a bottle open. Monty can also whip up whatever cocktail you'd like. I've got tea, too, sweet of course, and some sparkling water..."

"Tea would be great, thank you. And these are for y'all." I hold out the wine and the book.

"Well, doesn't this look inviting," Eliza says, taking the book. "I do like a man in a kilt. Have you watched that show *Outlander*?"

"Love it," I reply with a grin. "Did you read the books? I think the casting in the show is A-plus."

"I've read them all. Twice. Good Lord, is that Jamie Frasier a tall glass of water or what? I've half a mind to travel back to the eighteenth century to find him myself."

"And that's our cue to keep moving. Let's head inside." Greyson puts his hand on my back and guides me into the kitchen at the back of the house. It's open to a living room that's beautifully furnished and strewn with toys. Dolls, books, a red and blue tricycle.

No one seems to bat an eye at the mess. In fact, Eliza beams at the little girl in leggings who sits in the center of the toy hurricane. When the girl sees Greyson, she immediately leaps to her feet and heads our way, face lighting up.

"Uncle Grey!" she says, holding up her arms.

He leans down and swoops her into his arms, airplane-ing her over his head—noise effects and everything—before he bends his arms and presses a kiss to both her cheeks.

"Bryce!" He shifts her easily onto his hip, like he's done it a million times before. "Where have you been, girl?"

"Workin'."

"Workin' on what?"

"My computer"—she points to an iPad—"just like you and Daddy."

"Are you CEO of your own company yet?"

"I am." She nods proudly. "Can I be CBD of yours too?"

He laughs. Ford does, too, from his perch on the sofa.

"You must be a pretty chill boss, then," Grey replies.

"She is anything but chill," Ford says. "But you already know that."

Bryce crosses her arms. "You gonna make me the boss or what?"

"Hm. What are your qualifications?"

Bryce rolls her eyes dramatically, letting out an aggravated sigh. "Girls run the *world*, Uncle Grey."

"Yeah they do," Greyson says, looking at me.

I bite back a laugh while simultaneously fighting a joyous sense of *what the ever-living fuck*.

It's obvious Greyson is very close with his niece. Again, no awkwardness, no hesitation. Just sweetness and warmth and familiarity. He's literally radiating affection. Joy.

Not only that. He's already talking to Bryce about owning businesses and being a boss.

He's helping to raise a feminist in the making.

I mean. Stick a fork in me. I am *done*.

This isn't me heaping praise on a man for doing what's merely expected of a woman (and never, ever rewarded with said praise, by the way); it's not me giving him too much credit for being an involved, helpful family member, or being good with kids.

This is me seeing a whole new side of him. The warmth beneath the corporate, cold-hearted veneer that I've gotten glimpses of but have never witnessed in such unabashed, unafraid glory.

This is how I was with my family. Because I loved them and they loved me.

Greyson loves these people. *Loves* them.

Fiercely.

I'm gripped by a fierceness myself. It's a primal and possibly problematic longing, but it's there. Lodged in the very center of my being.

I want him to love me like that.

I want to have this man's baby.

Because I know he's going to love Charlie Brown this way.

The thought of starting a family with him fills me with this brimming happiness. One day that's going to be *our* baby on his hip.

One day *our* baby will be a part of this loving, tight-knit family.

I want to be a part of it, too. So badly it hurts.

Am I an idiot to even entertain the idea? I've known Grey for, what, six months? And his family all of six minutes?

But you can just tell. They're close. They're in each other's lives and help each other out.

They love each other. Unconditionally.

They belong to each other, too.

"You tell 'em, Bryce," Eliza cuts in. "And don't you let these boys forget it."

"She may not run the world yet, but she sure as hell runs this family," Ford says. He smiles and gets up, coming over to give me a hug. "Hey, Julia. Glad you could make it."

All this hugging. The toys. The sweating glass of deliciously sweet tea in my hand.

Amazing how I already feel right at home.

"It's good to see you," I say, tilting my head to look at Bryce. Greyson's got her on his shoulders now. "And who is this?"

"This is my daughter, Bryce. Bryce, can you say hello to Miss Julia?"

"Hi, Bryce," I say with a little wave.

Bryce looks at me for a full beat, brown eyes locked on mine. Serious and steady and smart. I struggle not to laugh. She's got this intensity about her that I immediately recognize, because she shares it with Grey.

"Hello," she says at last.

Grey grins. "Give her a little bit to warm up to you. She'll get there."

"Hey, boys, do y'all mind coming to help me outside?" Monty asks. "Time to put the steaks on."

Grey puts Bryce back on the ground. Then the three of them grab their cocktails and head out back. I join Eliza in the kitchen, where she checks on a huge pot of mashed sweet potatoes and some collards simmering with bacon and sugar in a dutch oven.

"What can I help with?" I ask.

Eliza waves me away. "You just sit, honey."

"Bryce is too stinking cute," I say, turning to look at her. She's playing quietly on her iPad, her wispy brown hair tucked neatly behind her ears.

"She's got my boys wrapped around her little finger, that's for sure."

"Greyson clearly adores her."

"Oh yeah. He's been a big part of Bryce's life since she was born." She lowers the lid onto the pot of potatoes. Lowers her voice, too. "Ford's wife died when Bryce was just a baby. Grey stepped up in a big way. We all did, but he took his role as surrogate parent very seriously. Same as he took his role as the responsible older brother seriously when they were growing up."

My heart has started to pound. I swallow to keep it from working its way into my throat.

"So Greyson was, like, the Prince William to Ford's Prince Harry."

"That's it exactly," Eliza replies, an easy smile breaking out on her face. "Ford wasn't wild, but he was definitely more of a free spirit than Greyson. More sensitive, too. When Rebecca died, Greyson knew Ford needed time to heal. Time to acclimate to being a single parent. So he told Ford to focus on his family while Grey focused on the business. He's been running Montgomery Partners single-handedly for a while now, supporting them both. I think that's what motivates Greyson more than anything—growing the business so he has a way of giving back to our family. Sweet of him, but I worry he's too hard on himself. He can be very intense about things, if you haven't noticed."

"I have," I say with a scoff.

Eliza's smile deepens. "Hard not to. He means well, Julia, even if it doesn't seem like it at times. When Grey isn't at work—not often, granted—he's over at Ford's. Bringing dinner. Hanging out with Bryce."

"Teaching her about leadership and girl power."

"He really does mean well."

I swallow again. This time to keep from tearing up.

I guessed at it Friday night, when he told me how his love of food was what spurred his interest in venture capital, and that he was close with his family. But now I'm seeing the proof firsthand: *this* is why Greyson is so obsessed with turning a profit.

Not because he's a greedy, egomaniacal asshole. But because he's been supporting his widowed brother and three-year-old niece.

Because he wants to give back to the people he loves. Do right by them.

Show his love by working to build them a stable, happy future. While *showing up* in every way that he can.

That's some kind of fierce love right there.

And such a beautiful idea that for a second I can't breathe.

If I wasn't falling for Grey before, I sure as hell am now.

My desire to know him, all of him, burns to need.

I get that Grey is the dutiful older brother, and I get that he takes said duty seriously. But I have this nagging feeling that maybe he's atoning for something, too.

His divorce? I imagine a high-achieving, dutiful, firstborn son would rather die than disappoint his parents. Disappoint anyone, his ex included.

I look up at the sound of masculine laughter. Greyson is shouldering the back door open, an enormous tray of steaks in his hands.

He's smiling, making the dimple in his chin really pop. When his eyes meet mine, they're warm and happy and as different from the icy eyes I first saw at the barn as shadow from light.

"Steaks are done," he says.

His mom claps her hands. "All right, y'all, let's start fixin' some plates."

"Mind if I play a little music?" Grey asks, setting the tray on the counter beside me. His elbow brushes mine.

"Music?" Ford's eyes go wide. "Since when do you like *music*?"

Grey shrugs, digging his phone out of his pocket and scrolling through what I can only assume is his music library. A second later, David Bowie starts to play on the speakers above our heads.

It's "Young Americans." One of my favorites.

"Ziggy Stardust?" Ford smiles. "Heck yeah."

My heart—my stomach—my feelings—

They all bottom out. In the best way.

Grey catches me staring at him. He winks.

"Just in case the exorcist doesn't show."

"What's an exorcist?" Bryce asks, trotting into the kitchen.

Ford picks her up, smoothing her shirt. "It's what we're going to need to make sure the kind alien life force that's taken up residence in Uncle Grey's body sticks around for a while longer."

"Let's eat," Monty says. "By the way, is this song about what I think it is?"

Chapter Twenty-Two

GREYSON

I can't take my eyes off her.

Julia doesn't know my family. Hardly knows Ford. I assume she doesn't regularly dine with three-year-olds who somehow always manage to get food in their hair and/or vomit whenever they eat.

But she's still fucking radiant at the table across from me. At ease. At home. Chatting with my dad. Charming my mom. Cleaning her plate and going back for seconds, and then thirds, of Mom's famous collards.

Julia and Ford wig out over their shared love of eighties rock and some poet named Paul Neruda (or maybe it was Pablo? Damn it, now I wish I paid more attention in lit class). She laughs, eyes lighting up mischievously, when he tells the story of my Jonas Brother-style tuxedo pants.

"So *are* you going to pull a Patrick Swayze?" she asks me. "You know I like to dance."

"Lordy do I love that man." Mom sighs. "I'll be his Baby anytime."

"I'm sitting right here," Dad says.

"Greyson hasn't danced in years." Ford looks at me, Bryce dangling from his knee. "Julia, you gonna help us change that?"

She grins. "Only if he promises to wear those tux pants."

It's obvious my family genuinely enjoys her company, too. They brighten any room. Any mood. But with Julia here, too, that brightness is almost blinding. She's witty and real and interesting, and they can't get enough of her thoughts, ideas, stories.

I can't, either. I just sit and stare like a slack-jawed, lovesick jackass. Soaking up her every word and every expression. The way she puckers her lips and pulls them to the side when she's thinking about something. How she surrenders to laughter, a whole-being exercise that involves eyes and mouth and belly.

The way her gaze always catches on mine. Like she's feeling this too.

This.

The stupid happy certainty that you're exactly where you should be, with exactly the right people.

Your people.

Julia is my person. At least I'd like her to be.

I am downright obsessed with this woman.

Bryce is drooling on Ford's shoulder by the time Dad brings out a dish of his brown sugar pecan bread pudding. He retired young and took up baking to keep busy. In the years since, he's become one hell of a scratch baker.

Bryce magically wakes up at the mention of the words *ice cream.* Dad piles a heaping scoop of vanilla bean onto bowls of the warm bread pudding, making the ice cream nice and melty, and passes them around the table.

Lord have mercy, Julia's definitely going to make noises while she eats that. And I'm definitely going to spring a very inconvenient boner unless I do something about it.

Shoveling a massive bite of bread pudding into my mouth, I swallow. Clear my throat.

"So. Y'all." I meet Julia's eyes across the table. "Julia and I have some news."

Julia blushes. Ford looks up from wiping regurgitated ice cream off Bryce's foot. Mom and Dad exchange a glance.

A happy, excited glance.

Lord, please don't let me get their hopes up just to disappoint them again.

My heart is thumping loud and clear inside my chest.

I'm scared shitless. This is the first time my parents are meeting Julia, for Christ's sake. First time I've brought a girl home in years. And we're about to announce that we're having a baby together.

But I'm reaching for Julia's hand and holding it in mine and doing this fucking thing anyway.

"You want to tell them?" I ask her softly.

She smiles.

Her eyes are wet.

"It's a bit of a surprise," she begins. "Trust me when I say no one was more surprised than we were. But Greyson and I are pregnant. We're going to have a baby."

Immediate pandemonium ensues. Mom launches across the table to wrap Julia in a hug. Dad bursts into tears and so does Bryce. She climbs into my arms, sobbing, and tells me she doesn't want a baby but will be nice to it if I ask her to.

And you know what? As overwhelming and as *loud* as it all is, it's pretty wonderful. I've never appreciated how non-judgmental my family is more than I do now. Julia and I don't get any questions about getting married. No sly comments about how fast we're moving or what idiots we are for not knowing how birth control works.

I wouldn't blame them if they judged us. Or at least had some hesitation about the suddenness of it all. The choices we're making.

But my family—my parents and Ford and even baby Bryce in her own way (who's not much of a baby any more, it kills me)—*trust that I'm making the right decision.*

Which makes me think—makes me hope—I can trust myself.

Ford pries Bryce off of me and gives me a tight hug.

"Congrats, brother. I don't know if you deserve Julia"—this makes her laugh—"but you do deserve to be happy."

I meet Julia's eyes over Ford's shoulder. She's crying and smiling all at once. Holding nothing in—hiding nothing—as usual.

My heart feels like it's about to burst.

Can I do this?

Do I deserve this?

And why does my mom always ask so many damn questions?

"Oh my God y'all!" Mom is saying. "Oh my God! Bless your heart, Julia, you kept that news in all this while. I don't know how you did it! How are you feeling? When are you due? Can I host a shower? What do you need? You've got to take all the leftovers tonight. Is my son cooking for you as often as he should be? Tell me your favorites, honey, and one of us will make 'em for you."

Julia laughs, wiping away tears.

She's glowing. Eating, too—she's almost finished with her bowl of bread pudding and dessert, a fact my eagle-eyed father doesn't miss.

He quietly refills her bowl. She thanks him with a smile.

I don't have answers to my questions. I guess in a way I never will. Life will play out the way it plays out.

But I do know I want this baby. I want a family.

I want Julia. I'm definitely hurting all three of us—her, the baby, me—by not letting her in.

I'm so fucking tired of denying myself. I'm gonna take what I want. Finally.

But first, I have to tell her the truth. I owe her that much.

I just hope she doesn't run after hearing it.

My heart is pounding on the drive home.

I'm also half hard. I keep catching whiffs of Julia's perfume. And the top she's wearing doesn't hide the fact that her nipples get hard every time I look at her. Like she's just as aroused by my attention as I am by hers.

One of the five hundred things I adore about her. She doesn't lie, and neither does her body. She's honest to a fault. Even when the truth is messy. Inconvenient.

I have so much to learn from her.

My hand shakes a little as I put the truck in park in my driveway. The sound of the engine shifts and so does the mood inside the car.

I look at Julia.

She looks at me.

"Julia."

That's it. That's all I say. Her name.

But it's enough to let her know what I'm about to say.

She reaches for my hand. Tangles her fingers in mine.

"Tell your inner villain not to worry," she says. "I'm not going to fix you. I'm definitely not going to save you. But I am going to listen."

The world tells us that men aren't supposed to have feelings. If we do, we damn well better not show them.

But I feel more like a man than I have in years when I look at Julia and pry open my chest, blood and guts and truth spilling out between us.

"Three years ago, I walked out on my wife. She was a good girl, and she loved me, and I broke her heart and destroyed her life."

Chapter Twenty-Three

GREYSON

I wait for Julia to recoil in horror.

Will her exit be dramatic, I wonder? Will she call me out and slap me across the face and slam the door on her way out? Or will her disgust be of a more quiet variety, where she silently judges me, slowly begins to loathe me as she stops answering my calls?

I wait.

But Julia just looks at me. Her fingers moving gently through mine.

In her eyes—

I don't see loathing.

I see sympathy.

Makes the throb inside my chest and ears lessen. Just the tiniest bit.

Just enough to encourage me to keep going.

"I've struggled to forgive myself for breaking the promises I made to a woman whose life I completely leveled."

"Understandable," Julia says, nodding. "I think that's a doozy by any standard."

"On paper, what Cameron and I had was perfect. Our families were old friends. We grew up in the same neighborhood, moved in the same circles. Both of us had successful careers. From the beginning, everyone loved that we were, well, falling in love. They called us the Barbie and Ken of Charleston."

Julia's lips twitch.

"I know, I know, totally gross," I say, scoffing. "But looking back, I see that I was swept up in it all. The fairy tale. How perfect everything looked from the outside. Now I understand that I was more in love with how happy that story made everyone else—my family especially—than I was with Cameron. I was in love with how it all looked on paper and in pictures."

"But your parents are so cool. They don't strike me as the type to be caught up in appearances. Pretty sure they didn't need you to be the picture perfect son who married the picture perfect girl."

"I know. My parents are awesome. Authentic. I love them for it. They didn't put that pressure on me to have, this, like, insanely perfect, insanely accomplished life. I put that pressure on myself. I wanted to be that son for them."

"Why?"

Lifting a shoulder in a shrug, I say, "Not sure. Maybe I thought that that was the kind of kid they deserved because they gave me every privilege imaginable. Maybe I, you know, wanted to save them from how stressed I remembered them being when I was growing up. They're pretty chill now. But they were overwhelmed a lot when Ford and I were younger. Like all parents, I imagine."

"I felt that too with my parents—the stress," Julia says. "Parenting is hard. As we're about to find out first-hand."

I give her hand a gentle squeeze. "I've said it before and I'll say it again—we'll figure it out, Julia. People way less prepared than we are do it every damn day."

"You're right." She gives me a smile. "I mean, I *hope* we'll figure it out, anyway."

A beat of silence passes between us. She's waiting for me to continue. Patiently.

"It became clear pretty quickly once Cameron and I were married that we wanted different things. We both worked a ton, which didn't help matters."

"Who, you? A workaholic?" Julia arches a brow. "Never."

"You don't do big things by working a nine to five."

"I don't disagree, although I want to challenge you a bit on that later. But I want you to keep telling me about Cameron. You've only blown me off, what, twice now?"

I grin. "Third time is a charm."

"Keep going."

"Right. Okay. So Cameron very much wanted to live the same life as her parents. Same white picket fence, same friends, same country club. It's how we both grew up. So I get it. But I began to get really bored doing the same things with the same people all the time. She was obsessed with always going out, always with just the right people at just the right places. It felt superficial. I began to wonder if that was all there really was. I thought it was the life I wanted. But it didn't...I don't know, it didn't feel right. Didn't feel like me. We grew apart. She wasn't happy, and neither was I. She still wanted to hold on, though. She really wanted that perfect, beautiful existence we promised everyone. Kids especially. But I knew—deep down I just knew—that was a big mistake." I let out a breath. "I was the one who called it quits after a year of therapy got us nowhere. I've always taken pride in being a workhorse. I make shit work. Literally. But I couldn't make my marriage work. I couldn't make myself fall back in love with her. And one day I just woke up and felt tired. I couldn't do it anymore. So I ended the perfect marriage."

"That wasn't actually so perfect."

"Right."

Julia's still looking at me. Sympathy still in her eyes. In the slight curve of her brow.

She is *still here*.

"So why the struggle to forgive yourself then for walking away?" Julia asks. "If you were unhappy and you knew that you and Cameron didn't want the same things? If you knew that being shallow and fake was...well, shallow and fake and wrong?"

I spear a hand through my hair. Let out another breath.

"I can't help but feel that I shouldn't have married her in the first place. I should've known better. I should've seen the signs for what they were. Why did I make that choice? I'm so methodical in all I do. I've been trained to consider every outcome. Look at things from every angle. How did I not see that I wasn't head over heels in love with the woman I promised my life to? I lied to her, Julia. Lied to our families and to myself."

She swipes her thumb across the back of my palm. "You said it yourself. You were blinded by the gorgeousness of it all. By your need to be the perfect son with the perfect, beautiful life. Why you did what you did—it makes terrible sense, Grey. And you made a terrible mistake that hurt people you cared about."

"Yup," I say, my throat swelling. "Cameron was devastated. So were my parents. I couldn't forgive myself for hurting them so deeply. Julia, I have never, *ever* felt so awful in my life. And I was once awake for seventy-two hours straight when I was put on a deal back in my banking days. While I had the flu. And pink eye. I was surrounded by a perimeter of trashcans I'd puke into between working on decks."

Julia laughs. "Bet your co-workers loved you."

"They hated me. I gave all of them the flu *and* pink eye."

"You really do destroy everything you touch."

"Whoa whoa whoa." I hold up my hands—one of hers, too, still clasped in mine—in mock consternation. "I'm pouring my shriveled black heart out to you, and you're gonna hit me below the belt? You play dirty."

Julia levels me with this saucy, simmering look. "You like it dirty."

"Well, yeah. But so do you."

"And I'm damn proud of it." She tilts her head. "So. Why you felt the way you have about your divorce is totally valid. You made a big mistake. But you also learned a big, important lesson. You learned *to tell the truth*, even when it hurts. That takes courage."

"I wasn't courageous. I was tired. And lonely."

"Of course you were tired. But you were also brave, Grey. And when you're brave like that, you're inevitably going to hurt people. By telling the truth, *your* truth, you're going to hurt them. But telling your truth, and living it, is always the right thing. Maybe it sucks. Maybe it complicates things beyond repair. Keeping it in, though? Smothering who you truly are to fit into some Instagram-sized box of what passes for happiness? That's much worse. You're not a liar. You're honest and brave, and I adore you because you did the hard thing when it would have been so much easier just to keep quiet. Keep pretending that everything was perfect. That's how tragedies happen—tragedies like spending the rest of your life pretending to be someone you aren't."

I look at her. Heart swelling now, too.

I love that she doesn't judge me. She doesn't absolve me of everything, either.

She's got a nuanced understanding of me. My story. The world.

Makes me want to judge less, too.

Judge myself less harshly.

"I had the fairy tale, but I walked away from it," I say hoarsely. "Why the hell do I deserve another shot at happiness?"

"Because that wasn't the right fairy tale for *you*. You say you were the villain in that story. And I say you were in the wrong story. Stop thinking of yourself as the big bad. Stop punishing yourself for not knowing better then, and start celebrating the fact that you know better now. Take that knowledge and live the life you risked your soul for."

I can only stare at her. "That's beautiful."

"Thanks," she says, the skin around her eyes crinkling with genuine pleasure. "I only study beautiful language for a living. Think about it, Grey. What's the worst that could happen if you give yourself another shot? You get to spend eternity with David Bowie and/or The Prince of Darkness. I think your inner werewolf would be *quite* content with that scenario."

I grin. Butterflies swarming inside my belly.

There have been few times in my life when I could pinpoint the moment that separated *before* and *after*. Before I knew my marriage was over, after. Before I became a lame thirty-something who spends his Friday nights building models or in meetings, after.

But I can tell that this is one of those moments. One that changes everything. The one that marks the time *before* I put down the gun I've been holding to my head, and *after*.

I am putting that fucking gun down.

Who the hell knows if it's the right call.

Who knows if I deserve another chance. Maybe I do. Maybe I don't.

But either way, I've been given that chance. She's sitting right here beside me, hand in mine. Clear blue eyes and trust and warmth.

I'd be an idiot not to take the leap. Every bone in my body is telling me to do it. Take Julia with me.

"My past doesn't excuse my behavior on the Rodgers' Farms project. I want you to know that this—you and me—it feels different. My feelings for you are so different." I lean down and brush my lips against her knuckles, inhaling her scent. Blood pulses through my cock, gathering in the head. It presses greedily against my fly. "I mean this in a good way—but I didn't want to want you like I did. I fought it. Resisted you as best as I could, because I didn't want to hurt you. Didn't want to involve you in my mess. But you still got under my skin, and staying away from you was agony. Agony that pissed me off to no fucking end. I'm sorry, Julia. Truly, deeply sorry. I guess I'm just...I was smothered by superficiality for so long that you—your real and your deep—felt like this huge breath of fresh air. I was insanely attracted to it. Still am. Although it pisses me off a lot less now."

She's smiling, eyes twinkling. "Well that's good news. Although I have to admit it was fun pushing your buttons. Now I get why you always rose to the occasion. You had a big old crush on me, didn't you?"

"The biggest fucking crush of my life. Also the most inconvenient." I kill the ignition. My cock is screaming, and I want to show Julia exactly how insane my attraction to her is. "Do you forgive me?"

"I do," she says. "I get why you acted the way you did. Doesn't excuse it, but I appreciate the apology nonetheless. Thank you for that."

I look at her. Heart thudding inside my chest.

"Come to bed."

She grins. A soft, wicked thing. "Only if the no-clothes policy is still in effect."

"Sweetheart, that policy will be in effect from now until forever as long as it's you in my bed."

I turn to open my door, but Julia catches me, giving my hand a tug.

"And thank you," she says. "For telling me. I know that wasn't easy."

My throat—my cock—they're all swelling now, and I can't fucking stand it. She makes me wild. The werewolf in me yawning awake inside my skin.

"Thank you for not running. For seeing the good in my bad."

"I've never been afraid of your werewolf side. Your growling. What made you think I was going to be afraid now?"

I laugh. "Good point."

"Shadows come with the light. You can't have one without the other. And you have to know by now that I believe they make the other more interesting. It's our shadows that give us depth. Literally and figuratively," she says, reaching up with her other hand to trail her thumb over the indent in my chin. "I like your depths. Same as you like mine."

It's rare that I'm rendered speechless.

But right now—

Fuck, I don't know what to say.

I do know that shit just got real. We don't have to talk about it yet. But I'm in this now. For the long haul. I promised Julia I'd be a real partner in raising the baby. Now I want to be her partner, period. In all things.

I want to grow a family with her. Grow old together. Is this happening fast? Yes and no. I was done for the second she and I met. I couldn't stay away from her, no matter how hard I tried. It's part of the reason why I showed up to all her meetings, whether or not I actually had to be there. I just wanted to see her. Soak up her laugh, her lust for real life.

Her way of being.

She's already made me a better man. A more honest one. I could never talk to Cameron the way I talk to Julia. Openly. Without fear of judgment. She hides nothing and neither do I.

I want to be the man she deserves. One who's real. Who takes care of his own and provides for his family.

I will work myself to the bone if it means keeping Julia and this baby happy and safe.

In the meantime, I'm going to make Julia come. A lot.

"Upstairs," I manage. "Now."

Julia shivers, drawing a breath through her teeth.

"Jesus, I like it when you growl like that."

Chapter Twenty-Four

JULIA

Is there anything sexier than a growly man who's raw with honest need and admiration and the desire to fuck you hard and well?

Watching Greyson tear off his sweater and undershirt as we head up to his bedroom, I think that no.

No, nothing sexier exists on this planet. Not by a long shot.

By the time we're in his bedroom, I'm shaking. The smell of him fills my head and my body. Bergamot. Leather.

I'm so turned on it hurts.

Grey spins around to face me, hands at work on his belt buckle. I can see the outline of his erect penis straining against his fly. The sight of his bare chest—all that skin, all that strength—

It's too much. Along with the strength he showed by sharing his pain with me, his shame and his truth, it's overwhelming.

It's beautiful.

He is so damn beautiful.

All of him. The hero and the villain. The good and the bad.

I love all of him.

I want to show him just how much I love his shadow and his light.

"Sit," I say, making quick work of my shirt and my jeans. "There, on the edge of the bed."

He looks up at me, bent over as he steps out of his pants one leg at a time.

"Baby, I gotta get my hands on you. I'm not gonna wait."

"You'll wait." In just my underwear and bra, I back up against the wall. "Sit down."

He shucks off his boxers, revealing an impressive erection. "Absolutely not."

"Sit the fuck down. Don't make me ask twice."

A flame ignites in his eyes. He takes himself in his hand and gives his cock a gentle tug.

"You playin' games with me, sweetheart?"

I step out of my underwear. Slip off my bra. Then, eyes still on his, I slide down the wall, my knees falling open as my ass meets the floor.

"This is a game you're gonna like."

His eyes dart to my pussy. Spread open and *wet*.

He swallows, making his Adam's apple bob.

"Okay," he says. And then he does as I tell him and sits on the edge of the bed. Legs spread, dick still in his hand. He swallows again. "Sweetheart, you are so—Jesus, baby, you are gorgeous. Everywhere. That pussy—"

"Bet you'd like to fuck it"—I reach down and touch myself, dragging my finger through my folds—"wouldn't you?"

He's rolling his palm over the head of his cock. "I'd very much like to fuck it. Hard. The way you like it."

I feel the low, rumbly timbre of his voice in my clit. My nipples pebble to hard points, the soles of my feet arching off the floor as I touch myself there, circling two fingers, circling in time to Grey's movements. Slow and steady.

"See how much you turn me on?" I manage, sinking one of my fingers inside me. The sinews in his neck pop when he gives himself a long, hard pull. "This is all you, Grey. You did this to me."

"I did"—he swallows, stroking himself some more—"what?"

I roll my hips against my hand, urging my clit against my palm. I want to make this last, but my orgasm is already close.

"Your bravery. It made me wild."

"Yeah?" He grits his teeth. Legs spreading wider, allowing me a glimpse of his asshole.

So lewd. Dirty.

My arousal spikes.

"Your honesty made me—" My breath catches when my thumb hits my clit. My nipples are screaming for attention. I start to play with my nipples with my other hand. He growls.

"It made you what?" he bites out. I can tell he's trying not to jack himself off too hard, too fast. He's on the verge—having your arousal continually stoked over an hours-long period will do that—but he wants to draw this out. Savor the moment.

"It made me hot. So hot for you, Grey. Your openness, too. Your vulnerability made me want you in ways I've never wanted anyone else. Ever."

"Fuck—Jesus Christ, Julia, you gotta let me have you. I want to be inside you. I want to feel you. You make me beg, and I'll make you pay. I'll punish you."

I bite my lip, allowing my fingers to amble back to my clit. Sensation winds tight tight *tight* in my core. I'm grinding against the wall, my skin burning.

I don't care.

Grey's eyes are hot and hard on my body. His nostrils flare as he tugs at his cock, running a thumb up the seam on the underside of his head.

"Maybe I want to be punished." I glide my fingers around and through my folds. "Show me the villain. Be the bad guy. And I'll show you how much I like him."

He growls, bolting to his feet. My eyes flick up to meet his.

He's enormous. Breathing hard.

Angry. Cock and eyes and muscles, drawn taut with frustration.

"How much bad do you want?"

My legs fall all the way open. I arch my back, offering him my tits.

My everything.

"All the bad you're willing to give me."

He takes a step forward. Nostrils still flaring.

"Take your fingers. Touch your clit," he bites out. When I hesitate, he takes another step forward. Towering over me. "Do what I fucking say, Julia."

I shiver. Shake.

I love this game. Switching up the power dynamic. I lead. Then he does.

I take charge.

Then he takes charge of me.

I meet his eyes and touch my clit. Both fingers. Pressing, pinching.

A tremble moves through my left leg. I'm close.

"Open your mouth," Grey says, taking his cock in his hand. Taking a step forward. "Wider."

I do as he tells me and open wide.

Without preamble, he puts himself inside my mouth. Sinking on a slow, deep thrust that induces the tiniest gag, making my eyes water. Lewd and lovely, all at once.

He lets out a pant.

Need spears me right through my middle. I moan, too, and Grey must feel the vibration, because he slams a palm against the wall above my head.

"Stay still," he grunts. "And don't you dare come. Your turn to wait, pretty girl."

Gliding a hand through my hair, he gives it a little tug. Tugs my head back so that my eyes meet his as he glides in and out of my mouth. In and out.

"That's it," he says softly, pulling out until his head is at my lips. "Play with me, sweetheart. Taste me. Show me how much you want this."

I wrap my lips around him, tugging and sucking and licking him. I taste the salt of his pre-cum, and use my tongue to smear it across my lips.

"Aw, fuck," he says, gently pushing my hair away from my face. "Fuck, you like that. You like the way I taste."

In reply, I swirl my tongue over his head and give the underside a long, lingering lick.

His control snaps. He jacks his hips and *howls*, this gravelly roar that makes my nipples tighten painfully.

Before I know what he's doing, Grey is wrapping a hand around my arm and yanking me to my feet, his cock bobbing as it falls out of my mouth.

"Can you stand?" he asks roughly.

"I—"

One of my legs gives out, but he's there to catch me. He hikes me over his shoulder, making me laugh. Then he sets me on the bed, the fluffy duvet sinking beneath my weight. The fabric feels cool and silky against my back.

My pussy is throbbing.

"Please," I say.

"Still want the villain?"

"I just want you. Whatever that looks like."

In reply, he takes my knees in his hands and parts them. Ducks down and licks my pussy with the broad flat of his tongue. Back to front, ducking inside my cunt before pressing against my clit.

I feel my orgasm rising up to meet me. I gasp. He growls.

"You'll get the villain," he says, and grabs a condom on the bedside table. "By the way—I'd really like to stop using these things. How about we get tested? Make sure it's safe before we..."

I bite my lip. "Fuck without them? I love that idea. I got tested when I found out I was pregnant—they test you for a lot of stuff to make sure you don't pass it on to your baby. I'm clean."

"I will schedule a new test first thing tomorrow."

Chapter Twenty-Five

GREYSON

I flip her over onto her stomach. The skin on her ass and back shines in the low light of the room. I lean down and kiss the outside of her neck, the underside of her ribcage. I kiss her ass cheek, giving it a playful smack.

I straighten, tearing open the foil packet.

"Get on your knees," I grunt, rolling the condom on. "But keep your head down."

She does as I tell her, ass up, head down, face turned to the side so I can just make out her features. Hair everywhere, pink lips swollen to a bright shade of red.

She's watching me, eyes bright with arousal and curiosity.

Scooting toward her, I nudge her legs wider with my knee. Ducking down, I sink my teeth into her ass cheek. Her muscles there tense.

"You're good," she says before I can ask. I cup her ass in my hands, kneading her cheeks before I use my thumbs to part them.

I love seeing her. All of her. Pussy, asshole.

She's trusting me with all this.

Pulling her ass cheek a little wider to spread the lips of her cunt open, I guide myself inside her. Sensation in my balls spiking as I sink into her tight heat.

"Fuck, you feel good," I groan.

"Grey," she pants. Pleads.

Wrapping my hand around the back of her neck, I pull my hips back. Roll them forward. Do it again. Harder this time, our bodies slapping when they meet.

She cries out with delight.

I reach around and play with her clit while I thrust deep. She's crying out again, her pussy just barely fluttering. I feel sparks at the base of my spine. I grit my teeth. I've always managed to get her off first. Not about to break that tradition.

I may be a villain, but I'm not a selfish bastard.

"How bad do you want?" I repeat, rolling the pads of my middle finger right where she needs it.

"Bad," she breathes.

I thrust into her at the same time I gently pluck her clit between my thumb and forefinger. I'm sweating with the effort to hold back. She's so wet. So soft. Clearly turned on by this side of me.

A tremor moves through her legs.

She's close.

Perfect.

I swipe my thumb across her clit one last time. Get it nice and wet.

And then I pull back.

"What the fuck?" she cries.

"You asked for bad," I say, drawing my thumb across her ass cheek. "So that's what you're gonna get."

I dip my thumb between her crack. Just above her pucker. I tug at her ass cheek, spreading her some more.

Carefully, I press the pad of my thumb to her asshole. Still pumping into her.

Her pussy contracts forcefully, once.

"Grey," she's saying. "My God, yes."

"Bad enough?"

"More."

I press a little harder. "Play with yourself, baby. It'll make the bad real good."

I play with her asshole and fuck her from behind while she reaches down and plays with her pussy.

I have to bite the inside of my cheek to keep from coming.

She starts to moan. Legs trembling, cunt fluttering. Hips rolling against me, seeking more.

My heart swells. She doesn't just like this.

She fucking loves it. She's playing along. Letting me in.

Showing me just how much she likes my dark side.

She comes and I come, a burst of light and feeling. I dig my fingers into her sides, holding her tight. She reaches back and grabs me by the wrist. Holding on for dear life as she clenches around me. Crying out my name.

I love it when she says my name.

I fall to my side and pull her down with me, curling her into my body so that we're face to face. She's shaking. Smiling.

"You're so beautiful," I murmur, kissing her lips.

"See?" she pants, brushing my hair out of my eyes. "Like you said—the bad is good."

"You mean that?"

"So fucking good. Dirty doesn't equal bad."

"Well, yeah. But it is a little taboo."

"Clearly I don't mind, Grey."

I grin. "Clearly, Jules."

She grins. "You've never called me that before."

"You like it?"

"I love it when you say my name. Any version of it."

I grin, too. "I noticed."

I kiss her. Keep kissing until we're making out like teenagers, right down to the dry humping.

We make out until the dry humping turns to real humping.

When we're done, we stay up talking. I get the answers to the questions I had before.

Where she comes from—born in Atlanta, moved to Charleston when she was a teenager.

Where was she in that picture of her with her dad at Hogwarts? She got a graduate degree at Cambridge.

The travel—she mostly travels with colleagues, but would love to travel with me. Maybe on a babymoon somewhere.

What about historical romance does she find so comforting?

She loves the reminder that no matter how difficult life can get, or how hopeless your story can feel, we all deserve our own happily ever after. And that sometimes, the more difficult the story, the happier the ending.

Underwear—does she wear it with those yoga pants? Or does she go commando?

Commando, always.

That alone has me rolling on top of her for one more round.

Julia

I wake up in Greyson's bed.

This time he's in it with me. Sleepily scrolling through his phone, running a hand over his face.

"Hi," I say.

He blinks, turning his head on the pillow. His face creases into a smile, and my heart does a back flip. Pussy pulses.

I've been awake for all of five seconds, and already I want him.

No time for bathroom or toothpaste. I need.

Now.

"Mornin', baby," he says, leaning over to press a scruffy kiss to my neck. My blood warms. "How're you feeling?"

We look at each other for a beat. Then another. I'm feeling all squishy and happy inside, and I kind of can't stand it.

I can't stand him. His smile and that cute fucking cleft in his chin and the goodness, the intelligence, of his heart.

Wordlessly I roll on top of him. His smile broadens, his hands gliding up my thighs.

"That good, huh?"

I shimmy down a little and reach for him. Grin when I find him rock hard.

"Uh-huh," I reply. I duck down, using my elbow to keep my face out of my hair.

I take his head in my mouth. Kiss it, tease it. Taste him. Just how he likes it.

His hands are in my hair. On my tits. I open my lips wider and take him deeper.

"Aw, baby," he says, voice still gravely with sleep. "Aw, Jules, I like this, but I think I'd like to make love to you more. Up, sweetheart."

He gently guides me up from his dick. Then he's reaching for his nightstand.

"Make love to me? That's new."

"It's what I want. That gonna be a problem?"

I'm grinning so hard my eyes start to water. "Not at all."

Open wrapper. Quick hands.

He curls one hand around my hips and the other around his cock. I lift up onto my knees, helping him settle himself between my legs.

I sink down onto him slowly. Quietly. Both of us rocking into one another. I'm sore and I'm tired and I probably have terrible morning breath, but this feels *so* nice. No rush, no madness.

His hands trail up my sides to cup my breasts, and he rubs the pads of his thumbs over my nipples.

I moan at the bolts of sensation that move between there and my clit. Reaching down, I play with myself, and Greyson's eyebrows come together. Like he's in pain.

"You take what you want," he says. "You know what you want. I love that about you. I can't—I can't fucking stand how much I want you, sweetheart. Let me—"

And then he's flipping me onto my back. Guiding one of my legs over his shoulder as he rolls on top of me, the weight of his body delicious and warm.

His smell is all over me, that masculine, clean scent I can't get enough of. I want to bite him. Devour him whole. Crawl inside his skin and live there for a week.

I reach between us and wrap my fingers around him. I guide him to my center and roll my hips a little. He sinks into me easily. This new angle with my leg over his shoulder allows me to take him deeper. He hits me right there, and my mouth falls open. Shit I'm sore.

Shit this feels lovely.

His eyes are locked on mine as he strokes into me. Slow, deep, muscular thrusts that I feel in every corner of my being. We watch each other, breathing softly. My hands marvel at the way the muscles along the sides of his torso ripple and bunch as he moves. I glide my fingers up his arms, catching on the nicotine patch on his shoulder. His brows curve upward, his gaze steady. Same as his thrusts.

He sees me.

I see him.

The soft, almost sticky sound of our bodies moving together fills the space between us. It smells like sex now. Sex and sheets and shared everything.

The wiry hair on his chest grazes my nipples. They're sore, too, but when he leans into me a little more, the heat of his skin feels nice pressed against them.

He reaches between us and thumbs my clit. I gasp. He replies with a low rumble that echoes in the barrel-sized cavity of his chest.

The moment is quiet and unbearably sweet.

This feels *so good*. So real and so right. Like I'm at home. Welcome and comfortable just as I am. I can't explain it. I just know there's this feeling that fills me. This fullness inside my chest and throat.

He's loving me.

This man is actually loving me. The one who was cold and cruel.

The one who was hurting. He's healing now.

Healing both of us.

My eyes blur with tears. I feel them leak out of the corners of my eyes. It's such a cliché, crying in the middle of sex. But I don't care.

Neither does Grey. He just silently wipes away my tears with his free hand and brings me to orgasm with the other. The muscles in my legs pull taut as the wave hits me. Rushes through my skin, flooding me with more feeling.

So much feeling I'm positive I'm going to burst. I close my eyes, overwhelmed.

"Grey," I plead, pulsing around him.

"I got you." He wraps a hand around the back of my neck and curls me into his body, thrusting through my orgasm. "I'm here."

He comes a thrust and a half later, letting out a low growl. His body going still above mine.

I don't know how he manages to hold himself up so he doesn't crush me. Maybe it's because he clings to me, same as I cling to him. The echoes of our orgasms leaving us sated and breathless and sweaty.

Grey pulls out of me with a wince and rolls onto his back. He takes care of the condom, and then he pulls me against his side. Kissing my forehead. I snuggle up against him, running my fingers through his chest hair.

"All right?"

"I liked that."

"Me too."

"Last night was good bad. This morning was just really, really good."

His lips curl into this cocky little smirk. "I'm good all around."

"What's my line again? The one about not stroking your ego?"

He laughs. Moves an arm across his torso to cup my breast, gently drawing his thumb across my nipple. "How's sex when you're pregnant? Any different?"

"Oh yeah. My orgasms are *insane* right now. One of the few perks so far."

"Well. Let's make you come a lot then. Try to even the score."

I grin. "I like the sound of that."

"I really am sorry you've been having a rough time," he says.

I snuggle a little closer. "Not gonna lie, this first trimester has really sucked. But now that the worst of it is over, I'm starting to feel the excitement everyone talks about. Seeing our baby on that ultrasound screen—that was pretty damn cool, wasn't it?"

"I just can't wait to meet this baby. Who is she going to be like? What will she love? Will she have a love/hate relationship with me the same way her mom does?"

I smile. "You think it's a she?"

"I do."

"Why?"

He shrugs. "Just have a feeling."

"I have that feeling, too." I glance up at him. "Do you want to find out? The gender?"

He looks down at me. "I'm down to do whatever you'd like. But if I had to pick, I'd like to be surprised."

I pull back. "Really? You, the control freak, *really* want to be surprised?"

"Maybe you're rubbing off on me," he says with a grin. "In every way."

"I like the sound of that, too."

Grey is quiet for a moment. His hand moves from my tit to my arm, where his fingers rove over my skin.

"I know you shot down the idea of us getting married," he says at last, making my heart skip a beat. "Which was the right call, by the way."

"I agree," I say slowly. "Don't get me wrong. I love love, and I love weddings. I can't wait for Olivia and Eli's. But why rush it, you know? If I'm with the right guy, in the right relationship, it will just feel... right. Whether or not a ring is on my finger."

He's quiet again. My heart is pounding. I glance up at him to see him looking at me intently. Softness in his eyes.

"Julia, I'd like to be that guy," he says. "The right guy. For you."

My heart is beating its way out of my chest now.

I want that, too.

I want that so badly I feel like I'm going to cry again.

But aren't we rushing? We went from enemies to friends to lovers in what feels like a flash.

Then again, getting pregnant will push things up a bit.

Finding out the guy you thought was a jackass is actually an excellent human being will *definitely* move things forward.

I love the way this man loves me.

I love the way he shared his family with me, knowing how much I miss mine.

I love the way he makes me feel. Like I belong. Like I'm sexy and admirable, just for being myself.

Cupping his face in my hand, I kiss him. Morning breath and everything.

"You already are that guy, Grey," I reply.

He looks at me. "Let me take care of you the way I want to. I want to be good to you, Julia, and the baby, too. I want to be your date to Olivia and Eli's wedding and every wedding after that. Even if we never end up having one of our own."

I smile. Smile and laugh.

He's opening up.

Putting himself out there.

This is not what I planned.

But it's still fucking beautiful.

"Yes. *Yes*. I'll take that leap with you," I say. "Gladly."

Chapter Twenty-Six

GREYSON

Julia: You know what I could go for right now?

Greyson: Please say an orgasm

Greyson: Please

Julia: Well that's a given. But you already gave me several of those this morning. And last night. And the night before that. I'm starting to forget what my place even looks like.

Greyson: My bed is bigger, but my backseat works too

Greyson: I have twenty minutes before my next meeting

Julia: I have back to back classes until five. Otherwise I would already be outside waiting for you.

Greyson: now I'm gonna have to summon satan to get rid of this hard on. Great.

Julia: #sorrynotsorry

Julia: But besides an orgasm. I could really go for one of Gracie's pumpkin scones. Like the one we split for breakfast that morning? Random craving, I know. But I've suddenly got this sweet tooth now that I can't have Chardonnay.

Greyson: you mean the scone we ate before I went down on you for the rest of the day?

Julia: Yup, that's the one. Also, if memory serves, you went down on me for approximately ten minutes, and spent the rest of the day in meetings.

Greyson: But it was a good ten minutes right?

Julia: Ugh the best.

Greyson: Can I take you to dinner tonight? Should wrap up by 8.

Julia: I'd love that.

Greyson: Don't forget to pack your stretchy pants

Julia: Let's be real do I even need pants? You're forgetting your no-clothes policy.

Greyson: touché my dear touché

But I can't wait until eight to see her.

Instead, I get through my meeting, and then I give Elijah Jackson a call. He puts me in touch with Olivia, who tells me Julia's 4 P.M. class is one on "Sex and Agency in Romance" with about thirty-five or so students.

I call Gracie and order forty pumpkin scones, just in case. I add an extra-large iced coffee, because I am wiped, and I still have a lot of shit to get through before dinner tonight.

Juggling real life and work life is no joke, y'all.

I park in a garage close to campus. Ask about twelve people how to get to the building where Julia is teaching her class.

I arrive breathless and a little sweaty. Gigantic box of freshly baked scones in tow, still so warm from the oven that I have to pass the box from one hand to the other.

Julia hasn't started class yet, thank God. But the room is already packed with students pulling laptops from bags and cracking open paperbacks with titles like *The Duke of Midnight* and *The Kiss Quotient*.

I catch the faintest whiff of weed as I move through the space. Bite back a smile.

College. Miss it. And don't.

Julia is at the front of the room. Standing behind a table as she sorts through several piles of papers.

My pulse hiccups. I feel my lips curling into an involuntary smile.

She's so fucking pretty. Full on Stevie Nicks today in a black dress with flowy sleeves and tall leather boots. Blond hair falling over her shoulders in unkempt waves.

She's also glowing. Color high, eyes bright.

She's feeling better. And she's happy.

The idea that I have something to do with that makes my chest swell.

I meant what I said when I told her she made the right call turning down my marriage proposal. Not only because the timing wasn't right. But also because I don't feel the need to show off our perfect, shiny relationship—symbolized by the perfect, shiny ring I would've bought her—the way I did with Cameron. I don't need that kind of outside validation when it comes to Julia. Same as I don't need to check off arbitrary boxes with her. Meet cute, date for two years, elaborate proposal, even more elaborate wedding. That's not what she's about.

That's not what we're about.

I just adore her. Being around her. I love when she's with me and miss her when she's gone.

Our story started with a less than stellar meeting and an unexpected pregnancy. But now it's just about us. Her and me. And isn't that how it should be?

I stick out like a sore thumb in my suit and tie.

A fact nobody misses. Immediately students start to whisper as I pass.

"Oh my God, who *is* that?"

"Did Professor Lassiter hire a cover model to come talk to us? I hope he takes his shirt off. Or at least unbuttons it a little."

"Bet he's got his dick in that box."

That last one makes me laugh. Julia looks up from her papers. She does a double take when she sees me, blue eyes going wide with delight.

"Grey?" she says, smiling. "What in the world are you doing here?"

I open the box.

"You said you were craving a pumpkin scone. Thought I'd bring some over for you and your students. This qualifies as brain food, right?"

"Everything qualifies as brain food!" someone calls out behind me.

Julia just looks at me. Digs her teeth into her bottom lip as she smiles at me with her eyes.

Gracious, this woman.

She does things to me.

Things I like but usually try to avoid when I'm standing in front of forty college students.

I'm not sure what the appropriate greeting here is. I don't want to embarrass Julia or make her appear unprofessional.

So I just smile back and hold out the box.

"Hi. Take one."

She gathers her hair in one hand to hold it back and leans toward the box. "Hi. This was very sweet of you."

"I was thinking about how good these things are," I say, watching as she lifts a scone from the box and brings it to her mouth. "I was also thinking that I'd love to see you in action. Teaching, I mean. Talking romance. Seemed like the perfect opportunity. Is it okay if I stay?"

"You can stay as long as you like," another student says.

Julia tilts her head to glance over my shoulder. "All right, Priya, don't make me assign extra reading this week."

A tingle sneaks its way up my spine. I *like* it when Professor Lassiter lays down the law.

Maybe she'll do it with me tonight.

"And of course you can stay," Julia says, turning back to me. "You're always welcome."

"Always."

"*Priya*."

"All right, all right. I'll stop."

Julia grins. "Cool if I introduce you? Then you can pass those around and we'll start class."

She introduces me as her boyfriend, which makes me smile harder than it should. It just feels so good. Being a part of things again.

Participating fully in life for the first time in years.

I don't have a ton of time to hang out. My phone vibrates like crazy in my pocket. But I manage to watch Julia teach for a solid half hour from a seat in the front row. The class and I munching on our scones while she lectures passionately—creatively—on how changing social norms have shaped romance and vice versa. She encourages her students to be active participants in the conversation, calling on people by name. I notice that, while the majority of her class is female, there are more than a handful of guys in the room.

Everyone is very engaged.

Julia reads excerpts. Asks questions. Pushes her students to move past clichéd answers. She's incredibly smart and capable and charismatic.

Competence porn is a real thing.

This is some of the best I've seen. Ever.

The class talks about sex positivity in romance. About power dynamics between heroes and heroines. Problematic tropes and the even more problematic lack of diversity in the genre.

One excerpt in particular grabs my attention. In more ways than one. It's from a book called *My Romp With the Rogue*, written by our very own Olivia.

Charlotte listened quietly as Callum told the story.

His brother William was a troubled man. Abused as a child, he in turn abused others as he grew into adulthood. He drank heavily. Callum did his best to help William. When those efforts were rebuffed, he settled for staying away from him. But when William turned his hand on their housekeeper—the woman who all but raised them—Callum could stand by no longer.

There was a fight. Mrs. Yardley lay bleeding at the foot of her bed. William drew a pistol, and Callum returned the favor.

He survived. His brother did not.

And that was the story of the murder.

Tears streamed down her face by the time Callum was done talking.

She realized then she didn't have to defeat the monster, or protect herself from him. She'd merely had to unmask him. See *him for the deeply pained, deeply lonely man beneath.*

Charlotte reached for him, but he was already climbing out of bed, ducking into his nightshirt.

"Don't go," she said.

He looked at her steadily. Eyes no longer hard but soft.

Soft with pain.

"I must. For now you know the truth about your husband. And the truth is an ugly thing."

No, Charlotte wanted to say. Truth is both ugly and beautiful. Terrible and courageous.

The truth was everything, and it meant more to her than she could say that he'd shared it with her.

But Callum had already stalked out of her chamber.

She had a sinking feeling he would not return.

I walk out of Julia's class with a whole new appreciation for romance. And for Julia.

Woman is a rockstar.

Scares me a little to think how close I came to keeping her at arm's length. If I hadn't gotten her pregnant, would I have risked getting to know her beyond our backseat hookups? Or would I have crushed on her from afar like the scorned scumbag I used to be?

I thought I was doing the world a favor by staying out of the way. Playing it safe.

But now I know better.

Thank God I chose better.

The weeks fly by in a whirl of good bad sex and good good sex, too. In meetings and Excel models and many, many episodes of *Game of Thrones* and *The Sopranos*. Breakfasts made while listening to Bowie and Queen. Sunday suppers at my parents' house.

Julia practically lives at my place. I love having her around. How could I not? I go to sleep with the taste of her on my mouth. Wake up with her warm and soft beside me. Juggling my two obsessions—my job and Julia—has left me exhausted to the point of borderline narcolepsy. I'm feeling a new kind of pressure at work now. It's not just my family on the line anymore—Bryce and Ford.

It's the family I'm going to have with Julia, too.

I wasn't kidding when I told Julia I want her and our baby to have the best of everything. It's what I'm good at—providing. It's what I take pride in. I may not be great at this intimacy thing yet. It's still new, and still scary sometimes. But I am good at making the people I love feel safe and secure.

Julia made it clear she doesn't want or need my money. And that's fine. But I still need to pull my weight. Still need to feel like I'm contributing something.

And it's not like I can phone it in at work. I own the company, for Christ's sake. I call the shots. Our success or failure rests entirely on my shoulders.

The nicotine patches I've been wearing have curbed most of my appetite for cigarettes. But I still sneak one every so often when I'm especially zonked or the stress gets to me.

For the most part, though, things are good.

Really good. Charlie Brown looked perfect at our twelve week ultrasound. She was more baby than blob this time, and even had her little legs crossed and moved around for us.

Julia laughed. I cried.

She's feeling better, too, which is a big relief for us both.

"Fourteen weeks today," Julia says one night at dinner. "I'm officially in my second trimester."

We're at Julia's favorite fried seafood place. It's a teeny tiny spot on a corner in Elliotborough, a cute neighborhood in the Upper King Street area. The restaurant has been owned by the same family for two generations now. The space and menu are straightforward—no frills—but they serve up some of the best fried seafood platters on the peninsula.

Julia's sitting across from me in a vinyl booth. Going to town on her locally caught fried shrimp basket, complete with sides of lima beans and Carolina gold rice and a deviled crab, just because.

"Fourteen weeks." I wipe my hands on my napkin, then get back to work on my fish. "That went fast."

"No it didn't," Julia replies cheerfully, dipping a shrimp into a small plastic container of tartar sauce. "I've been pregnant for a fucking year. How did you not know?"

"Must feel that way when you're sober, huh?"

"Whole new appreciation for those in recovery, I'll say that much."

She swallows. Eats another shrimp and reaches for her tea, looking up at me. "Have you thought about our registry at all?"

"Shit." I blink. Feel a wave of exhaustion move through me. "I completely forgot. Between the Moore Foods storefront opening and that champagne bar we're trying to get the permits for—just. Shit. I have no excuse. I'm really sorry, Jules."

"Did you do any research? You know, have you looked into what we're going to need when this tiny human comes? How we're going to survive The Battle of The Newborn Baby?"

"No," I reply, sheepish. I take a long pull from my own tea. "But nice *Game of Thrones* reference. Have you? Given it any thought, I mean?"

"Well, yeah. I've read a couple great books on pregnancy and motherhood. I've reached out to some friends who have kids and picked their brains. I mean, I get that we have a lot of time, but still...I'm a little disappointed, Grey. I'm not the only one becoming a parent for the first time here. I'm also not the only one working. I'm busy, but I still make time for what's important."

I tug a hand through my hair. Let out a sigh. "I know, I know. Work's just been insane lately."

"When is it ever *not* insane for you?"

"It's for us, you know," I reply. "I work hard for us."

Julia tilts her head and gives me a look.

"I'll read some books, I promise. I'll try harder. I'm sorry, Julia. It's been a while since I did this." I motion between us. "Also, give me some credit. I've helped out a lot with Ford and Bryce over the years. I have some firsthand knowledge of what it means to be around. Be present, as much as I'm able to, anyway."

She nods. "That's fair. But promise me you'll learn? That you'll make the effort with me and our baby?"

I nod. "Absolutely."

"Good. The girls are meeting me in February—the weekend of the twentieth—at Hello Baby to pick some stuff out. You'll be there, right?"

"I'll be there," I say, even as a hand grips my heart and squeezes. That weekend is the grand opening of a champagne bar we've been working on with a local sommelier. Whatever. I'll figure it out. "I promise I'll learn. I learned to make love to you pretty damn quickly, didn't I?"

Julia lifts her brows, one quick, saucy bounce, and grins. "I have to say you've gotten really great at that."

"Finish your food." I nod at her plate. "I'd like to take lessons from the Professor in how I can make it even better for her. She's an excellent teacher."

Chapter Twenty-Seven

JULIA

Eli and Olivia aren't having bridal parties—no bridesmaids or groomsmen—but she requested that Gracie and I get our hair and makeup done with her the day of the wedding.

Saturday morning dawns cold and clear. Beautifully so, the sun scrubbing the sky clean of any clouds. Grey and I decided to treat ourselves to a room for the weekend at the hotel downtown where Olivia and her family are staying. We grab coffee and breakfast biscuits at the cafe off the lobby for breakfast, and then I head upstairs to meet the bride.

I tear up the second I enter the suite. Gracie is already in the makeup chair, eyes glued to the ceiling as an artist carefully applies mascara to her bottom lashes.

The scents of coffee and hairspray fill the room.

Fill my heart to bursting. I love my girlfriends. My village. So much.

Olivia's wedding dress hangs in front of a window, the morning light streaming through the gauzy material.

She's sitting on the sofa, finishing off a bowl of what looks like cheesy grits with eggs and scallions.

I grin. Elijah has turned our New York girl into a proper southerner. Olivia has come so, so far since she arrived in Charleston a couple years ago, confused and burnt out and broken.

When she sees me, her whole face lights up. Smile broadening, she leaps off the couch and wraps me in a hug.

I laugh, tearing up all over again. She is nothing short of radiant. Happiness and excitement coming off her in waves.

"Happy wedding day, friend," I say, giving her a squeeze. "How's it going so far?"

Olivia pulls back, still smiling. "I woke up with Elijah beside me. Had a cup of my favorite coffee from Gracie's and a grits bowl, made Elijah's way. My parents are entertaining themselves and their friends at the restaurant downstairs. And I get to hang out with my favorite women in the world while someone else blow dries my hair. Needless to say, it's the best day ever."

"You are *glowing*. I'm so happy for y'all. And excited to celebrate! I feel like I haven't been out or danced in forever."

"The band we hired is kind of the best," Olivia says. "There's a horn section, backup singers, the whole nine yards. I told Eli my number one request for our wedding was to see him shaking his ass on a dance floor. Everything else was secondary."

Gracie grins. "This is already my favorite wedding, and it hasn't even happened yet. Wait 'til y'all see the barn."

"Is it magical?" I ask.

"I took a peek this morning—Luke was up with the sun and has been helping out over there ever since—and it is gorgeous," she says, looking at me. "You and Greyson did such a fabulous job with the space. Now that they're dolling it up, it's nothing short of spectacular. So, so romantic."

I look at Olivia. Wrap her in another hug. "Sounds perfect for our resident romance novelist."

"I just can't wait to marry him," she replies. "I never thought I'd feel this way about someone, you know? Least of all a Southern chef covered in tattoos."

"It's always the guys you don't expect that end up making you the happiest," Gracie says. "I think all three of us can attest to that."

"Amen, sister," I say.

Olivia looks at me. "Greyson's making you pretty damn happy."

It's not a question.

It's a statement. She *knows*.

I put a hand on my face. "Is it that obvious?"

"Oh yeah," Gracie says, pointing to Olivia and me. "*Both* of you are glowing."

"Things are good," I reply. "Not perfect. But they're really good, y'all. I'm with you, Olivia—not that I never thought I'd feel this way about someone. But I never thought that I could feel this *excited* after the start Grey and I had. Could be the fact that I'm feeling like myself again now that I'm out of my first trimester, but I'm kind of in love with him. In love with our life together."

"Aw." Olivia wraps an arm around my waist. "I'm happy for you guys. Truly. Told you Greyson was a stand-up guy."

"Just had to peel back all the growly, grumpy layers," Gracie says.

I smile. "I don't mind the growling."

"Now *that* sounds like an interesting kink," Olivia says.

"Almost as interesting as Charlotte's broody kilted Scotsman kink," I say. "I finished my fourth re-read of *My Romp With the Rogue*. Safe to say I'm obsessed. I don't know how you do it, but I saw so much of myself—and my own story—in the characters."

Olivia smiles. Her eyes twinkle, the way they always do when she talks about her books. "The magic of romance. It's a real thing."

"Totally," Gracie agrees. "*My Deal with the Duke* was the book that gave me the idea—and the balls—to approach Luke about a little sexual deal of our own."

I laugh. "You fell for his penis, and then you fell for him."

"I think it happened all at once. Fortunately, there's no separating one from the other when it comes to Luke."

"The Luke Lady Dagger claims its last victim," Olivia says.

We spend the morning and part of the afternoon in the suite. Chatting. Drinking mimosas (mine are, sadly, very light on the champagne) while getting fake eyelashes applied. Generally basking in our love for each other and our shared love for the happy couple.

My heart is so full and swollen it feels tender to the touch. It's all I can do not to wince whenever I breathe.

The photographers arrive just as we're finishing up a late lunch. Gracie and I, along with Olivia's mom and aunt, help her into her dress and shoes.

We board a bus and head thirty minutes west of the city, to Wadmalaw Island where Rodgers' Farms is located. I'm buzzing with excitement at the prospect of seeing Grey. I've been away from him for all of, what, six hours, but I miss him.

I step off the bus when we get to the farm, and there he is. The late afternoon light painting him in gauzy tones.

Greyson.

Standing by the barn door, like he's waiting for someone. Hands clasped in front of him.

Oozing George Clooney deliciousness in a crisply cut tux. Broad shoulders filling out the jacket to perfection. Satin lapels giving his look an Old Hollywood-meets-hipster vibe. Dark hair combed in a classic swoop to the side.

Just enough scruff to make the insides of my thighs tingle. His scruff always catches me there as he makes his way down to my pussy.

Ford is beside him. A tattoo peeking out of the sleeve of his jacket as he reaches up and runs a hand through his hair. The motion reminds me so much of Greyson. The two of them are different—Ford is warmer, chiller, freer with his thoughts and emotions—but very much alike, too.

As an only child, I can't help but be intrigued by that. Tickled by it, too.

My eyes move back to Grey. I notice the cut of his tuxedo—the pants especially—is different from the suits he usually wears. It's... tighter. A bit more daring.

Makes me smile. Small thing, but it still shows Grey's taking a chance. Putting himself out there.

I love it.

I love him.

I drink him in for a full beat. Heart twirling inside my chest like it's being spun around the room in a *My Romp With the Rogue*-style waltz. I can't believe I just thought those words. *I love him.*

I can't believe this is happening. It's bewildering. And wonderful.

That's my man right there.

Never in a million years would I have picked him out of a lineup. But I'm pretty damn glad he's mine.

I move toward him, careful not to let my heels sink into the grass. He turns his head and our eyes meet.

"Hey," he says, lips parting as his eyebrows shoot up. "Jules, you look stunning. Wow."

My heart rises. Through my chest, throat. Mouth.

It's outside my body.

It doesn't belong to me anymore.

Grey holds it in his hands as he kisses me. As he takes my hand and walks me into the barn, Ford waving us off with a smile. As the two of us marvel at how gorgeous the space is. Modern and romantic and full of character.

The cabinets and countertops look amazing. So does the hardware I selected. Rustic with a modern, sophisticated edge. Layout is spacious without feeling empty. The beams we installed in the ceiling are statement pieces, especially with simple wrought iron chandeliers, decked out with greenery and flowers. A bar is being set up on the massive countertop at the back of the barn. The reclaimed floorboards are just the right amount of roughed up, a perfect counterpoint to the strings of fairy lights and swoops of gauze that hang overhead.

New windows let in the pretty autumn light, bathing everything in shades of amber and gold. People mill around the space, admiring the details, the flowers. The cute programs, bound in green ribbon, that dot the long benches at the front of the barn.

I'm smiling so hard my face aches.

I look at Grey. He looks back.

"Your work is magic, you know," he says. "This place is fucking unbelievable."

Nudging him with my elbow, I reply, "You're the one who gave Luke's business a fighting chance. This is your work, too. Although mine is *clearly* more beautiful. Especially when it's been *zhuzh-ed* up by a team of wedding planners and florists."

He grins. Blue eyes lighting up. "I'm proud of you, Jules."

"I'm proud of us."

"You think Charlie Brown is, too?"

I curl my hands around his neck and pull him in for a kiss. His hands go to my waist, his thumbs working small, soft arcs across the just-barely-there swell of my abdomen.

"I think Charlie Brown is a lucky kid to have parents like us. She's going to be just fine."

The ceremony is beautiful. Grey's hand wrapped around mine, I beam the entire time. I've always loved weddings. But witnessing one of my best friends marry the man who helped make her dreams come true fills me to the brim with joy. She looks gorgeous in her dress and heels. Eli looks handsome as hell in his tuxedo as he pledges "to provide all the inspiration you'll ever need for your books—the sex scenes and all the other scenes, too."

Sitting next to Grey, the broad expanse of his thigh pressed against mine, doesn't hurt.

I notice he keeps his jacket buttoned so that his crotch is covered.

"What's that about?" I whisper, nodding at it.

His eyes slide to meet mine. He's blushing a little bit. "You'll see. Or hopefully you won't. But it's kind of—well. Never mind."

It's over too quickly, and all of a sudden we're standing and clapping and hollering as Eli and Olivia make their way back down the aisle, this time as man and wife. Passing by, she catches my gaze.

She looks so happy, eyes glistening, that for a second I can't breathe.

We head to the counter at the back of the barn for cocktail hour. Grey grabs me a mock gin and tonic—ice, soda water, lime—while he gets himself the real deal.

"How freaking happy were Eli and Olivia up there?" he says, handing me my mocktail. "I think their smiles had their own force fields."

I look at him. Grin. "So does yours."

"Everyone keeps telling me I'm smiling. I have to figure out how to stop, damn it. It's not good for my reputation. It's just...what we have feels real. I like it."

"Real and right."

He's smiling that smile now. The kind with a force field.

"Real and right. I love that idea." His eyes search mine. "I love you, Julia. I am so crazy in love with you it terrifies me. But you and David Bowie showed me that can be a good thing."

My heart is pounding.

Fluttering.

Sighing.

All those things. Grey is making me feel all the things I always hoped I would about a guy. The excitement and the lust and the respect.

The way heroines in all the romance I've read feel about their heroes.

"I'm crazy in love with you, too," I say.

And then he leans down and kisses the shit out of me. Tongue and everything. Right there in front of the bar for all of Olivia's hundred and twenty guests to see.

"Y'all best watch yourselves," I hear Ford say. "I don't mind y'alls' PDA. In fact, I'm a big proponent of public displays of affection. But with Grey's pants situation...there's not a lot of room in there for, you know...growth."

I break the kiss, laughing, and turn to see Ford smirking at us as he lifts his drink to his mouth.

"Pants situation?" I glance at Grey.

He does this little shimmy thing, clearing his throat. Clasping his hands in front of his groin again.

"Nuh-uh," I say. "Show me."

"You said you liked it when I wear tighter stuff," he begins.

"Better tailored. Yeah. Why?"

"Well." He lets out an uncomfortable grunt. Glancing around, he quickly unbuttons his jacket and holds it away from his crotch. "Think we went with a look that's a little *too* tailored."

I pull back with a gasp, eyes going wide. I can see the outline of Grey's dick through the fine fabric of his pants. The head, the ridge that separates it from the shaft. The shaft itself.

A pulse of heat moves between my legs.

"Too tailored to the wrong body part, anyway," Ford says.

Luke happens to appear at that moment. He claps Grey on the shoulder.

"Way to steal the spotlight," he says, grinning. "All anyone can talk about is what a handsome couple the bride and groom make and that guy wearing the pants that show his dick."

"Oh my God," I breathe, looking at Grey. "You're Tuxedo Dick Pants."

Ford lets out a bark of laughter. "TDP. Classic."

I hold up my hand to Grey. "Way to go, baby. You're already the toast of this party and it's barely even started."

Laughing, Grey gives me a high five, curling his fingers around mine.

"I was thinking about you when I had these pants made," he says. "I wasn't thinking about—"

"Showing your dick to Olivia's grandma?" Ford says, raising his brows.

"No, you jerk off, I wasn't thinking about that," Grey shoots back. He turns to me. "I'm sorry."

"Don't be," I say, grinning. "I just can't wait to see you dance in those TDPs."

"But Grey doesn't dance," Ford says, teasing.

I look at Greyson. "We'll see about that."

Chapter Twenty-Eight

GREYSON

Despite my unfortunate pants situation, I manage to enjoy myself through cocktail hour and dinner, too.

Julia doesn't exactly make things easy in her tight little black dress and sexy high heels. Her bump really popped over the past week, and she's enjoying showing it off.

Another thing that dress shows off? Her tits. And ass. And legs.

Everything, basically. When catching sight of just *one* of those things is enough to make me hard.

The combination is gloriously infuriating.

Julia in a nutshell.

Goddamn I love this girl.

I keep things under control by focusing on the food. The conversation Julia and I have with our table mates. The fact that people love the barn and seem to appreciate the work and money we put into the property.

But when the band starts to play—first song is Al Green's "All Night Long," fuck me for life—I know I'm in trouble.

Julia is on her feet before the first verse is over.

"Wanna dance?" she asks, running a hand through her hair. The movement is slow and sensuous, and it makes me think about how slow she moves when she's on top. Riding my cock like she's got all day. Hands on my chest, head thrown back, tits bouncing. Back arched.

Pussy spread open. Soft and slick.

Jesus Christ.

I grab my water. How long until we go back to the hotel? An hour? A year?

Why the fuck did I think these pants were a good idea?

"I'll be there in a minute," I say. "Just gonna—"

Find that exorcist we keep talking about.

Gargle some gin.

You know, anything to keep my dick from literally tearing a hole in my pants until I can get this woman naked.

Julia smiles. "Okay. I'll go find Gracie. But don't think I'm going to let you off easy. You *will* get out on that dance floor tonight."

Ford tips his glass in my direction. "You heard her, TDP."

"I will," I say.

If I don't take a swim in the marsh nearby to cool the fuck off first.

I head to the bar for that gin. Order a double and turn around, leaning against the counter. Watch the dance floor fill up.

Doesn't take long. The band is excellent, and people are just happy enough—just drunk enough—to let loose. Eli twirls Olivia to Queen's "You're My Best Friend." During the next song, Gracie, Olivia, and a few older women—Olivia's mom, maybe, and her friends—groove together, laughing.

Julia is with them. She's kicked off her heels and is wiggling her ass, her sweet little belly along for the ride as she shimmies her hips in time to the beat.

She is so damn adorable. And sexy. And fun.

Makes me want to be fun, too. Makes me want to have a good time. It's just been so long—

Then again, who cares? Why not celebrate? Life is *good* right now.

Things are good. And I'm just tipsy enough to really pull a Patrick Swayze. Or Chris Farley, depending on how it goes.

Julia is singing now, head thrown back as she belts out the lyrics to "Mustang Sally." Shaking that thing like she doesn't have a care in the world.

Her energy—zero fucks given—is contagious.

"Dude," Luke says, sidling up to the bar. "You all right?"

I take a sip of gin, my eyes not leaving Julia. She's doing the twist now with somebody's grandma. I can't help it. I smile.

"I'm fine. Why?"

Luke looks at me for a beat. Then he grins, tapping the neck of his beer bottle against my glass.

"Cheers, Greyson. Congrats. On the baby." He motions to Julia. "And on her. Y'all look real happy together."

"Thanks," I say. "I appreciate that."

"Can't say I'm surprised y'all ended up together. I knew it the second y'all met—you two had some special kinda connection."

I pull back. "But we didn't get along. Like, at all."

Luke wags his eyebrows. "Exactly. Look, even your sperm knew y'all were meant to be. I knew I'd either end up callin' the cops on you or callin' it love. Either way, y'all two couldn't take your eyes off each other. That first day I had half a mind to just slip on out of there to give y'all some privacy."

If only he knew Julia and I found all the privacy we needed in the back seat of my truck.

"Be good to her, you hear?" Luke says.

"That's all I care about," I say. "Her and that baby. Taking care of them. Making them happy."

Luke nods, looking at the dance floor. Looking at Gracie.

"I know how that goes," he says.

I catch Julia's eyes. She smiles. Motions for me to come join her.

Luke sets his beer down on the bar.

"Let's get to it," he says.

I follow him to the dance floor, grateful I don't have to weather the approach alone. Immediately Gracie loops her arms around his neck and pulls him down for a messy, wet kiss. The two of them disappear into the crowd, his hands sliding to her ass as they swing their hips to the beat.

Damn him, he makes it look so easy.

"Stop thinking," Julia says, curling an arm around my waist. Pressing her body to mine. Oh, Lord. "You're at a wedding where the average age is fifty-seven. Trust me, you're going to look good out here no matter what."

For one heartbeat, then another, I kind of just...stand there. Swaying slightly from one foot to the other. The gin loosened me up a bit, but I still feel awkward and stupid.

I'm also worried about scaring people with my TDP.

But then Julia is slipping her hands underneath my jacket. She's pulling me even closer, grinding her hips against me.

My dick screams.

I start.

"Jules—"

"It's all right." She bites her lip. "No one will see but me."

And then she grinds against me again. And again.

My body starts to move. Pure instinct and need. I'm hard but I don't care. I just keep up with Julia. My hands on her waist, her sides. Her ass when no one is looking.

We dance to Donna Summer and The Village People. She laughs when I spin her, and I laugh when she spins me and I completely fuck the whole thing up, nearly taking us both down when I bend my back too much.

I stop thinking about what people will think.

I stop thinking about my pants. Even though they're getting really fucking tight.

I stop thinking about my past. About work.

I just dance. Like an idiot. I let go and throw my hands up when the band plays "Shout." Julia falls on her butt when she tries to go low, and the two of us are laughing so hard we're crying as I pick her up off the ground.

I'm sweating. Smiling. Moving.

Julia is right there with me, bumping into me with welcome regularity. She's got her fingers in my hair. She's turning around and rolling her ass into my crotch.

I pull her to me, her back to my front, and trail my lips over her neck.

She turns her head to look at me. Grins. Eyes alive with mischief. Arousal.

I wonder how wet she is.

"I'm happy," she says.

"Me too," I say.

We continue our dance floor dry humping until the very last song.

Back at the hotel, Julia comes out of the bathroom wearing a bathrobe tied at the waist.

I'm waiting for her just outside the door. She startles, eyes going wide.

"Are you okay?" she asks.

In reply I pick her up and turn around, setting her on top of the tall boy dresser on the opposite wall.

"I need you," I say, using my hand to part her knees. Her robe falls open a little, revealing her red satin thong. "How bad do you need me?"

She bites her lip. "You mean how much did your Patrick Swayze dancing turn me on? Why don't you find out for yourself?"

Keeping my eyes trained on hers, I use my first two fingers to glide her thong to the side. Revealing the slick folds of her pussy.

I press my thumb to her center. Groan when I find her hot and swollen and *fuck* so soft.

She's this hot for me.

She's this hot despite the fact that I looked like an idiot on the dance floor.

Or maybe because of it.

Julia's mouth falls open. She looks at me through heavy lids, breath starting to come in pants.

I play with her for a minute, drawing my thumb lightly up her cunt. Across it. Staring at her in wonder. Her legs fall open a little wider.

I step between them and, gliding my hand from her pussy up to her waist, reach for the knot there and give it a tug. Her robe falls open. I guide the robe over her shoulders, baring her tits.

She shivers. I groan.

Her breasts are fucking perfect. They've gotten heavier. Fuller. Her nipples have darkened, gorgeous, raspberry-colored circles.

I lean down and trail my mouth over her belly. Up to one nipple. I give it a gentle suck, holding her bare waist in my hands, and Julia arches against me, fingers slicing into my hair.

"You looked so beautiful tonight," I say, carefully giving the underside of her tit a small bite. "I've wanted to fuck you since you stepped off that bus. And when you started dancing—sweetheart, I was done."

When I hook my fingers around the straps of her panties and pull them over her legs, she falls back against the wall. Face flushed, tits firm and high, cunt bared to me.

I want her bared to me. All of her. The way I've bared myself to her.

"I'm glad you decided to dance, Grey," she says. "Really, really glad. You know, you're not half bad."

I grin. "Hey. I was better than that, wasn't I?"

"Show me," she says, a wicked little smirk on her lips. "Show me how good you are, baby."

I cup her breast in my hand. Draw my thumb over the hardened point at the same moment I press two of my fingers down over her clit, then back up again.

Julia's head falls back.

I toy with her nipples. Toy with her pussy, circling my fingertips through her folds, taking my time while she eggs me on by bucking her hips.

All the while I watch her. Eyes on her face. Taking in every sigh, every small smile, every time her breath catches.

My dick presses painfully against the front of my pants. At this point, I could care less if they tear open. Seems fitting for the evening we're having.

I lean in and kiss her chest, her throat, moving both my hands to her pussy. Holding her lips open with my thumbs, I duck down and give her a quick, firm lick, back to front.

"Grey," she moans. "I'm close. Please."

Smiling, I sink two fingers of one hand inside her. I circle my thumb over her clit.

And then, straightening, I tickle her asshole with my pinkie finger.

Like clockwork, she *comes*.

With a shout. Her legs clamp around my torso and she bolts upright, arms wrapped around my head as her cunt pulses around my fingers.

I wait for her orgasm to subside and her breathing to slow.

Then I make quick work of my pants and boxers. I lift her off the dresser and press her up against the wall. She slides down my torso, the heat of her bare pussy meeting with the head of my cock as I wrap her legs around my waist.

"I love having you like this," I say softly, pressing my thumb to her clit. "Bare."

After my screen came back negative, we stopped using condoms.

The feel of her raw—it's heaven.

She runs a hand through my hair, smoothing it back from my face.

Without a word, she reaches down and positions me at her entrance. Rocking her hips, she welcomes me inside her. Just my head.

Just enough to make me see stars. The sensation of feeling her raw —hot, sweet, soft—

The knowledge that she trusts me, that she's letting me in—

I growl, burying my head in the crook of her shoulder. I move my hands to her ass cheeks and guide her farther down onto my shaft. I can just feel the final echoes of her orgasm in small, sweet flutters.

Fucking hell.

I gotta *have* her. This woman who trusts me and knows me and keeps me, despite everything.

Rocking back my hips, I surge forward, impaling her in one strong, measured motion. Her tits bounce; her mouth is open again, and I cover it with mine. Biting her, claiming her as I rock back, thrust forward, again and again and again. Each time harder and faster. Gliding through her slick heat with ease. Mindless with lust and love and my God look how far we've come.

Look how good this has gotten.

The dresser beside us rocks against the wall in time to my movements. Neighbors can definitely hear us fucking like animals but I don't care.

She sucks on my lower lip. Tears at my back with her fingernails, even as she spreads her legs wider, asking for more, wanting me to go deeper.

I come. Hard. Going still as I empty myself inside her.

Always.

This is always how I want it to be between us.

Open and raw and real.

Vulnerable.

This is what I've been after. This is what I've been looking for my whole life without even knowing it.

The truth. The trust. The connection.

Seeing and being seen. It's a risk.

But now I understand it's one worth taking.

Julia

I wake up early the next morning. Beside me, Grey is still sleeping. I peek underneath the covers and smile when I see his bare ass, pale and thickly muscled.

A pulse of desire flares between my legs.

Will I ever get over how sexy this man is?

I contemplate waking Grey up, but then I decide against it. The man danced that cute ass off last night. He needs his rest.

So I head to the bathroom, then grab my book and settle back into bed. Nothing like some quiet Sunday morning reading time.

I'm barely through a paragraph before I feel something, a flutter, low in my abdomen.

At first I think it's just gas. It feels like little bubbles. A ripple of air moving through my stomach.

But then I feel it again. Stronger this time. Feels more like a distinct roll. Not the kind of stomach roll you get on a rollercoaster. But more of a sense of pressure, slight but insistent.

I feel it *again*.

My heart skips a beat. I put my hand over my stomach. I can't feel anything from the outside, but I can feel another roll from within.

It's Charlie Brown. Has to be. I'm feeling him or her move for the first time.

My heart starts to pound, and I smile. Hard.

Holy shit, there is a *live baby* inside me. And she's doing backflips first thing in the morning.

The fact that I'm having a baby becomes suddenly—terrifyingly—real.

My smile fades as panic rises inside my chest, making my heart pound harder. Grey and I are going to be responsible for another human life. There's no going back.

In a few months, life as we know it is going to be forever altered. Sexy nights spent in hotels? Quiet weekend mornings in bed together?

Yeah, we can kiss those goodbye.

The baby does another backflip. I try my best to breathe deeply, the way Katie taught us in yoga class.

"Hey." I almost start when I feel a hand move down my leg. "Hey, Jules, you all right?"

Blinking, I turn to see Grey looking up at me from his pillow, brow furrowed.

I take his hand and move it to my belly.

"Baby's moving."

His eyes go wide. He bolts upright, the covers falling from the broad expanse of his chest.

"You can't feel it from the outside," I say, even though I keep his hand on my stomach. "But she's definitely moving around in there."

"Does it hurt? The way you were breathing—"

"Nah. Feels like bubbles. I'm just having a teeny tiny panic attack over the fact that we're having a baby, and that she's coming so soon."

Grey nods his head, pressing his hand a bit more firmly against me. "That's fair. It's terrifying, isn't it? The permanence of it. The idea that we're going to be responsible for keeping her alive."

"Yes. Exactly."

"But." Grey leans in and grazes his lips across my bare shoulder. "It's also really, really exciting. What is her laugh going to sound like? Will she have hair, or will she be a sweet little bald peanut? Most importantly, is she going to be smart and beautiful like her mother—"

"Or growly and demanding like her father?"

He grins. "Let's hope she takes after you."

I manage a tight smile. "You don't get the excitement without the terror, I guess."

"Parenthood in a nutshell?"

My smile grows. Of course he'd get me back to smiling.

"Whatever the case, I'm grateful I get to do it with you," I reply.

Grey nods, his mouth moving to my chest.

"Show me how grateful, exactly."

Chapter Twenty-Nine

JULIA

After slogging through my first trimester, I feel like I'm riding a high in my second.

Not only am I back to feeling like myself, both mentally and physically, I've also made some new mom-to-be friends through the yoga classes I've been taking. Hallie, Fiona and I meet once a week for coffee. We commiserate—swollen ankles, shitty sleep—and chat about babies and breast feeding and normal, non-pregnancy related stuff, too. Stressful jobs and sick parents and not-so-secret dreams that don't disappear when you become a mother.

Neither does your desire to connect with the world. Other people. New ideas. I always leave our coffee dates feeling energized and at ease. Like everything is going to be okay.

I'm back to feeling like myself at work, too. I begin the spring semester on a high note, with the English department head approving a "Romance Summit" Olivia and I are planning for spring of next year. We're inviting authors, agents, publishers, and other academics to campus for a weekend of all things romance related. It's part of our ongoing effort to get the genre the recognition it deserves.

I'm also in love. Head over heels in love with Grey. I spent the holidays with his family, which was wonderful. He's been pretty great himself. A little distracted, yes. But he makes a real effort to ensure that I'm comfortable and looked after. He's thoughtful. He makes me come at least once a day.

He's trying to find a balance between life and work.

And I am content with that. The *trying*. It's enough.

Until it isn't.

Olivia, Gracie and I arrive at Hello Baby right on time on a sunny Saturday morning. We wait for Grey to show. And wait some more.

"You sure you gave him the right date?" Olivia asks, glancing at my phone.

I've sent Grey three texts and called him twice. No answer.

"I'm sure. I reminded him this morning," I say. I run through our conversations in my head, just to be certain. "He's late sometimes, but never this late. I'm really sorry."

My annoyance, simmering up until now, flares to full blown anger. Why am I the one apologizing for Grey's fuck up? It's not my fault he forgot. Or was too busy at work to make it.

Makes me wonder if he ever did that research or read any books yet. He's on his laptop in bed pretty much every night. I'd hoped—maybe stupidly—he was doing the research and reading then.

I'm twenty-one weeks. While we still have time, we definitely need to start thinking about things like what car seat we'll bring Charlie Brown home in, and where she'll sleep as a newborn and beyond. I don't want to be unprepared or feel rushed. I imagine having a new baby will be stressful enough. Adding disorganization to the mix feels like a recipe for disaster.

I've done my research. I've consulted half a dozen books on the stuff we'll need, and I've copied a bunch of ideas from my fellow mamas-to-be's registries. Case in point: I carry a literal folder of information with me into the store.

Gracie glances at her watch. "Well. Why don't we get started? Greyson can give us his thoughts when he gets here."

"Sounds good," I say, and grab her hand. "Thanks, y'all. For being here. Clearly I'd be doing this alone without you."

Olivia gives me a sympathetic smile and runs a hand across my back.

"He'll show, Julia. It was probably just a mix up. And if it wasn't, I will personally go kick his ass."

"I'll go too," Gracie says. "Luke taught me how to properly swing a baseball bat. I keep one in my trunk, just in case."

But Grey doesn't show. The girls and I spend hours in the store. Scanner guns in hand, the three of us debating the merits of various bottle nipples and whether or not I'll need a wipe warmer.

It's not super fun picking everything out. Studying the various safety features of car seats is only so exciting. But it is fun being with my girlfriends for the morning. I always love their company. And it *is* exciting to think about using all this stuff when Charlie Brown arrives. Now that I can feel him or her moving, the whole thing is starting to feel thrillingly—terrifyingly—real.

Still. There's a lump lodged in my throat the entire time as my anger and disappointment and frustration grow.

I feel like I've asked very, very little of Grey up to this point when it comes to the baby. Yes, he's cooked. Yes, he's been to a couple doctor appointments, and he's taken me to Jeni's when I'm craving Chardonnay but settle for ice cream instead.

But he hasn't dedicated real time to really un-fun baby things like I have. The bottle nipples and car seats are case in point. I'd much rather read romance than books on breastfeeding, or spend the afternoon recruiting panel members and keynote speakers for next year's summit.

Grey promised to be an equal partner in this. But the baby is barely the size of a spaghetti squash, and already I feel like I'm the one doing the heavy lifting.

It's not fair. And it hurts my feelings that he'd put me in this position. That he'd let me do more, full well knowing how important it is to me that we share the work as equally as we're able.

Grey calls just as we're walking out of Hello Baby.

"Jules," he says before I can say hello.

"Hey," I manage.

"Oh my God, I am so fucking sorry, sweetheart. Shit really hit the fan over at The Champagne Bar this morning. A server stole three cases of Cristal and six of Veuve Cliquot—some of the most expensive stuff we have on the menu. Over ten grand, just gone. The cops came and we filed a report. I was on the phone for a fucking hour with our insurance agent trying to figure out what to do. It was a total clusterfuck. I couldn't get away, and I'm sorry. Really, really sorry. But I—"

"Had to work," I reply tightly. "Right."

"Sweetheart."

"Look, I really am sorry that happened at the bar. That sucks, and I hate that you had to deal with it. But we've had registry shopping on the calendar for months. Olivia and Gracie are here. This is important, Grey. Couldn't, I don't know, Ford or that sommelier who owns the bar have handled the situation over there? Why do you always have to be the one on the ground?"

"Because." He lets out a breath. "This is my company, Julia. I have a lot of people depending on me to get these things right."

I swallow. Let a beat of uncomfortable silence bloom between us.

"Grey, I'm disappointed. And embarrassed. And angry."

"I know, I know, and that's completely fair. I deserve all that and then some. I'm sorry, Julia. Let me make it up to you. Please. I swear I'll make this right."

I swallow. "Just like you swore to show up today?"

He lets out a breath. "I deserve that. I mean it this time. Please. Give me another chance. I've been sitting on something exciting for a bit—been waiting for the right time to share it."

"Share what?"

"You'll see. Can I pick you up in a bit? Your place?"

My turn to let out a breath. I cross one arm over my chest. Glance at Olivia and Gracie. They're pretending not to listen to my call.

I think about that baseball bat in Gracie's trunk.

I think about Greyson dancing at Olivia's wedding.

"Please, Julia," Grey is saying. "I feel like a fucking idiot. I messed up. I know that. But I want to show you that I am doing my homework—I am doing stuff to get ready for Charlie Brown's arrival."

"All right," I say. "I should be home in an hour or so."

"I'll be there."

Greyson is waiting for me in the driveway when I get back into town. When I climb into his truck, I notice he kind of looks like hell.

His hair, usually neatly combed, is a mess. There are purple thumbprints underneath his eyes.

My anger softens. He's wiped. We both are.

"Sweetheart." He glances at me. "I really am sorry. If there was any other way...you know I would've been there with you. Did y'all pick out some good stuff?"

I reach back for my seatbelt and look down to buckle it. "We did."

"You all right?" he asks, putting a hand on my leg.

I look back up. "I understand you got stuck dealing with an emergency this morning. But I'm struggling with you, Grey. I feel like I'm doing the lion's share of the work for this baby."

"I've been doing work, too." He takes my hand and runs his thumb across my knuckles. "Can I show you how?"

I give his hand a squeeze. "I'd like that."

He tangles his fingers with mine as we make a right onto East Bay Street. We pass the famous Rainbow Row on the right, its colors vibrant against the grey February afternoon.

We continue on as East Bay Street turns into East Battery. Charleston Harbor stretches out to our left, the murky green water smooth as glass.

We don't go far. Grey slows, pulling into a gravel driveway immediately off South Battery. There's a For Sale sign on the wrought iron fence that encloses the property.

My heart begins to pound.

The drive winds under a canopy of palm trees. A gorgeous—and very large—house comes into view. It's red brick with black shutters. Two stories, very classic Georgian design. It's shiny and perfect. Too perfect. It's brand new, as evidenced by the full dumpster by the garage and the barren landscaping. The yard is big but bare.

Grey puts the truck into park in front of the house. There's a woman in a long skirt and sweater at the glossy front door. She smiles and waves.

I feel queasy all of a sudden.

"Grey," I say, staring at the house. "What's going on?"

He cuts the engine. Untangles our fingers and unbuckles his seat belt.

He's grinning.

"You'll see."

I follow him to the door, where he introduces me to his real estate agent, Vanessa.

I swear my heart is going to beat its way through my chest.

A creeping realization comes over me.

Grey wants to buy this house. For us.

Our family.

I don't say a word as Vanessa takes us on a tour of many thousands of square feet. The place smells new, like paint. More bedrooms and bathrooms than I can count, everything white and clean and trendy. The kitchen is enormous, with two islands and a scullery.

It's beautiful, don't get me wrong. But it has no character. No story to tell.

I love properties that are a little rough around the edges, like Luke's barn. Properties that I'm able to transform with my own touch, my own style.

When I flip through a sales brochure I find on the kitchen counter and see the asking price, my eyes almost pop out of my head.

It hits me.

This.

This is Grey's way of being an equal partner. By spending obscene amounts of money on things I didn't ask for. Things we certainly don't need.

"So," Vanessa says brightly. "What do y'all think?"

I look up to see Grey's eyes glued to my face. They've got a hopeful gleam in them.

"Do you like it?" he asks. "I thought you'd appreciate the amazing architectural details. I know it's new, but everything is top of the line, and the house is built with Charleston's history and architecture in mind. The exterior, the wood doors, the brass hardware. The molding. I've been searching high and low for just the right house. A family place. You know, with a yard and stuff. Neither of our places have anywhere for the baby to play."

"Grey," I say. Heart breaking a little.

He's trying to be sweet. Thoughtful.

But this is wrong.

This isn't me. This house—this big, insanely perfect house—is not *us*. This is not the life I wanted or asked for.

It's a poor substitute for what this baby and I really need—for Greyson to be around. Be present.

He's Christian Grey-ing me again. Only not in a good way this time.

"Do you mind giving us a minute?" I ask Vanessa.

She smiles. "Sure. Y'all take your time."

She heads out of the kitchen, leaving Grey and I alone.

"You don't like it," he says matter-of-factly.

I take a breath. Look away. Look back at him. Look down at the brochure.

"Don't get me wrong, this is a dream house," I say. "It's—Jesus, Grey, it's like something out of a magazine. Everything is new. The location is A-plus. It's a huge lot for this part of town."

He smiles. A tight thing.

"But."

"For starters, it's a whole comma out of my price range."

"I'd take care of it."

My pulse skips a beat.

"You don't have to do that. In fact, I don't want you to. I want to contribute at least something to a huge purchase like this."

"What if I want to buy this house for you?"

"I appreciate the sentiment. And I see what you're trying to do here. But when you said you wanted only the best for me and the baby—Grey, you don't have to buy a house like this to prove that. You can just stick to ice cream and I'd be perfectly content." I put a hand on my belly. "Same with Charlie Brown. I mean, I've been contemplating where she'd sleep. Like whether or not we'd need two cribs, one at my place and one at yours. Now you just want to up and buy a house without ever asking me if I want to move in with you?"

Slipping his hands into the pockets of his slacks, he takes a step toward me. "Do you not want to live with me?"

I blink. "I mean, I'd definitely consider it. Yeah. But we've never really talked about it before."

"What if I want to treat y'all? I have money, Julia. I work hard to be able to afford stuff like this. Let me treat you. Buying this house—having you move in with me—it's my way of contributing. My way of making you feel safe and taken care of."

I take a sharp breath. My eyes prick with tears. Shit.

Shit shit shit.

"I love how safe you make me feel," I say. "But you can take care of me by showing up. You'd make me feel taken care of if you helped me with the registry. If you did the research and read those books you promised you would. I needed you this morning, Greyson. I'm going to need you to be around when this baby comes. More than I'll ever need a house like this."

His brows curve upward.

"Please don't cry," he says, taking his hands out of his pockets. "I just—this is all I know, baby. This is what I do. I provide. I'm really good at it."

"You are. I see how you look after Ford. I see that you want to take care of Bryce. But I think you and I have different opinions about what being an equal partner means. This"—I motion to the house—"isn't what I meant when I said I wanted you to contribute. I've told you many times that I'm perfectly capable of providing for myself. This baby, too. Of course your financial contribution is an important piece of the co-parenting puzzle. But so is *showing up*. And you're not doing that enough, Grey."

"I disagree," he says. "How is this not showing up? I've spent a lot of time trying to find this place. Real estate in this town is a tricky endeavor—it's tough finding just the right spot. I'm putting in the time, Julia. Just in my own way."

My frustration gathers in a lump in my throat. "You're not listening."

"And neither are you!" he says, throwing up his arms. "I have a plan here. It's not like I'm flying by the seat of my pants. I'm intentional in all that I do, especially when it comes to you and the baby. I think about y'all all the time. This house is exhibit A. The yard, the space. The location. We'd be close to family and friends—the people who are going to help us out the most when Charlie Brown comes. Why can't you see that?"

"Why can't you see that there's got to be a balance? This house..."

He looks at me. "What? What about this house I spent months searching for?"

Swallowing, I say, "I appreciate the effort, Grey. But it's not my dream house. Not by a long shot. If you were listening, you'd know that. It's too new. Too perfect. And way too big. I imagine you'd have to keep working like you do now to afford it. Working all the time, I mean. Yeah, we'd have this big fabulous family home, but we'd never see you. You wouldn't be around to help, which would mean most of the work of raising this kid would fall on my lap. It's already happening, and it's not fair. I work too. I want to keep working—I love my job. But if you don't start showing up, my life is going to turn into a living hell once this baby comes. I'll be stuck trying to do it all. All by myself. All the time. I want you around more, Grey. I need you. I love you, and I love spending time with you. But you made me a promise, and if you can't keep it..."

Greyson takes another step forward.

"What am I supposed to do, Julia? You know full well I don't work a typical nine to five job. To be honest, I don't think you'd be into me if I did."

"Ouch." I pull back, stung. "What does that mean?"

"It means you're not interested in normal. You're bored by the usual. You're passionate and fiery and different, and you're drawn to other people who are the same. My passion is my work. Does it take up a lot of my time? Yes. But I love my job, too. I worked really fucking hard to get where I am. I can't just walk away. Not after I've come so far."

"You've come so far," I reply steadily. "How much further do you need to go? What are you trying to prove, Grey? What are you really trying to buy here?"

He pulls back, pink creeping up his neck onto his face. "What do I want to buy? I want to buy you a house that has a yard with enough room for a swing set. A house that our family can grow into. That's what. Total dick move, I know."

I shake my head, my anger growing. "That's not what I mean, and you know it. You have my love. I love you. I trust you. I'm offended you'd ever think I could be bought like this."

His eyes search mine. Anger's in them now too, along with the hurt.

I've hit a nerve.

"I'm not trying to buy you," he says, nostrils flaring as he ducks to get in my face. "I'm trying to do something nice. If you don't like the damn house, then fuck it. We don't have to buy it. We can just tell our kid to go play in the street in front of your garage apartment or something. I'm sure that's safe."

I'm breathing hard. Blinking back tears.

"Don't be stupid," I bite out. "Yes, we need a place that's better suited to kids. But we don't need a place that's *this* big or *this* new or *this* expensive. We need one that we can afford without you working eighty hour weeks."

"Jesus Christ, Julia, what do you want me to do?"

"Our lives are about to change, Grey. Our priorities should, too. Work is important. But it's not everything. It can't be." I blink. Hard. "Please. Meet me halfway here."

He scoffs. "Is buying our family a house not meeting you halfway? Is that not showing you I'm committed to you and this baby?"

"It's showing me your priorities are fucked up. You don't contribute by throwing money at us. You do it by participating in our lives in a meaningful, consistent way. You show up to doctor appointments on time. You spend Saturdays in bed with me instead of in meetings. You don't blow off important dates. You say you've searched for a house for months. But have you even looked at your paternity leave yet? Are you planning on taking any? You keep saying we'll figure things out, but I think that's just your way of blowing me off. I've spent *hours* in meetings with HR and my bosses and mentors trying to figure out how to make my maternity leave work without damaging my career. Days coordinating appointments and ultrasounds and reading books. Days researching registries and working on budgets for when I go on leave. And what have you done? Honestly, Grey, tell me what heavy lifting *you've* done for this baby."

He lets out a growl and spears a hand through his hair. Looks away.

"I work. A lot. In a very stressful environment. You can't tell me that's not heavy lifting."

I just shake my head. "It is. Of course it is. I know you work hard. That's not the point I'm trying to make. I'm trying to say working like that isn't the *right* kind of lifting. Working like that is exactly what's keeping you from being the partner I need. You're stressed. Worn out. Buying this place is only going to make that worse. Do you see what I'm saying here, Grey? Do you understand where I'm coming from?"

He shoots me a look. It's murderous. Angry.

"The money I make won't just pay for a house like this. It can pay for childcare. College. Whatever this baby needs, I can give them."

"Except quality time. That, you can't spare."

Yeah. Think it's safe to say he doesn't see. He's too angry. Too entrenched in old ways of thinking, maybe.

All I know is I can't reach him. Which fills me with a crushing sense of loss.

"You don't want the house," he grunts. "I get it."

He turns and stalks out of the kitchen.

Chapter Thirty

GREYSON

The space between Julia and I rings with silence on the drive home.

I'm worried I'll say shit I'll regret if I open my mouth. I already did enough damage back at that house.

Somewhere in the back of my mind, I know she's right. But so am I. I worked really hard to find that house. Time spent on the phone with Vanessa, touring properties, thinking about what my family will need going forward.

I'm too wound up, maybe. It's not like I didn't want to go registry shopping with Julia. Hell, I would've loved to have spent the morning with her. Way more than I enjoyed dealing with cops and crises and all the other un-fun crap that comes with opening a new bar or restaurant, that's for damn sure.

But who else was supposed to deal with that stuff? What was I supposed to do? Tell my business partners—my investors—*hey, sorry, can't open the bar we've all poured tons of money into because someone stole our stock but I couldn't handle it because I had to run out to buy some baby bottles we won't need for another four months?*

I've been the point person on this project since the bar's inception. I had to be there. It would've been irresponsible to leave. Not to mention stupid.

"Drop me off at my place," Julia says. Eyes glued to the passenger side window.

I adjust my hand on the steering wheel.

Great. Now she's going to ice me out.

God*damn* it.

"You sure?"

"I'm sure."

A voice inside my head tells me to pull over and put the car in park and fix this. Apologize. Try to figure out what the fuck's going on with me together by walking through what just happened.

But I can't.

I know I'm fucking up. But because I'm apparently a pathological masochist, I can't stop.

Instead, my throat tightens with anger. Thoughts spinning out of control. Why do I always have to be the one that does all the talking? Why am I the one who has to do all the explaining?

I pull into her driveway.

"I'm sorry that turned into a fight," I manage.

She looks at me. Finally.

"That's what you're sorry for?"

"Julia. I'm trying—"

"That doesn't mean anything to me anymore." She shakes her head. "I'm done with your trying."

"Jules—"

"Listen. Remember when you told me you felt this pressure to be the perfect son? The perfect partner? I think you still feel that pressure, even though I've told you countless times you don't need to be perfect for me to love you. I just want you *here*. I just want *you*. Not your money. Not the prestige that comes with who you are and the name of your firm and all the fancy restaurants and bars you're involved with. I just want you to be around. Period. That's all I'm asking for, Grey."

I open my mouth to reply—*that's not true, I put the gun down*—but she's already shoving the door open and launching out of my car like it's on fire.

I hate that I'm upsetting her like this. I hate that she's hurting on my account.

What is *wrong* with me?

"Can I call you? Later?" I ask.

She turns. Meets my eyes.

"If you're ready," she says.

What the fuck does that mean, I want to shout.

What the fuck is happening?

Heading back out onto East Bay, I unbutton the neck of my shirt and reach inside for my nicotine patch. I rip it off my shoulder and ball it up in my palm.

I grab a pack of Marlboros from a nearby grocery store. Smoke one in the parking lot while I think about what I should do next. I don't want to be with anyone, but I also don't want to be alone.

Bryce is still awake at Ford's house. She can't see me like this. Maybe he can come over to my place. Have Mom or Dad watch Bryce.

I shoot him a text.

I think I really fucked up with Julia and I don't know what to do.

I head home and get into my stretchy pants. Head out onto the patio for another cigarette.

Ford appears on my front walkway below.

Looking up at me, he lifts a bottle of brown liquor.

"I come bearing gifts," he says, squinting against the early evening light. "C'mon, let me in."

I put out my cigarette and head downstairs.

"Who'd you get to watch Bryce?" I ask when we're in my kitchen.

Ford unwinds the plastic from around the whiskey's bottle cap. "Mom. I told her you and Julia were fighting and I had to do some triage before you chased Julia off for good. She was at my house in five minutes flat with instructions that I get the two of you back together or else."

I set two rocks glasses on the counter.

"Dude, why do you have to tell Mom everything?"

He lifts a shoulder and pours us each a few generous fingers. "Because I like being her favorite. So what happened?"

"I don't know." I bring my glass to my lips. Take a sip, the liquor snaking a line of fire down my middle. "I mean, I do know. But I don't. You know?"

Ford just looks at me. "Sounds bad. As bad as you look."

"Do you always have to be a dick?"

"I always have to be honest. If that makes me a dick, then, well." He shrugs, taking a sip of whiskey. "So be it. You look tired."

"I am tired."

"Tell me what happened with Julia."

He listens while I tell him what went down. The registry, the disaster of my morning, the house on South Battery.

"I'm trying to do the right thing. I want to be Julia's dream partner. She means the world to me. That baby in her belly means the world to me, Ford." Ah, fuck, my throat's tightening up again. I take a slug of whiskey. Doesn't help. "Just lately—I feel like I've been drowning trying to keep up with work and the baby and Julia. Don't get me wrong, I'm happy. Genuinely happy being with her. But I'm struggling to show up at work the way I need to while showing up for her the way *she* needs me to. That make sense? Everything just feels so real and so... urgent. I'm overwhelmed."

Ford ducks his head in a nod, swallowing his sip. "Makes perfect sense. I think I see what's going on here."

I let out a breath. "Thank God. Help me, Ford. Please."

"Work has always been important to you. But why do you think it became your life after your divorce?" he asks.

"Because," I say, searching for the right words. "For one thing, I didn't have a personal life anymore. I had no one to go home to. For another, Rebecca passed. I wanted to provide for you and the baby so *you* were able to take the time and space you needed to grieve. I wanted you to be there for your daughter. So I stepped up to the plate and covered for us both. I took over. Once I was in at the firm, I was *in*. Doesn't hurt that I like the work, and that I've gotten really fucking good at it. Being there kept me busy. Kept me distracted."

"Keep digging."

I shoot him an annoyed glance.

"Okay. I guess I also wanted to..." I swallow. "Give back to y'all.

You and Bryce and Mom and Dad. After the hell I put you through with my divorce."

"So you were trying to earn something by working like you did."

"I guess, yeah. Earn y'all's forgiveness. Show y'all I cared. Maybe punish myself a little, too. I felt such shame...I mean, in my mind, I didn't deserve another shot at a happy life. I broke Cameron's heart, and I broke Mom and Dad's, too. You know how much they adored her. I couldn't give them the daughter-in-law or grandchildren they always wanted. But I could crush it at work. I could give back that way. So that's what I did."

Ford's brows jump. "Aha. There it is."

"How much Dr. Phil have you watched since you started working part-time?"

"I'm telling you, Oprah's *Super Soul Sunday* podcast is life changing. I know you've opened up a lot since you've been with Julia. A lot lot. You're smiling. You're not smoking. Well. You weren't smoking until tonight. You're wearing inappropriately tight pants. Grey, those are mostly good things. I would say you've completely transformed. Only you haven't." He touches the heel of his glass to mine. His voice softens. "I think you're still hanging on to this last shred of that misbelief that you can't be loved just as you are. You still think you have to earn love. Work for it. Because you've fucked up so bad that's the only way you're going to get it."

I slurp the rest of my liquor. It does nothing to clear the blur in my eyes.

He's right.

Damn my brother, he knows what he's talking about.

"Forgive yourself for everything. All of it. Julia's already gotten you ninety percent of the way there. But you have to go that extra ten percent, or you're going to lose everything that's good in your life right now."

"Makes sense," I say.

"You think you have to buy Julia and the baby this enormous house —splash out tons of money—to be the kind of partner she's looking for. When really she just wants you to go shopping with her. Spend time with her. *Be there.* You're doing the right thing by anticipating her needs. But I think you're just mixing up what she needs with what you think you need to provide."

"But how do I do that?" I say, pouring myself more whiskey. "How can I spend time with her when I have so little of it to begin with? Money—I have a lot of that. But time?"

Ford turns to face me, resting his elbow on the counter. "I say this lovingly. But you do that by letting me step back up at Montgomery Partners, you big idiot. Just like I've been asking to do for the past six months. Why do you think I was ordering all those new suits from Brumley's? You let me take the reins so you can take a step back. It's your turn to focus on things outside of work. You know I'm capable. Bryce is older and more self-sufficient. I've got great childcare lined up, and Mom's already offered to help when I need to travel. It's done."

I blink. But that's too simple. Too easy.

It makes too much sense.

"But—"

"But nothing. You're forgiven, Grey. We've all forgiven you for what happened. The only person who hasn't forgiven you—not fully—is you. So forgive yourself. For real. Let me be a full-time employee again. And then go get your girl back. I don't know how she does it, but she puts up with you. She loves you for you. She sees you—the real you—and hasn't run. Yet. That's something worth fighting for."

I lift a hand to my face and wipe at my eyes with the back of my first knuckle.

"It can't be that simple."

"It is, though. No offense, the world—and Montgomery Partners—aren't going to collapse if you're not there to run the show."

I run through the scenario in my head. The one where I bring Ford back up to speed so that he's an equal partner in the business again. It won't be easy for me to let go of some things. But yeah—if Ford could help handle snafus like the one this morning, obviously that'd be huge.

Am I ready to let go? Am I ready to step back?

Yes and no.

But more than anything, I want to be with Julia. Have a family with her. Be the man she needs.

If that means stepping back at work, I'll do it.

I'll do anything for her.

I also have a nice chunk of change in savings. *Really* nice. Enough to get a healthy college fund started for the baby. Plenty for whatever else she'll need.

"Thank you," I manage. "I don't know what to say, Ford. But thank you. For listening. For being *you*."

"Hey. You were there when I needed you, Grey. You went above and beyond to help me put my life back together after I lost Rebecca. I'll always be there for you in any way that I can. Always."

"I love you, brother."

He grins. Claps me on the shoulder. "I love you too. Just promise me one thing."

"What's that?"

"You'll never wear those tuxedo pants again. If Mom ever saw—"

"Pants are gone," I say, laughing. "I promise."

"Good. I was worried there for a second I'd have to pretend not to know you at weddings from now on. Although I did love how you danced. Granted, it was definitely more Farley than Swayze—"

I give him a shove. "Not according to Julia. I have it on very good authority she thought my Swayze was sexy as fuck."

"Ew." Ford holds up his hands. "Please don't finish that thought."

"What? You don't want me to tell me you that she and I got complaints at the hotel for being too loud?"

"And it's time for me to head back home. I'll see you at the office first thing Monday morning?"

I look at him. "You sure you're ready?"

"I'm ready. I have been for a while. Put me back in, coach."

"If you stop with the terrible sports metaphors, I'll consider it," I say. Letting out a breath.

"All right," he says.

"All right."

Everything's going to be all right.

I hope.

I can only pray Julia will forgive me for the things I said and the way I acted.

I give Ford a hug. Tell him to give a kiss to the baby.

Then I head upstairs to do some serious reading. As much as I want to literally run to Julia's place and beg her forgiveness, my gut's telling me not to rush this. She needs time to cool down. Get some rest. And I need time to 1) download a bunch of baby books and read them (thank God for e-readers), and 2) figure out what I'm going to say to Julia.

Listening to that Oprah podcast might be a good place to start.

Chapter Thirty-One

JULIA

I have a lunch date with Eliza the next day.

Part of me wants to cancel. Has she heard about my fight with Grey? I don't want to put either of us in an awkward or uncomfortable position.

I *do* want to stay in my pajamas and wallow in self-pity all day.

But the more I stew, the angrier—sadder—I get. It'll be good for me to get out. And I genuinely enjoy spending time with Eliza. She's nothing if nonjudgmental. Maybe she'll have a nugget of wisdom or two to pass along.

Because I miss Grey. I want more than anything for us to make up. I feel horrible about how things went yesterday, and spent the night and the entire morning crying about it.

I hated going to bed alone.

I hated waking up alone even more. I love our Sunday morning routine of sex and coffee and breakfast at home.

Grey's gotten my body trained to crave him the second I'm awake. It's like clockwork. I open my eyes, smell him on my pillow, and *poof*.

I'm raring and ready to go.

I think about reaching out to him as I shower and get dressed.

I think about why he hasn't reached out to me. His silence is deafening.

Then again, part of me appreciates the fact that I've had some space and time to work through my feelings. To, yes, wallow a bit in my self-righteous anger.

But now I just *miss him*. Even though I have no idea how to work things out. That urge to provide, to give the best to the people he loves—I can tell it runs deep in Greyson.

I never set out to change him. Like I told Grey, I'm not in the business of fixing or saving men.

But something has to change for us to work.

Something's got to give if we're going to be together for the long haul.

I'm scared we won't be able to find common ground. What would that mean for Charlie Brown? What would our lives look like as co-parents? If we fucked up a relationship, are we going to fuck up parenting, too?

I meet Eliza at Craft Cafe. It's a super cute—and super tiny—spot in an old Charleston single just off bustling Market Street.

Stepping inside, I slide my sunglasses onto my head. Eliza is waiting by the door. Her face creases into a warm smile as she holds out her arms.

"Hey, honey! How are you feeling?"

"I'm all right," I say, my throat welling as she wraps me in a tight, familiar hug.

She pulls back. Hands still on my arms as she looks at me, brow furrowed.

"You sure? You sound a little upset."

Jesus, why does she have to be so wonderful?

Why does Greyson's entire family have to be so freaking wonderful?

"I'm...yeah. I'm not doing so great."

"Aw, sweetheart, come here." Eliza hugs me again, running a hand over my back. "I'm so sorry you're upset. You don't have to tell me anything. But just know I'm here to listen. Or just to sit with you. Whatever you need, Julia, I'm here."

"I'm sorry." I blink hard and turn to dig through my bag for a tissue. But Eliza's already holding one out to me. The simple gesture—how *familiar* it feels—makes me cry harder. "I'm sorry I'm such a mess."

"No need to apologize. Why don't we sit down and order some food? I always feel a bit better after I eat."

I wipe my nose on the tissue. "That sounds great. Thank you, Eliza."

We're seated at a two-top by a window. I don't get upset like this often. When I do, I usually can't eat much. But just because I'm bumming out doesn't mean Charlie Brown is. I've been ravenous for pretty much the entirety of my second trimester, and today is no exception.

I inhale my pimento cheese and fried green tomato BLT. It's delicious.

And Eliza is right. I do feel the tiniest bit better with a full stomach.

Leaning back in my chair, I put a hand on my belly. Look at Eliza, who's quietly working through her shrimp and kale salad.

"Oh!" she says suddenly. "I forgot to tell you."

She reaches behind her and pulls a dog-eared copy of *My Romp With the Rogue* out of her purse.

"I loved it!" she exclaims. "So much so that I read it twice, then suggested it to my book club. We'll be discussing Lord Callum and Lady Charlotte at our next meeting."

I manage a grin. "I'm so glad y'all enjoyed it. Olivia is absolutely killing it with that series. I'm determined to help her reach bestseller status."

"I'll do what I can to help. She's got a new fan in me, that's for sure. You know how I feel about men in kilts."

"I do, because I feel the same," I say with a laugh. "Speaking of—well, not men in kilts. But speaking of romance and plot points and black moments—"

Eliza grins. "The professor of romance is coming out to play. I adore it."

"Thank you. I really appreciate that. But I don't know if you heard

—I think Greyson and I are kind of having our own black moment right now."

She nods, picking up her napkin. "I did hear y'all got into an argument. I hate to see you two hurting like this, obviously, but again, if you don't want to talk about it, no problem. Just know if there's anything I can do...anything at all to help y'all work things out, I'm here. We really do adore you. I mean that, Julia. You've made my son very happy. I hope he's done the same for you."

I take a deep breath. Let it out.

"How did y'all do it?" I ask. "You and Monty. How did you make this family thing work? I admire the relationship you have with your husband. You really seem to have it figured out. *How*?"

Eliza smiles and takes a sip of her tea.

"For starters, we may put on a good show. But Monty and I don't have a damn thing figured out. Just last night we were running around like our hair was on fire when neither of us could get Bryce to go to bed. She screamed for an *hour*, Julia. An entire hour. No matter what we tried, it didn't work. And we are experienced parents who raised two kids of our own! A three year old made us feel like complete idiots. Relationships—and parenthood—are always a work in progress. You learn as you go. And I won't lie to you, it's not easy. Parenting requires constant renegotiation. Constant communication."

I wince. I've been open with Grey about my expectations and needs since the day I told him I was pregnant. But I definitely should've been much better about communicating what I meant, exactly, when I said I needed him to be a real co-parent. I should've talked to him more about it after that first conversation we had when I told him I was pregnant.

I just assumed he'd know that meant showing up and helping out with the big stuff and the small stuff. The fun things and the tedious things, too.

I assumed he'd get it right on the first try.

Both bad—not to mention unfair—assumptions.

He also clearly put a lot of time and thought into his house search, however misguided it might have been. Even though he did it in the wrong way, he *is* taking his co-parent duties seriously. He does have a plan for us. He is thinking about our future.

He's been doing the work. It's just the wrong kind of work.

"Although I have to say I'm proud of the fact that Monty and I were able to be ourselves in our relationship while still being open—and willing—to change in order to be what the other needed," Eliza continues. "To make our relationship and our family work. He never asked me to change who I was deep down, or what I wanted. But he did ask me to work on my patience because I'd hurt him when I snapped. I asked him to help me more in the kitchen, because meal planning, grocery shopping, and cooking for four people seven days a week was a full time job, and I already had one of those."

Nodding, I swallow. Hard.

"That's exactly what I want for Grey and I—the ability to be ourselves while still being willing to change to make our relationship work. But Grey just has these deeply entrenched beliefs that I'm not sure he's willing to budge on. He wants to contribute. Wants to give our family what he believes we want and need. 'The best of the best' as he says. But I need something different. We need him to be there, Eliza. I need him to be around more."

Eliza takes a bite of salad. Chews thoughtfully for a moment.

"I hope there's a way for y'all to compromise. A way for you to meet halfway, so Grey can scratch that itch of his to do the best of the best thing and still be around the way you'd like him to be. I've said it before, and I'll say it again. Grey means well. That's as much a part of him as his drive."

Yes, I think to myself. And I need to acknowledge that. I need to give that part of him space to thrive, because it *is* a good thing.

I just don't know how.

"I hope we can get there," I say, tearing up again. "I just don't know how."

She reaches across the table and puts a hand over mine.

"I know my son, Julia. And I know he's head over heels in love with you. He'll try his damndest to make you happy, and make your family work."

Yep, definitely crying now.

"I'd do the same," I say. "Honestly, Eliza. We're just...different."

"Talk to him. I'm sure he's working on this, same as you are right now. And once you've talked, keep talking. Make it a habit. Show you can change, same as him, while still remaining true to who you are. The woman he fell in love with."

I don't know what else to do. I reach across the table and pull Eliza in for the awkwardest, sweetest hug.

Who knows what will happen next. If Grey and I can work things out. If we can't.

But I do know I feel better just talking to Eliza. Being with her.

"I really appreciate the words of wisdom," I say. "I miss my parents like crazy. But y'all have welcomed me like a daughter, and that means more to me than you'll ever know."

She kisses my cheek. "I'd be lucky to call you a daughter, Julia. Not only did you bring my son back from the dead. You also have excellent taste in literature."

That makes me laugh, even as my eyes flood with a fresh round of tears.

"Men in kilts," she continues. "Men in suits. They're not so different, are they? They have their uniform, and they're confident enough to rock the hell out of it."

"They have sexy accents," I add. "At least our men in suits do."

"They're the ultimate alphas. But the taller they are..."

I grin. "The harder they fall."

"Exactly." Eliza meets my eyes. "Believe it or not, Monty was the tall guy in the power suit when we first met. As cocky and self-important as they come. Now look at him. He bakes cakes from scratch for his granddaughter's birthday parties. He loves *Outlander* as much as I do. He's still Monty. Still the man I married."

"He's still who he is. You've just rubbed off on him."

She grins. This sly, almost secret thing.

"I have." She motions for the check. "Now you go rub off on Grey. And let him rub up on you."

I laugh. Blush. Cry.

I hope Greyson and I have as happy an ending as Eliza and Monty's.

Chapter Thirty-Two

GREYSON

I make a million calls. My employees. My partners.

I call Olivia. Gracie, too.

The West Ashley location of Hello Baby. The downtown location of Rainbow Row Books, Charleston's most well-known Indie bookstore. I somehow, through a combination of shameless flattery and even more shameless desperation, convince the owner, Louise, to open the store for me this morning so I can check out a few things and pick her brain.

Once I have that shit somewhat settled, I take a deep breath and call Julia last. I bring my phone to my ear. Heart thumping inside my chest.

She doesn't answer. I check my watch. She told me a few days ago that she was meeting my mom for lunch today. I was hoping they'd have wrapped it up by now.

Should I be worried they're still talking?

Did lunch even happen?

I leave a voicemail, apologizing and asking Julia to call me back. Then, because I can't help myself, I send her a text.

Many texts.

Because I can't fucking stand being apart from her like this. Physically. Emotionally.

I hadn't realized exactly how much I valued our connection until it wasn't there anymore. When I'm with Julia, I feel seen. Safe. Plugged in to something greater than myself.

I've only ever felt that way with my family and close friends. I'm not sure if I've ever felt it in a romantic relationship before.

Greyson: Can we talk?

Greyson: I'm so fucking sorry baby

Greyson: I miss you

Greyson: and I feel horrible about the things I said.

Greyson: meet me? Anywhere

Greyson: I'm going to see Luke at the barn later today (its not work related I promise)

Greyson: but I'll work my schedule around yors

Greyson: I'm sorry

Greyson: even bowie isn't making me feel better

Greyson: how the hell do I dance without you?

Julia calls me half an hour later.

"Sweetheart," I say. "Hi."

"Hi, Grey," she says. She sounds stuffed up. Quiet. Like she's been crying.

I let out an anguished breath. "Please. Let's talk."

"I'd like that."

"How about now?"

"Like right now?" I hear the smile in her voice.

"Right now. I can't—" I swallow. "I can't stand this, Julia. It's killing me. Being away from you. Knowing you're hurt."

"Right now works. Where?"

"I'm in my car. I'll come get you."

"Okay," she says. "I'm at home."

"Be there in five. Less than that."

She's waiting for me in her driveway. Looks up as I approach and put the car in park.

I can't see her eyes; she's wearing sunglasses.

My heart feels like it's about to burst.

It leaps to my throat when she starts walking toward me. At first I think she's going to open the passenger side door.

Instead, she opens the door behind mine.

Slides into the backseat.

She pushes her sunglasses onto her head and meets my eyes in the rearview mirror.

My stomach dips. Hers are bloodshot, ringed with dark circles.

But there's a spark in them. I could be imagining it. Wanting so badly for her to forgive me that my brain conjured the hopeful glint I see there.

Or maybe—just maybe—she's willing to give me another chance.

"How are you feeling?"

She puts a hand on her belly. "Your mom just fed Charlie Brown and me. So we're pretty content at the moment. Minus, you know, the whole heart-that's-been-torn-to-pieces thing."

"Jules," I say. The word coming out as a tight growl. "I want to make this right."

"I want to make it right too," she says. Her throat working as she swallows.

"Can I come back there?"

Her lips twitch. "But I told you I don't fuck assholes."

"I've deserved that. Both times you've said it."

"You sure as hell have. But I'm not blameless here either." She pats the bench. "Come. Sit, I mean. No coming."

Not yet, I silently reply.

I cut the ignition and slide into the backseat. Feels familiar and foreign, all at once.

Our gazes lock. My pulse marches in my ears.

"I'm sorry," I say. "So sorry for the things I said. The way I behaved. But more than that, I'm sorry for not being the partner I promised I'd be. The man you needed. I thought I was doing the right thing by providing in my own way. I see now that I was wrong. You and

I had different interpretations of what being a true partner meant. I thought that meant providing for y'all financially. Giving y'all the best of the best."

Julia nods. Reaches for my hand.

"And I was wrong not to tell you what I meant by 'real partner' in more honest terms. I thought it was universally understood what that meant, you know? I thought everyone had the same understanding of what co-parents did and how the whole thing worked. Turns out we all have *very* different definitions. Which makes perfect sense now that I think about it. We all come from different families. We have different needs. I'm sorry I made such a dumbass assumption."

I give her hand a squeeze. "Not dumbass. But thank you for saying that."

"I recognize that you were trying in your own way to be there for me and Charlie Brown. That house search you did—I get that it took a lot of time and effort, and I sincerely appreciate what you did. You *do* think about us. You love us deeply, and you do work your ass off to show it. So thank you. I'm sorry I didn't say that at the house—*thank you*."

He nods. "You're welcome."

"I really do appreciate you putting that time in. The effort. Even though it was a bit..."

"Off," he says. "I get it. Since my divorce, I've felt this pressing need to be a workhorse. I caused everyone so much pain, Julia. So much fucking grief. I guess I kind of wanted to make up for that the only way I knew how—by working my ass off so Ford could be there for his daughter, and my parents could be there for Ford. I'd take care of the financial piece of the puzzle so they could take care of each other."

Julia's brow curves upward. "And you thought you'd do the same for Charlie Brown and me."

"Exactly."

"Grey," she says. Voice rough with anguish. "I hate how much you've beaten yourself up. I hate that you've put yourself through hell these past few years."

"But something needs to change."

She swallows. "Yeah. Yeah, it does. For us to work..."

I wrap my hand around hers. "And it will. Things are going to change, Julia. No more trying. No more empty promises. I'm making real changes. Big ones. So I can be there for you and the baby the way you need."

She raises her brows. "Really?"

"Really. I'm stepping back at Montgomery Partners."

Now Julia's eyes are wide. So wide I have half a mind to hold my hand out to catch them when they pop out of her head.

"Shut the fuck up! Stepping back? My God, Grey. What does that mean?"

"Means Ford is returning as a full-time employee. We've always been partners—technically, anyway—but he's going to be taking on more work so I can ease up a bit. More than a bit. A lot. Enough so that I don't have to work nights or weekends. And I'm taking eight weeks of paternity leave. I'll obviously coordinate the dates with your maternity leave."

She just looks at me for a full beat. Finally, when I think my heart is going to explode, she smiles. A wide, radiant thing.

"That's really happening," she says, more a question than a statement. "Right now, you're already working on the transition."

I nod. "Yup. I was on the phone all morning making arrangements. We'll spend the next few weeks getting Ford up to speed on all our current projects, but he's already familiar with a handful of them. Plus he's a fucking smart guy, so. Yeah. Shouldn't take long at all."

"You'd do that." Her voice shakes. "For me. And the baby. You'd change your entire life for us. Everything. You'd change everything, Grey."

Now it's my voice that's shaking. "Of course I would. Y'all are my life now, Julia. I *love* our life together. I didn't even like my life before. I wasn't living. I was just existing. Too afraid—too ashamed—to give myself another chance. I was hiding from the world and from myself. But you showed me the risk to try again was worth it. That taking a chance on myself, and forgiving myself, was so fucking worth it."

A tear slips down Julia's cheek. Her smile is in her eyes now. Just how I like it.

I glance around the truck.

Shit, I wanted to do this differently. Make more of a grand gesture in, like, the rain or something.

But now that I'm here with Julia, in the exact spot where this whole thing began, it feels...right.

Mostly.

"Don't freak out," I say, shoving open the door. "I'm not proposing or anything."

"What? Grey, you don't—"

But I'm already doing it.

I climb out of the car and get on my knees. The concrete biting into them through my jeans.

"You've helped me to forgive myself. And now I ask that you forgive me." I take her hand again, squinting against the afternoon sun. "I'm on my knees, Julia. You and Charlie Brown have brought me to my knees. Please give our happily ever after another shot. Whatever that looks like—wherever we end up—I'll be there every step of the way. Just let me ask you two questions. First, will you move in with me? We'll start the house search all over again. Find something that's you—something you love. And second, will you be my partner? In all things?"

Julia's crying and smiling and biting her lip, all at once.

"Yes," she breathes. "And absolutely *yes*!"

She pulls me up into a hug. I hold her in my arms and hold her tight, kissing her hair, her mouth, her neck.

"You lost your family," I murmur into her ear. "I will never presume or try to replace them. But let's start our own family. A new one. Together. In Charleston or Paris or where the fuck ever. We'll dance to David Bowie and wear our stretchy pants and watch Tony and Carm. As long as you're there, it will be home."

She pulls back to look at me. Tired, but relieved now, and happy.

"That's all I've ever wanted," she says. "To dance with someone like you. This—you—us—it's what I've been looking for without even knowing it."

I grin. "Can I make a point though?"

"Of course."

"I really would like a backyard for Charlie Brown. Bryce lives in Ford's. We don't have to buy a house like the one we looked at. But I would eventually like to have a place with some grass."

She nods. "I hear you. I agree we probably need a new place in the long run, so I'd be happy to undertake the search for one with you. I'd just like it to be something a little closer to what I'd always pictured my dream house looking like."

"Tell me more."

"It'd be something we can afford without you working all the time, for starters," she replies. "And I'd love a house that's got some history and plenty of character. A spot in a great neighborhood with lots of trees we could hang a swing from. Something that needs work—something we could put our mark on, and make our own."

"I love that idea," I say. "I love you. I am so in love with you, sweetheart."

"And I am so in love with you. All of you. The good parts and the bad. The gentleman and the villain. Don't you dare hide any of who you are from me, Grey."

I grin. "Because you don't scare easy."

"Because I adore you. All of you. Your truth. I want it all. And now I want you." She gives my hand a hard tug, pulling me to my feet. "Get in here."

"Yes ma'am."

I glide back onto the bench and shut the door.

She climbs on top of me.

She straddles my lap, nearly falling over when her belly gets caught between us. I catch her, just in time.

"A little different from when we first did this," she says, laughing.

"Don't worry, Charlie Brown, we'll keep you safe. Here Julia—try leaning back," I say, putting my hands on her hips. "I got you. See? Yeah, that's better."

She puts her hands on my shoulders to steady herself. I glide my hands up her sides, gathering the material of her dress in my fists.

But instead of tearing her dress off and kissing her neck, I kiss her mouth.

Hard.

Well.

She kisses me back. Hands on my face and in my hair. Tilting her head, her mouth soft and slick and hot on mine.

Needy.

She needs me as much as I need her.

Then—and only then—do I tear the dress off. Right there in her driveway in broad daylight.

Good thing my windows are tinted.

I work my mouth down her neck, her chest. Reach up and use my fingers to coax her breast out of her bra. Her nipple hardens to a point that I take in my mouth.

Julia arches into my caress with a moan, digging her fingernails into my skin.

"Grey," she pants.

My name.

It sounds so good—so right—when she says it.

Still holding on to me with one hand, she works the zipper of my jeans down with the other. Taking my cock, aching and hard, in her hand.

I'm already leaking cum. She uses her thumb to swirl it over the head. Lust rips through me.

Lust and love and so much life I can hardly breathe.

I lean in and kiss her. Tongue licking into her mouth.

"Put me inside you, baby," I say, lips brushing against hers. "How ready are you?"

Julia spreads her legs a little wider. "Feel for yourself."

Reaching between us, I pull her panties to the side and gently glide my first finger between her lips.

I growl.

Wet. Hot. Soft.

For me.

She rises up on her knees. Eyes locked on mine as she settles me at her entrance. My head meets with the slick heat of her, and for a second I see stars.

I see her, and she sees me.

Julia sinks, slow and steady, onto my cock. Swallowing me to the root.

Her blue eyes locked on mine—that cute little belly pressed against mine—heart so full—

For so long I was in hell.

But now, for no reason at all other than that I love and am loved, I'm in heaven.

This is heaven.

Julia rolls her hips, and I rock into her. She's tight and bare and mine, and I could shout with gratitude.

I play with her pussy the way she likes. The way she needs. Thumbing her clit. Sucking on her nipples.

The scent of her skin surrounds me.

I actually do shout when she comes and I come, too. Our orgasms separated by a handful of heartbeats.

There's an extra heartbeat between us now. One that we created.

One that we'll love and raise together.

Being together—that really is everything, isn't it?

Julia collapses against me, burying her head in the crook of my neck.

"No cigarette this time," she says. "What should we do instead?"

I kiss her temple. "I'll reschedule with Luke. How about a super cheesy dance party, followed by dinner, ice cream, and *Always Be My Maybe*? That's another good one about family."

She laughs. Kisses me.

"Sounds perfect."

Chapter Thirty-Three

JULIA

"Y'all, where are we going?" I ask, peering out the window.

Olivia just grins, taking a turn onto 17 South. "You'll see."

I turn to look at Gracie in the backseat.

"But I thought the shower was at Holy City Roasters."

She shakes her head. She's wearing the same secretive, knowing smile Olivia is.

"We had a change of venue," she replies.

My heart skips a beat. "Wait a second. Wait. Does Greyson have anything to do with this?"

Gracie makes a zipping motion across her lips. "I know nothing."

"How about some music?" Olivia turns the knob on her Honda's stereo. "Ah, Gucci Mane. This will get us in the baby shower mood."

Eva shimmies beside Gracie in the backseat. "Hey, I'm a fan."

We listen to "Freaky Gurl" as we make our way out of the city. Twenty minutes and many early 2000s R&B hits later, we cross onto Wadmalaw Island.

I smile.

I know exactly where we're headed.

Grey *definitely* had a hand in this. I remember what he texted me the day we made up—that he was meeting with Luke at the barn to discuss something non-work related.

This had to have been it.

I smile harder. Things have been *good* with us. We moved in together about a month ago—I'm living at his place while we search for a new home together. He's working a lot less, just like he promised. He's home most nights and weekends, and has really stepped up to do his fair share of life and baby stuff. He cooks a lot, and helps clean up when I'm too tired or too sore to stand at the sink (the baby is putting *a lot* of pressure on my pelvic floor these days.) We show up to doctor's appointments on time. He's helped me pack my bag for the hospital, and together we've done way too much research on college savings accounts and co-sleeping and pediatricians. It's a lot of work, but we dork out over it. That stuff can be kinda-sorta fun when you have someone to do it with.

Olivia takes a turn onto a familiar dirt driveway, and my pulse takes off at a sprint.

She pulls into the lot beside the Rodgers' Farms barn. I see a familiar figure waiting beside the barn door.

Greyson breaks out in a smile when he sees us. He hustles over to the car and opens my door, helping me out.

I'm grinning ear to ear.

"Don't you look gorgeous," he says, a familiar spark of heat igniting in his eyes as he takes in my floral dress and sandals.

I'm getting huge—thirty-four weeks yesterday—so my wardrobe options were limited. I'm big and unwieldy, but Greyson still manages to make me feel sexy.

"No tuxedo dick pants this time?" I say.

He ducks his head to plant a quick kiss on my mouth. "Saving that for later. I think my mom might faint if, you know, she saw it. Them. The whole thing."

"Right. Good call." I glance at the barn. "So this was your idea, huh?"

Grey nods. "I wanted to show off your work, for starters. Let all your friends see just how amazingly talented you are. I also wanted to be involved. And yeah, maybe I'm getting sentimental in my old age.

Seemed right to host your shower where our story—yours, mine, and Charlie Brown's—began."

"That's the fucking sweetest thing I have ever heard," Eva says as she passes by with an enormous cake in her arms.

"So sweet," I say, kissing him back. I twine my fingers through his.

He nods at the barn. "Can I show you what we've done?"

"Can't wait."

We walk into the barn, and immediately the breath leaves my lungs. The decor is simple but pretty, the space filled with rustic wooden tables set with white flowers and pretty glassware. I laugh when I see that the centerpieces are books. Picture books, more specifically. I move closer to take a peek at the titles.

Pride and Prejudice: The Newborn Edition

My Deal with the Duke, G-Rated Version

Baby's Guide to Virginia Woolf & The Bloomsbury Group

Olivia appears at my elbow. Arms crossed, still wearing that smile.

I just stare at her.

"You wrote all these, didn't you?" I ask.

Her smile grows. "I did. And Grey had them illustrated. The whole thing was his idea, actually."

My head snaps in his direction. "It was?"

Grey shrugs shyly. "I was trying to think of something thoughtful to get you for the shower. I saw firsthand how passionate you are about romance and feminism and history. So I called up Olivia and floated the idea, and then we went and talked to Louise, the owner of Rainbow Row Books. She put us in touch with an illustrator."

"Needless to say, I loved it," Olivia replies. "We got to work straightaway. I think they came out beautifully."

I smile at her. Smile at Grey.

Do my friends know me, or do they know me? One of the five thousand things I adore about them.

One of the five thousand things I adore about Grey.

I loop my arm around her waist and give her a squeeze. "I love them. Thank you both for such a lovely gift. And for hosting this shower. Y'all went above and beyond. This place looks amazing."

Grey nudges me with his elbow. "Thanks to you."

"And you."

"You two make a great team," Olivia says. "And you're going to make a beautiful baby, too."

People start to arrive. A slow trickle at first. Eliza and Monty arrive with Ford and Bryce in tow. She giggles with delight when I hand her a "best big cousin" gift wrapped in giraffe paper. She's warming up to me, slowly but surely, and I want to keep the momentum going.

"Thank you, Julia," Ford says when he hugs me.

"No problem. Figured she'd like something to open while we open gifts for the baby."

He grins. "You know my daughter well. She hates not being the center of attention."

The flood gates open shortly thereafter. My TA Irene, Hallie and Fiona from yoga class. Luke's mother and her wife, the two of them cackling over hilariously inappropriate vegetable innuendos.

Grey and I both notice Eva and Ford chatting together in a corner.

Friends, old and new, crowd the barn, chatting over mimosas and small plates of Elijah's ham and brown sugar biscuits, pimento cheese finger sandwiches, and fried oyster salad. The food is absolutely divine, but then again, Elijah's food always is.

We also devour Monty's homemade cupcakes and insane chocolate chip cookies dusted with sea salt. He made enough to feed a small army, but by the time we're ready to open presents, everything is gone.

Gracie and Eliza herd Grey and I to the front of the room, where an embarrassingly huge pile of gifts waits for us. Olivia leads the room in a champagne toast to me, Grey, and Charlie Brown.

Grey grabs my hand. I look at him. Look out at all the smiling faces beaming at us. Colleagues. Friends from college. The women I've met through yoga, some of them with their babies in their arms.

"This is overwhelming," I whisper. "The amount of love in this room."

He grins. "We're lucky, aren't we? To have a support system this big and this awesome?"

"So damn lucky," I say, shaking my head. "Makes me want to help women who aren't so lucky. I'm new to this mom thing, but I can already tell support is *everything*."

He tilts his head. "Let's do it then. Let's help those women."

"You want in?" I ask, smiling. So much freaking smiling these days.

"Of course," he replies. "Let's talk about it when we get home."

We sit in a pair of chairs and start to open gifts. Eliza records everything in a small pink notebook—we're all still convinced it's a girl —while Grey drapes onesies across his chest, and I hold up fuzzy blankets and stuffed animals for everyone to see.

Eliza wants me to open her gift. It's an adorable grey gingham baby bubble romper. Smocked, just begging for a monogram. As southern and sweet as it gets.

Exactly the kind of thing *my* Southern mama would get her grand baby.

"Thank you," I say, eyes welling with tears. "It's beautiful."

She pulls me into a tight hug. "We couldn't be more excited to welcome you and this baby into our family."

Grey looks on, tears in his eyes, too.

It takes an obscene amount of time to open our obscene amount of gifts. As soon as the last gift is opened and carefully packed back up, a stream of helpers already loading up Grey's car, he is on his feet and heading for the back of the room.

I notice the tables have been cleared over there, and Ford is crouched beside a pair of speakers, cursing quietly as he tries to plug them into the floor.

Putting my hands on my low back—Lord does it ache—I pad over.

"What's all this?" I ask.

Ford looks up at me. "If I can ever get these motherfucking speakers figured out, it's going to be a dance floor. Mr. Boogie Nights over there"—he nods at Grey, who's pouring himself another glass of champagne—"insisted on having one."

I smile. Again. For the seven hundredth time today.

"I didn't know there was dancing at baby showers," I say.

"Why not? You love it. I love it. Pretty sure Charlie Brown's going to love it, too," Grey says breezily, sidling up to me. He clanks his champagne against my flute of OJ. "If there's any excuse at all to dance, I'm going to take it. I have a lot of lost time to make up for."

Ford shakes his head, grinning. "Y'all are so cute it's gross, you know that? I love it."

"We love you," I say, meeting his eyes. "Seriously. I don't think we'd be here right now if you hadn't talked some sense into Grey so he'd let you come back to Montgomery Partners full time. Charlie Brown and I appreciate that more than you know."

"I appreciate it more than you know," Grey says. "Thank you, brother."

Ford waves us away, turning back to the speaker situation. "Y'all are welcome. Just save the dirty dancing for behind closed doors, all right?"

"I make no guarantees. Do you?" I ask Grey.

He takes a sip of his champagne and smacks his lips. "Nope."

It takes a couple minutes and some help from Greyson, but Ford eventually figures the speakers out. Grey plugs in a laptop, and few seconds later, "Let's Dance" starts to play.

My heart flutters inside my chest.

There's no way I could pick a favorite Bowie song. But if I had to, this one would be a top contender.

Grey extends his hand. "Wanna?"

"Like you even need to ask."

I take his hand, and he sweeps me onto the dance floor. I'm awkward and unwieldy and my center of gravity is God knows where, but Grey doesn't seem to mind. He pulls out all the moves—lawnmower, sprinkler, shopping cart—and I do my best to keep up, laughing the whole time.

I end up in his arms again. Mine looped around his neck, his looped around my back (they barely reach all the way around me anymore!). My big old belly keeps us farther apart than I'd like, but Grey still bumps and grinds against me like the best of them. Turning me around so my back is to his front.

A pulse of heat moves through me when his hands slip to my ass.

"Inappropriate!" Ford says as he passes by, Bryce on his hip.

Laughing, I turn back around to kiss Grey on the cheek.

As I turn, I see that everyone has joined us on the dance floor. They surround us. Bumping hips, elbows. Faces lifted as we all sing the words to the song.

A swell of joy bowls me over. Here I am, shaking my ass like I'm not eight months pregnant, surrounded by so much love and support and happiness it almost hurts.

I never in a million years would've guessed my story and Grey's would end like this—on such a high, happy note.

But then I realize that this isn't the end.

It's the beginning.

The beginning of something bigger than ourselves.

The beginning of a new story.

One that feels so very right.

This won't be our last joyful moment. Just like we haven't experienced our last painful one. There are more to come.

Many, many more. And I get to experience them all, good and bad, with Grey and Charlie Brown. I'll have them by my side through it all.

We dance until our feet hurt. And then we go home and dance some more.

The behind-closed-doors kind.

EPILOGUE

Julia

Six Weeks Later

Greyson Parker Montgomery IV—I know, I know, the fourth thing is a little much, but Grey and I loved the idea of continuing a family tradition—came roaring into the world right on time on June twenty-third. Eight pounds, twelve ounces of pure scrumptious baby chunk.

I thought I'd die of shock when the doctor held him up and said, "It's a boy!"

Greyson looked at the baby. Looked at me. Mouth agape, wide blue eyes welling with tears.

He kissed me, hard, and we both burst into the most gutting, most relieved, happiest sobs ever.

Grey opted not to cut the cord—"I won't lie, y'all, I think I might pass the fuck out"—and then I held the baby skin to skin on my chest. One hand on Parker (that's what we're calling him), the other holding an orange popsicle.

I just stared at him. Shocked that he was a boy. Shocked that *I had a baby*.

A real live human baby.

Hard to believe this whole thing started nine months ago in the backseat of Grey's truck.

Now here we are. A family of three.

Wild the turns life can take.

I traced the features of Parker's face with the tip of my finger. Blue eyes, wrinkly forehead, the Montgomery dimpled chin. Same one Greyson shares with his dad.

My heart was so full in that moment I could barely breathe.

That was magic.

The not so magical parts? The two stitches I had to get after I suffered a second degree tear. How the baby gnawed on my nipples for two days straight after we got home from the hospital.

The pain was unreal. So is the appearance of my nipples.

"They look like taco meat!" I wailed after an especially long and frustrating attempt at nursing.

Greyson, patting the baby's back on his shoulder, shrugged. "I like tacos."

"I'm never having sex with you again," I replied. "Your sperm has superhuman strength, and right now the thought of having another baby makes me want to stab someone."

"Hopefully not me," Grey says cheerfully.

Parker farts. A second later, shit leaks out of his diaper all over Grey's shirt.

Grey gags. I bite back a laugh.

"That's what you get for your smart ass reply," I say. "And for your smart ass sperm!"

We brought the baby home to our new house. After months of searching, we finally found the perfect spot. We moved in a week before Parker was born. It's a light blue Charleston single not far from Ford's—we loved the idea of our kids growing up together, although Bryce has yet to warm up to the baby—with plenty of trees in the backyard, a kitchen that needs a lot of work, and tons of character.

The best part? Neither of us has to work like a dog to be able to afford it.

Grey has taken his promise to step back at Montgomery Partners seriously. He's got his eight weeks of paternity leave, and I have to say I am incredibly grateful we both have the privilege of paid time off.

He's lucky that he had a partner who was willing to cover for him. And I'm lucky I work for an institution that provides excellent benefits.

We're *lucky*. Beyond belief. And it's made us realize that having this time together—having the time to heal and bond with Parker—shouldn't come down to luck.

We're even luckier to have the help and support of an incredible village of family and friends. Eliza comes over every day to do laundry, make coffee, and drop off groceries. Monty supplies all the pound cake and cookies I need to satisfy my voracious appetite. Plus, he does the dishes, loads and unloads the dishwasher, and pours us wine without judgment.

Meals arrive in a steady stream. I cry each and every time one is dropped off. Not having to worry about dinner—or lunch the next day, thanks to leftovers—is so, so nice when you're sleep deprived, bleeding from your vagina and nipples, and so terrified to poop you give yourself stomachaches over it.

I'm sincerely touched by the outpouring of support we get. Meals, gifts, flowers. It's overwhelming in the best way. And just the vote of confidence I need when my mood or body or both are flagging.

Gracie, Olivia, and Eva come over a week after we leave the hospital. They also bring gifts.

Only the gifts are for me, not the baby.

"Stop it," I say when I open the body butter Eva got me. "You are too damn sweet!"

She gives me a hug. "It's important that mama is taken care of so she can take care of baby."

Olivia gifts me a Kindle Fire.

"So you can read during night feedings," she explains. "Figure you'd need some entertainment to keep you awake."

I grin. "Besides a baby sucking on my boob?"

"That's not entertainment," she says, laughing. "I already gifted you a few of my favorite recent reads to download on there—check your email. I hope you enjoy them."

"So how is everything going?" Gracie asks after I open the specialty tea she made just for me.

Handing Eva the baby, I sit back on the sofa. Watch as she smiles down at him, tapping his little nose with her finger.

"We're surviving," I reply honestly. "The first couple days were really rough. But we're learning each other. Bit by bit. The pain is constant. So is the sleep deprivation. Not to scare y'all—"

"Please," Olivia says, waving me away. "If it makes you feel better to talk about it, give us all the gory details you want."

"But yeah. The postpartum struggle is real. And graphic. And intense. I swear I've almost had panic attacks thinking about what my vagina must look like right now. I don't know if I've ever been through anything this intense in my life."

Gracie grins. "And you've worked with Greyson Montgomery."

"I heard that!" Grey shouts from the kitchen.

Eva tilts her head in his direction. Lowers her voice.

"How's he doing?"

My turn to grin. "He's doing pretty great, all things considered. I'm really glad to have him around right now. Makes me really feel like we're a team. Even though breastfeeding kind of fucks up the division of labor. I'm feeding that baby every two hours at least. So yeah, that's been a lot of work. But Grey's up with me to change diapers and clean up poop and puke. He's a champ at swaddling. And he takes care of all the pediatrician stuff—making appointments, getting the paperwork ready, calling when we have questions."

Eva coos at Parker. He gurgles in reply. "Aw, y'all really are a team."

I grab her hand. "We all are. I know I keep saying this, but there's no way we could do this without y'all. Your love and support has made all the difference. Thank you guys, sincerely."

"You'll let us know if you need anything, right?" Olivia says. "We're only a phone call away."

I nod. "Of course. But enough about me and baby poop and pediatricians. What have I missed? What's going on with y'all?"

Gracie glances at Eva. "Have you told her yet?"

"Told me what?" I say, perking up at the hint of juicy gossip.

Eva blushes. Looks away. Looks down at Parker.

"Has Grey said anything to you?" she asks.

I blink. "Oh, girl, you'd better spill the beans *right now*. And no, Grey hasn't said anything to me non-baby related in eight days. What's going on?"

"Nothing," she says, careful to keep her eyes glued on the baby. Voice still low. "I just, um. May have seen Ford."

"Seen?" Gracie says. "Is that what we're calling it now?"

Eva shoots her a look. Then looks at me.

"We may have hung out. Once."

"Just once?"

"Once." She shrugs. "Twice. Something like that."

My eyes nearly pop out of my head. "Eva! What the hell? Why didn't you tell me? How? Why? When? I saw y'all talking at the shower. Wow. I knew the two of you had history, but I didn't know you still held a torch for him."

"I don't," she replies. "It just sort of...happened, I guess. I'm back in Charleston for the time being. We started talking at the shower. Then we...well. One thing led to another...God, I should've known the guy would charm my pants off."

I'm grinning. "The Montgomery men tend to have that effect."

"They certainly do," she says under her breath. "Anyway. It's not serious. Just a summer fling."

"How very Danny and Sandy of you," Gracie says.

"Welp," I say, patting Eva's knee. "You know I won't say a word. But I really do love Ford like a brother. Doesn't mean I won't kick his ass if he breaks your heart."

"He's already done that once," she says. "Won't be happening again, trust me."

I meet eyes with Gracie. She grins. So do I.

"Whatever you do, just be sure to use *two* forms of birth control," I say. "Don't do like I did and rely on only one. That's how accidents happen."

"Hey," Eva replies, nodding at baby in her arms. "I'd say things turned out all right for you guys."

I look up to see Grey standing in the doorway. Looking as handsome as ever in his stretchy pants—tight, just how I like 'em—and scruff, a burp cloth draped over one shoulder.

He's smiling. At me.

Making my heart and my stomach and everything else do backflips.

I may have taco meat nipples.

I may be wearing mesh underwear.

But that doesn't stop me from feeling a rush of emotion.

Desire. Joy. That very fine man is mine.

So is that very little man in Eva's arms.

Later that night, Grey and I take the baby outside and sit on the rocking chairs on our new front porch.

Well, Grey sits. And I do this kinda-sorta half sit that, when I get it just right, doesn't make me want to cry.

The three of us rock in silence for several minutes. Parker on Grey's shoulder.

Seeing them together like this makes me smile. So hard.

"You know, I forgot to ask you how that book ended," Grey says. "The one you read in your class—*Romp with the Rake*? I forget what it was called. But I remember really liking it."

I furrow my brow, smile deepening. "What made you think of that?"

"I don't know. Seeing Olivia today, maybe. Those girls love you, by the way."

"They're pretty awesome."

"I know. But yeah. Last I heard, Callum the Scot was walking out on Charlotte because he didn't want to taint her with his terrible truth."

"Sound familiar?"

He grins. "Yes."

"Welp. Callum finally sees the light, he begs for Charlotte's forgiveness, and then they get back to—well, getting busy in the comfort of his castle."

"Sounds like a solid ending."

"Castle sex usually is. But! They never end up conceiving an heir. Which crushes them both, because Callum really wanted to start a new family. He missed his terribly—Charlotte was dead on about that—and so they end up taking in orphans. Five of them, to be exact."

"Five! Holy shit. One kid is enough to push me over the edge," he says, nodding at Parker.

"No kidding. But Charlotte has this beautiful line at the end of the book—she says something like taking in five orphans was not the future she and Callum had planned. But it was beautiful and full nonetheless. So beautiful she couldn't help but feel it was a happily ever after that was very much meant to be."

Grey reaches over. Offers me his hand.

"Just like the three of us?"

I take it. The warm, solid, dry feel of it is familiar now.

"Yeah," I say. "Yeah, I do think we were meant to be. Because even though this is fucking *hard*, I'm still all right to do it, you know? I'm all right because I get to do it with you."

He gives my hand a squeeze. "Out of all the beautiful words you've spoken to me, I think those might be the prettiest."

"Thanks," I say. "I'm telling you, romance is where it's at. I learned all that and more from it."

"You've certainly taught me the power of love stories," he replies. "Callum and Charlotte's. Ours."

"I know I'm biased, but I kind of think ours is the best."

He looks at me. "Because it's perfect?"

"Because it's not. I told you—I'm all about the cracks in perfection. Give me the real." I look back at him. "Give me you."

He tilts his head. "You already have me."

"And you have me."

"And now *we* have a kid. When did that happen?"

I laugh. "I don't know. But I'm glad it did."

I mean that.

I do.

Thank you so much for reading SOUTHERN GENTLEMAN! Want to find out how Greyson proposes? Get your FREE bonus epilogue (complete with Julia and Grey's belated

Hawaiian babymoon!) by signing up for my newsletter at www.jessicapeterson.com!

Flip the page for an exclusive excerpt from SOUTHERN CHARMER, the first book in the Charleston Heat series! This is Olivia and Eli's story. If you've already burned through that series (thank you!), be sure to check out the first book in my super sexy Thorne Monarchs series, ROYAL RUIN!

SOUTHERN CHARMER EXCERPT

Eli

Olivia gives her hips a tiny little roll. Just enough to meet me at the crest of my own roll, so the head of my dick hits her center just right.

I grunt, biting down on her bottom lip.

Leaning all my weight onto one elbow, I hold myself up and reach between her legs. Even through the thick, wet fabric of her jeans, I can feel how hot she is.

I can feel the beat of her pulse, too. It's going wild.

She's clawing at my chest. Digging her nails into my skin when I press my two fingers against the length of her slit.

She is *burning*.

Olivia does this thing—she lets out these little moans, so quiet I can hardly hear them over the rain outside, whenever I do something she likes.

She's moaning now into my mouth.

I feel like I died and went to heaven.

I want to unbutton these jeans and touch her for real. Slide my fingers into her soft, sweet heat. Spread her wide and taste her. See if she's as hot and bothered as I am.

Because good *Lord* am I hard. My dick feels swollen and huge inside my jeans. I'd like to unbutton them, too.

But I don't.

For starters, I don't want our first time to be some wet, thoughtless fuck after a couple beers at The Spotted Wolf. Olivia means more to me than that.

I want to give her more than that.

But more important, she's letting me in. She let the fire in her eyes spread to her body. She's feeling the passionate things she writes about in *My Enemy The Earl,* and she's trusting me to keep them from burning her to a crisp.

She's being truly vulnerable with me for the first time. Her trust wraps around my heart like a hand and squeezes, making me feel—

Capable. Strong.

Things I haven't felt since this whole business with The Jam began.

And if I'm as capable as Olivia seems to think, then I'd know not to reward her trust by pushing her. Even though I'm on top, she's the one in charge.

She's the one calling the shots.

So as much as I want to get her naked and give her an orgasm or five and make love to her the way Gunnar would make love to Cate, I'm not going to.

Not unless she specifically asks for it.

We'll stick to making out for the time being. Which I certainly don't mind.

Actually, all this dry humping takes me back to my teenage days in the backseat of my old beat up Ford. It's fun. I feel like I'm seventeen again, doing all this shit for the first time.

The way Olivia froze when I kissed her—the way she went boneless not long after—makes me think this *is* the first time she's been properly kissed. The first time she's been overwhelmed by desire.

Or maybe it's just been a while for her.

Whatever the case, I follow her lead, and do my best to give her what she wants. When her hands rove over my body, touching every inch of my skin with reverence and care and curiosity, I do the same to her. I walk my fingers over her belly, her breasts, her neck.

Olivia really likes it when I touch her neck. Especially when it's my mouth that's doing the touching. My mouth and tongue and teeth.

She's as soft as I imagined her to be.

My heart—that's soft, too. Soft and already sore from so much *wanting*.

I want to make this girl mine.

I think we're finally moving in the right direction. Thank fuck.

We make out for hours.

My lips are raw. So is my dick from rubbing up against the zipper of my fly all night.

But I still fight a pang of disappointment when Olivia's kisses become less ardent, and then stop altogether. I look down to see her nodding off, head lolling on my shoulder.

Her breathing evens out. I tuck her hair behind her ears. My arm is falling asleep, but I don't move. I don't want to wake her. Not yet.

I know I need to go. Olivia hasn't asked me to stay. Even though I want to.

Lord, do I want to stay. Curl her body into mine and fall asleep breathing in the scent of her skin. Wake up together. Make breakfast. Talk books. Maybe get to third base before I have to go in to the restaurant.

With a sigh, I give my arm a little shake.

"Olivia," I murmur in her ear. "I'm gonna go. But you should take off your jeans. They're still wet, and I don't want you catchin' a chill."

She nods, not opening her eyes. "Okay."

"Can I see you day after next?" I ask. "I have a long day at The Jam tomorrow, but I should have some time the day after."

A pause. She rolls her lips between her teeth.

My heart contracts as I wait for her reply.

"Yeah," she says at last. "I'd like that."

I let out the breath I'd been holding. I gently roll her off my shoulder and sit up. Roll off the bed, careful not to disturb her.

"Promise me you'll take off the jeans. I'd do it for you, but..."

Her eyes are still closed when she nods again. Her fingers move sleepily to her fly. She undoes the button, raising her hips.

Even in the dark, I can see her nipples, puffy and perfect, straining against the sheer cups of her bra.

F-u-u-c-k.

"Two days." I quickly kiss her mouth. "I want to see you."

Wiggling out of her jeans, Olivia offers me a lazy smile. I glimpse the teeny tiny strap of a thong—red, too—and force myself to turn around. My cock is screaming bloody murder.

"Good night, Eli."

"Night, sweetheart."

Thank y'all so much for reading SOUTHERN GENTLEMAN! I started writing this book the day I found out I was pregnant, and it turned out to be a really great way of working through my own complicated feelings about pregnancy and motherhood. In a way, it was the best kind of therapy! Julia + Grey's story is very personal and very special to me, and I sincerely hope you enjoyed it. Look out for SOUTHERN HEARTBREAKER, Eva + Ford's book, next!

Check out the other books in the Charleston Heat series if you haven't yet. Like all my books, SOUTHERN CHARMER and SOUTHERN PLAYER can absolutely be read as standalones. If you've already burned through this series (thank you!), check out my steamy THORNE MONARCHS series, starting with ROYAL RUIN.

I love nothing more than hanging out with readers, and I'm very active on social media. Here's how you can get in on the fun:

- Join my Facebook reader group, The City Girls, for exclusive excerpts of upcoming books plus giveaways galore!
- Follow my not-so-glamorous life as a romance author on Instagram @JessicaPAuthor
- Check out my website at www.jessicapeterson.com
- Follow me on Goodreads
- Follow me on Bookbub
- Like my Facebook Author Page

ACKNOWLEDGMENTS

This book would not exist without the help and encouragement of a small army of people. Writing can be a difficult and lonely endeavor, but the lovely romance community I'm lucky to be a part of makes the whole thing worth it. THANK Y'ALL.

Thanks to my right hand woman, Jodi, for your patience, your ideas, and your honesty. I adore you and have so much to learn from you.

Thanks to Monica, my model hunter, my group admin, and my character namer (namer of characters?). It's been a total joy getting to know you over the past year, and I'm lucky to call you a friend.

Thanks to my Facebook group admins, Ingrid and Raquel. The City Girls is my favorite corner of the internet, all thanks to y'all.

Thanks to my beta readers, Jodi, Monica, Quinn, Julia, and Heather. You amazingly smart ladies have saved my ass so many times now I've lost count. I sincerely value your feedback, and my books are all the better for it.

Thanks to Pippa for being so open and honest and taking the time to answer my million questions. You are #authorgoals for sure!

Thanks to Mika for taking the time to talk to me about the tricky ins and outs of the accidental pregnancy trope. I appreciate your thoughts and guidance!

Thanks to my author friends, my ARC team, and the hundreds (well, thousands now I guess!) readers in my reader group. Your support truly has changed my life in all the best ways. Special shout out to Kenysha, Joyce, Tammy, Kenysha, Judy, Maria, Sophia, Terra, Kathryn, Pippa, Lucy, Stephanie, Maya, Kelsey...my God, there are so many of you now, and I am feeling so grateful I'm tearing up! Thank you guys for all the love you've shown me and my books.

Thanks to my editor, Kristin, and my copyeditor, Tandy. Thanks also to my amazing, and amazingly patient, cover artist, Najla Qamber. As usual, you knocked it out of the park with this one.

Thanks to Ryan for the TDP story/idea. Let's hope you started a trend!

Thanks to the cover photographer, Rafa Catala, and the cover model, Fabián Castro. You are both a dream to work with.

Finally, my biggest thanks to my husband (and soon-to-be best dad in the world!) Ben. You made all my dreams come true. I hope to return the favor. Love you.

ALSO BY JESSICA PETERSON

THE CHARLESTON HEAT SERIES

The Weather's Not the Only Thing Steamy Down South...

Available for FREE in Kindle Unlimited!

Southern Charmer (Charleston Heat #1)

Southern Player (Charleston Heat #2)

Southern Gentleman (Charleston Heat #3)

Southern Heartbreaker (Charleston Heat #4) Coming Fall 2019!

THE THORNE MONARCHS SERIES

Royal. Ridiculously Hot. Totally Off Limits...

Available for FREE in Kindle Unlimited!

Royal Ruin (Flings With Kings #1)

Royal Rebel (Flings With Kings #2)

Royal Rogue (Flings With Kings #3)

THE STUDY ABROAD SERIES

Studying Abroad Just Got a Whole Lot Sexier...

A Series of Sexy Interconnected Standalone Romances

Read Them All for FREE in Kindle Unlimited!

Lessons in Love (Study Abroad #1)

Lessons in Gravity (Study Abroad #2)

Lessons in Letting Go (Study Abroad #3)

Lessons in Losing It (Study Abroad #4)

ABOUT THE AUTHOR

Jessica Peterson writes smokin' hot romance set in her favorite cities around the world. She grew up on a steady diet of Mr. Darcy, Edward Cullen, and Jamie Frasier, and it wasn't long before she started writing swoon-worthy heroes of her own. She loves strong coffee, stronger heroines, and heroes with hot accents.

She lives in Charlotte, NC with her husband Ben and her smelly Goldendoodle, Martha Bean. You can check out her books at www.jessicapeterson.com.